The biggest trial…

DEATH
BY DANGEROUS

is yet to come…

OLLY JARVIS

Matador
9 Priory Business Park,
Wistow Road, Kibworth Beauchamp,
Leicestershire. LE8 0RX
Tel: (+44) 116 279 2299
Fax: (+44) 116 279 2277
Email: books@troubador.co.uk
Web: www.troubador.co.uk/matador

ISBN 978 1784623 494

British Library Cataloguing in Publication Data.
A catalogue record for this book is available from the British Library.

Printed and bound in the UK by TJ International, Padstow, Cornwall
Typeset in Adobe Garamond Pro by Troubador Publishing Ltd, Leicester, UK

Matador is an imprint of Troubador Publishing Ltd

For Amber and Ben

'A person often meets his destiny on the road he took to avoid it.'

Jean de La Fontaine 1621–1695

Causing death by dangerous driving
(Section 1 Road Traffic Act 1988):

A person who causes the death of another person by driving a mechanically propelled vehicle dangerously on a road or other public place is guilty of an offence.

Sentence – imprisonment not exceeding 14 years.

PROLOGUE

Spring 2003

Watching. Waiting. Always waiting. That was part of it. The build up. Thinking about what was to come. Of how he was going to change her life – forever.

She would always remember it.

To have that connection with a woman meant everything. Even if only for one stolen night.

He skipped through the cemetery, drunk with excitement. Which grave would be theirs? A place that only they would know. Eeny meeny miny moe.

Headlights.

He with hood pulled up. Crouched down behind the wall. Waiting.

The bus drew into the stop. Doors opened. There she was. Just like clockwork. A beautiful young lady. She stood for a moment, silhouetted by the red tail lights fading into a distant blur. Raising a hand to adjust an earphone, she set off along the road.

They were alone now, blanketed together in the darkness. Waiting. Waiting.

Now!

A hand over her throat, grabbed from behind. He could feel her body jolt – shock – as he pulled her to him. He pressed the blade against her throat. 'If you make a sound, I'll kill you.'

Frozen with fear. Pushed and dragged over the railings. Thrown to the ground amongst the moss-covered stone slabs.

Lying on her back, motionless but for her eyes, dancing with terror. 'Please don't!' Then a whimper.

He knelt astride her, brandishing the knife. 'See this?' He ran his tongue along the serrated edge. 'It will help you remember tonight. Our night.'

PART I

PART I

CHAPTER 1

Present Day

John Anderson was awake, in that no man's land between sleep and remembering. Remembering what day it was. Weekend, or was he in court? It would only take a split second to find his place, for his brain to get in gear and start focusing on the trial; tactics, a cross-examination, or was it speeches? Strangely, today he couldn't recall. Something was different.

He opened his eyes, squinting. An unfamiliar ceiling. Where was he? Pain, like nothing he had felt before. His whole body ached. Head throbbing. So weak, he could hardly lift his arms off the bed. A mask over his face – to breathe. Some kind of tube – a drip – on the back of his hand. What the hell was going on?

'Oh my God! He's awake!' A female – Mia – his wife, leaned over the bed. She looked into his eyes, hers watering. Mia's expression flickered between concern and curiosity. She pressed a button above the bed. 'How are you feeling?' She didn't wait for a reply. 'We thought we'd lost you, John.'

He stared at her blankly, confused.

'Doctor, he woke up, just now,' she announced to a man in a white coat entering the room.

'Hello, Mr Anderson. I'm Dr Nesbitt,' he explained as he monitored various screens by the bed whilst a nurse fussed around him. 'How much do you remember?' he asked, pulling down the breathing apparatus.

Anderson couldn't remember anything. Only finishing in court, going for a coffee, then… nothing. 'Where am I?'

'Wythenshawe Hospital. You were involved in a car crash.' The doctor added: 'A serious one.'

'Car crash?' Anderson had no recollection. His head ached. The conversation took all his strength. 'What happened?' The barrister in him took over – there were questions that needed answers. 'Where?'

'One thing at a time, Mr Anderson,' the doctor replied.

Anderson's lawyer's nous sensed more bad news.

'You've seriously injured your right leg.'

Why was he saying *you've* injured, as if somehow Anderson had done it to himself? He noticed things like that in people's speech.

'And you have a severe facial laceration.'

Anderson became aware of the bandage on his cheek. He lifted his hand.

'Try not to touch it. Mr Anderson, you've been unconscious for three days.'

'Three days?' He made to sit up but his body refused. 'What about the trial?'

Mia touched his shoulder and gently settled him back down. 'Sam Connor, your junior, took over.' She paused, then flicked back some wayward strands of her long brown hair. 'But, John, that's the least of your worries.' She exchanged glances with the doctor. Anderson wasn't the sort of man to be kept in the dark. A deep breath, then she said: 'They're saying it was your fault.'

'What?'

4

Tears – Mia could hardly bear to tell him. 'Someone died.'

Anderson's mouth went dry. His body felt cold, numb. 'No!' Was he dreaming. A nightmare? 'There must be some mistake!'

Mia shook her head. 'A woman.'

Silence.

The words sank in.

'And a little girl lost her legs. She's here in the hospital. Still critical.'

Too much to comprehend.

A commotion, outside the room. Voices getting louder. 'He's somewhere down 'ere, the bastard.' A female voice. Louder. 'Here he is, in 'ere.'

The nurse left what she was doing and attempted to block someone's entrance, to no avail. Nearly at the bed, Anderson glimpsed her eyes, bloodshot and full of hate. 'Do you know what you've done?' Sobbing, shouting again: 'Do you know what you've done?'

'Please, Sandra, come away.' Sandra's husband pulled her back out and into the corridor with the assistance of the nurse.

Screaming: 'She's dead! Not five minutes ago. You killed my baby.' Gut-wrenching sobs. 'My little Molly. My beautiful Molly.'

Anderson closed his eyes tight, wishing he could open them again in his old life.

CHAPTER 2

Four Days Earlier

'Our final and arguably most prestigious award is for the north of England's junior barrister of the year.' The master of ceremonies bestowed a supercilious grin on the audience, relishing his role, and at such a prestigious location – Manchester's Midland Hotel. A symbol of the city's great industrial history, built by the Midland Railway at the turn of the last century to service their northern terminus, the terracotta baroque building was a suitably grand venue to honour the region's greatest lawyers.

The clinking of glasses and background chatter dipped as attention switched to the stage.

Circular tables crammed the banqueting hall. The occupants of each represented a set of barristers' chambers. Only one chair remained empty.

'Where the hell is Anderson?' whispered Head of Chambers, Orlando West QC, not wishing to be heard beyond the confines of his party – colleagues from Spinningfields Chambers.

'History tells us,' the host continued, twisting a silver cuff link embedded in his pristine white dress shirt, 'that the winner invariably goes on to take silk, followed by a career on the bench.' A conspiratorial smile. 'An indicator of great things to come.'

Gary, the senior clerk, held his phone below the table and banged furiously at the keys. 'He's not responding.'

'He'll be working in chambers,' offered Sam Connor, Anderson's contemporary at Spinningfields. 'He doesn't do social functions.'

'Even if he's up for a bloody award?' laughed West, full of admiration for his former pupil.

Connor snatched at his wine glass and took a slurp. Anything to distract his mouth from saying something publicly about John Anderson that he might regret. He turned to the pretty young blond beside him and stole a glance at her breasts, erupting out of a shimmering black evening dress. At least he had the best-looking pupil in Manchester, and she seemed to worship him, despite his middle-aged spread. Thank goodness for Tilly. Anything to break the monotony of his crappy marriage. Tilly Henley-Smith was definitely worth the risk of being caught out by Connor's bitch of a wife. Maybe this was the push he needed. He only stayed for the kids. Another ten years before they were off his hands. Sticking it out for that long was unthinkable. Virtually a life sentence.

'The recipient of this award has enjoyed an extraordinary year, successfully prosecuting a series of complicated VAT frauds in the crown courts of both Manchester and Liverpool. A versatile performer, he is just as much at home prosecuting gang violence – fast becoming the scourge of the criminal gangs that so blight our inner cities.'

'Evening all,' said John Anderson, taking his seat.

'Where've you been, sir?' asked Gary, his clerk. 'Been pulling my hair out.'

'Working. Have I missed anything?' His humourless

persona seemed out of sync with the excitement of the evening. That was John Anderson. He kept it all inside, behind the armour. Emotion was weakness. He'd learnt that from his father.

'The presenter of this award needs little introduction. A glittering career at the Bar, an eminent silk, and now a circuit judge in Preston. Ladies and gentlemen, please welcome former winner of this award, His Honour, Judge Howard Anderson.'

Everyone at the table watched John Anderson for a reaction.

He was poker-faced.

'Did you know your father was presenting it?' Tilly asked, wide-eyed and smouldering.

'No,' Anderson replied, without further explanation.

'Yeah, right,' said Connor, almost in a sneer, the drink having loosened his tongue.

Orlando West gave his protégé a wink. 'A good sign, I think, John.'

Anderson remained cool.

Howard Anderson was at the microphone. Sprightly and distinguished looking at sixty-three, further judicial elevation was still possible. No way would he settle for the lowly honour of being a crown court judge. Nothing less than the red dressing gown of a high court judge would do.

Howard Anderson opened the envelope. 'And the winner is…' He took a pair of glasses out of the top pocket of his dinner jacket to prolong his time in the spotlight, before flashing a broad grin for the audience. 'John Anderson.'

His son.

Orlando West QC was the first to slap Anderson on the

back, followed by hearty handshakes from other members of Spinningfields Chambers, all clamouring to rub shoulders with the man of the moment.

Anderson rose to his feet and set off towards the stage. Another step nearer his goal – Queen's Counsel – a silk gown. He could almost feel it around his shoulders.

The applause pushed him up the steps and onto the stage where his father was waiting with the silver trinket.

Their eyes met, if only for a second.

John Anderson couldn't read his father's face, though he knew it so well. An unfamiliar expression. What was it? Not adoration or even love. Both emotions were alien to Howard Anderson. John reached out to take the prize, then it clicked: envy. His own father was jealous. Of his son's success. Jealous that John had it all before him, and that he, Howard, was in the autumn of his career.

It pained John Anderson that his father should think like that. He shook it off.

'Let's hope this bodes well for your silk application,' Howard whispered.

Nothing was ever enough. Howard Anderson was unable to just enjoy the achievement, bask in the reflected glory and be proud. Always a better view from the next hill. This had been the way of it ever since John could remember. Instilled in him from an early age – relentless ambition.

Quickly burying his unhappy thoughts and feelings deep below, John Anderson moved across to the microphone and began his acceptance speech.

'Firstly I would like to thank my father, without whose guidance and support I would never…'

Whilst all eyes were on Anderson, Connor took the

9

opportunity to pour the dregs of a bottle of Chardonnay into his glass. Not bothering to top up Tilly's glass, or anyone else's, he muttered: 'Cold fish. Just like his dad.'

'Quite good-looking though,' Tilly replied with a mischievous smile.

Connor gave a nonchalant harrumph, though her words had cut like a knife.

'And to my former pupil-master, Orlando West QC, I would like to…' Anderson went on, thanking all the right people. An efficient speech, nothing flamboyant, just like his advocacy.

Anderson finished with a few words of praise for the judiciary before weaving his way back through the hall to his table. He was now the most celebrated junior barrister in the north of England. A shoo-in for Queen's Counsel.

As Head of Chambers, Orlando West had already ordered champagne. A coup of this magnitude for Spinningfields had to be celebrated properly.

As Anderson retook his seat, a waiter opened the bottle and plonked it down before scurrying off to take more orders.

'Shall I do the honours?' asked Connor, without waiting for a reply. He splashed champagne into the empty flutes, eager to arrive at his own.

Just as he was about to pour, Anderson leaned across the table and whispered: 'Better not have any more. You did agree to schedule the billing records for my cross tomorrow.'

'What?' Had Connor heard right? 'You want me to go to chambers, *now*?' he slurred. 'To prepare a document for your cross-examination?'

'It needs to be done, Connor. And you are my junior,'

Anderson replied, hoping to avoid a confrontation. Anderson didn't want to embarrass his colleague but the case came first. 'You know I'd rather do it myself, but—'

'But he's needed here, old chap,' said West, having overheard some of the conversation.

An uncomfortable silence descended over the table.

Connor's eyes bored into Anderson. It was the humiliation of being led by someone of the same call. He needed every last ounce of strength to stop himself exploding, from letting rip at his chambers rival. But he couldn't afford to make an enemy of West's protégé. Connor's career was already in the doldrums.

Reluctantly, he got to his feet and, without another word, staggered towards the exit.

Sam Connor wasn't going to forget this in a hurry.

'A toast,' declared Orlando West.

They all raised a glass.

'To John Anderson.'

'John Anderson.'

CHAPTER 3

Lost in thought, Anderson sheltered from the winter downpour in the hotel entrance. Streetlights illuminated a deserted St Peter's Square. The trams had long since stopped for the day. Rods of northern rain crashed into the great dome of Manchester's central library, then bounced off and slid down the grey Portland stone pillars.

The taxi rank was empty. Five more minutes, then he'd make a dash for Albert Square and catch one from there. Anderson didn't want West or his father to realise he'd snuck off and come looking for him. John Anderson loathed these events. He'd never been good at having fun – relaxing. Boozy nights out with colleagues were to be avoided at all costs. Nothing made him more uncomfortable. Only the potential receipt of an award had made his attendance that evening unavoidable.

It was the job he loved. The courtroom. Working to a script. Somehow, in court, he always knew what to say. Within a framework, everything had its place. Everyone had a role. The awkward silences were always someone else's.

'Penny for them?' A female voice.

Anderson turned. That girl from chambers. Connor's pupil. He recognised her, but hadn't really noticed her before. She'd made the odd appearance at court during the trial to see her pupil-master, but Anderson had been focused on the job in hand. Now, seeing her properly for the first time, her figure silhouetted against the lights from the lobby, he could see how attractive she was. Beautiful, even. Hair groomed. Soft features and definitely a twinkle in her eye. Defensively, Anderson replied: 'I'm just waiting for a taxi.'

She returned an impish smile. Already in control. Holding out her hand: 'Tilly Henley-Smith.'

Reciprocating, Anderson enjoyed the physical contact. 'John Anderson.'

'I know who *you* are. Anyway, I thought barristers weren't supposed to shake hands?' she teased.

Without humour, Anderson replied: 'Only when robed.' No one knew the etiquette of the courtroom better than him.

What was she thinking? Why was she smiling? Was she flirting with him? In a moment the great prize-winning barrister had been replaced by a nervous adolescent.

'I live two minutes away, in Spinningfields. You can call a cab from mine if you like?'

He gave her a double take. She had some nerve – to make a pass at a senior member of chambers. The confidence that came from being well-bred. Almost arrogance. Anderson felt a rush of excitement. He looked down Quay Street towards Spinningfields, contemplating the offer. 'Must be handy for chambers?'

Still smiling: 'Yes. That's why I got it.'

An awkward silence – only for Anderson. She was enjoying her dominance.

A black cab pulled into the rank.

Relief. 'Here we go. That's me,' he said. 'Do you want a lift?'

Coyly: 'Yes, please.'

Holding the door open, Anderson caught sight of her lightly tanned calves as she stepped up and into the taxi. She slid across the back seat, leaving a place for her new friend.

Anderson climbed in and gave her a meaningless smile, unintentionally conveying anxiety. Filling the silence, he said: 'How's the pupillage going?'

'Very demanding of course, but fascinating.' Wasting no time, she swivelled round to face him as the cab made its thirty-second journey down the street. 'I'm so lucky that Connor's been on the Ahmed trial.' She paused. 'So I could see the great John Anderson in action.'

Deeply flattered, Anderson laughed off the praise.

'This is me. Just here, please.'

Suddenly disappointed, he said: 'Oh, of course. Right. See you tomorrow?'

'See you tomorrow, John Anderson.'

Anderson watched her take an extendable umbrella out of her handbag, then skip delicately around the puddles and into her building. She didn't look back.

Waking from the reverie of their brief encounter, Anderson said to the driver: 'M56, please. To Wilmslow.'

CHAPTER 4

5.45am. John Anderson was already up, thinking about the case. Tredwell was going in the box today, turning Queen's evidence in the case of the Crown versus Waqar Ahmed. Tredwell had been a subordinate and latest victim of local gangster Waqar Ahmed. His evidence could seal victory for the prosecution. The success of Ahmed's various illicit activities had catapulted him from small-time pimp to undisputed king of Manchester's Curry Mile in only a few short years. Those that knew him believed Ahmed to be untouchable.

Anderson had other ideas. Studying himself in the bathroom mirror, he thought of Tredwell's face – grotesquely disfigured. Anderson had no sympathy or compassion for the man, but considered the effect the sight would undoubtedly have on the jury. It could only help the prosecution. John Anderson was a cold-blooded prosecutor, almost a machine. He knew how to get a conviction better than any barrister in the north. His determination and uncompromising approach to his cases had earned him a great deal of respect over the years. He had plenty of acquaintances, but few real friends. Some of his contemporaries mistook his shyness for arrogance.

'John?' Mia was awake.

A conversation would be required, taking his mind off the day's work.

'You're up early, John. Are you staying for breakfast?'

She must want something.

Anderson left the en suite for the bedroom and started the excuses. 'I can't, Mia, I need to be in chambers before court. It's a big day.'

'Isn't it always?'

'You know I'm against that dodgy bastard, Hussain. I'm going to have my hands full.' He took his day collar out of a drawer and put it on the stud.

She watched him slip a link expertly through the cuff of his tunic shirt. A handsome man, especially in a suit. He never seemed to look quite right in anything else. 'Will has got his first match tonight. You will be there, won't you?'

Anderson took too long to reply: 'What time?'

'Six, on the school field.'

'I'll do my best.'

She waited for the usual caveat.

It came: 'But I can't control the judge. He decides when we rise.'

'Shut up, John. I know it's always by around 4.30.'

'Look, Mia, you know how important this case is for me – for all of us.'

'How could I not, John. It's the only thing you ever talk about. You need to do a good job… you've put in for silk… if you're going to get it before your fortieth birthday… blah, blah, blah.'

'We might run over. Like I said, I'll do what I can.' He took the opportunity to exit the bedroom. Paradoxically, a master at dealing with confrontations in the courtroom, he would do anything to avoid them at home.

'I need some money, John. There's nothing in the joint.'

'What for?' he replied, stopping at the door.

'Clothes. You want me to look like a silk's wife, don't you?'

He couldn't face another argument. 'Use the Visa.'

'Hi, Dad!' His boys had trapped him on the landing. Still in pyjamas, the argument had woken them. His eldest, Will, gazed adoringly up at him. 'Dad. It's my first game tonight. You will come, won't you?'

'I'll certainly do my best, Will.'

Will's head dropped slightly. He knew what *do my best* meant.

Angus, four years younger than his twelve-year-old brother, held up a red toy car – his best attempt at communication with his father at such short notice.

'Wow! I bet that's fast,' said Anderson, crouching down. Something made him pull the boys into an embrace. Motionless; for a brief, delicious moment, time stood still. 'I'm sorry I've been so busy at work lately, boys. Just a few more weeks, OK?'

'Yes, Dad,' replied Will, hugging tighter.

'Have a great day at school. I'll see you tonight.'

If only they understood. A month from now and he would be in silk, then things would be easier. More time with them. And Mia could buy whatever she wanted. That would take the pressure off; change everything.

Anderson shut the front door then cursed as he saw the smattering of snow that covered the path. Pulling up the bottoms of his pinstripe, he trudged towards his car and started scraping the frost off the windscreen. An old Volvo, he couldn't afford anything newer or more exciting. Not after the latest slashing of legal aid rates for criminal barristers. Mortgaged to

17

the hilt, he'd be lucky if they could hold on to the house. Silk would change everything. His only way out.

Despite only just making ends meet, the boys were at private school. His father – His Honour Judge Anderson QC – who had enjoyed a career at the Bar in more affluent times, paid the fees. It had given him an unspoken control over them. Anderson had wanted them to go to the local primary, but their grandfather, with Mia's support, had got his way. No Anderson had ever been to a state school. It was unthinkable.

John had learnt from an early age that it was much easier to adopt the opinions of those around him. That's why he was so good in court. Putting forward someone else's point of view. He didn't need an opinion of his own.

Oxford at eighteen had been his first taste of freedom. He joined the student union and began to think for himself about politics. One Saturday, his parents made a surprise visit, only to find him selling copies of *Socialist Worker* on campus. His father cut off his allowance, refusing to support a communist. Only a promise to join the Young Conservatives restored the equilibrium. That's the way it had always been; following a well-trodden path and living up to expectations. A career at the criminal Bar and, as the years rolled by, all energies became focused on winning trials. That made a difference, gave him meaning.

Anderson set off through Wilmslow on the road that snaked down the hill past open fields towards the M56 and Manchester. Driving on autopilot, his mind wandered. Thoughts of Mia. Was he happy, had he ever really been happy? Had she? He'd met her at university. From good stock, as his father would say; they got on well, had lots in common. They seemed the perfect match. His parents encouraged it. Mia happily swapped a History of Art degree for nappies, coffee mornings and hair appointments.

Uncomfortable with these reflections Anderson addressed his mind to safer things: the trial, his examination-in-chief.

Adrenalin was building, just how he liked it.

Out of nowhere, something on the road – a figure – crossed Anderson's path. A school boy.

No time to think, he braked hard. The rear end of his car sat up and lurched from side to side, skidding over the wet surface towards the youngster. Anderson's hands gripped the wheel so hard his knuckles turned white. Consequences flashed before his eyes: career, jail, to have killed someone.

Eventually he came to a stop with only inches to spare, collision avoided.

An embarrassed wave from the pedestrian as he reached the other side.

Cursing, then a deep breath from Anderson.

Hoots from the vehicles behind.

Anderson checked his mirrors, then, after a moment, went back on his way. It was over in the blink of an eye.

Already forgotten.

CHAPTER 5

Anderson parked his car behind chambers and walked into Spinningfields to buy a coffee. Rain had turned the dawn snowfall to slush, making the pavements treacherous. A quick browse through the local paper whilst waiting for his drink, just in case he got a mention, then on tiptoe back through the sludge to chambers.

'Morning, John,' came a choir of enthusiastic young voices – junior tenants and pupils, waiting around in reception for a late brief. Deep in thought, he hardly noticed them and headed straight to the clerks' room, the heart of chambers. In its usual state of organised chaos, phones were ringing, bookings being taken and fees agreed.

Senior clerk, Gary Arnold, stood almost to attention on seeing the rising star. 'Morning, Mr Anderson. Another new case just came in for you. A one-punch manslaughter.'

'Prosecuting?'

'Of course. God knows when you'll read it. Conference Thursday evening in chambers.'

'Don't you worry about that. I'll find the time,' Anderson replied.

'Good man.' Nothing pleased a barrister's clerk more than a workhorse. In that regard, Anderson had no equal. 'How are you getting on with Mr Hussain, sir?' Gary asked with a grin on his face.

'Badly, as ever. I can't stomach bent defence barristers. Gives us all a bad name.'

'Well, don't let him throw you off your game, sir. This is a very important year for you.'

Anderson nodded.

'Of course you do know, sir, if you take silk this year,' Gary whispered with a smile, 'you would be younger than your father and grandfather were when they took it?'

'That hadn't escaped me, Gary,' Anderson replied. The pressures of living up to the achievements of his family, alive and dead, had been with him since prep school.

'You've got a con at court with the CPS. They just want to go over a few things before you put Tredwell in the box.'

'Right, where's my junior?'

'He does have a name, sir,' Gary replied in a gentle rebuke. 'When all is said and done, he is a chambers colleague. We all know how much you expect when you are lead counsel, but try and go easy on him, especially in front of his pupil.'

'Of course,' Anderson replied, conscious that his single-minded approach to cases could sometimes appear insensitive.

Orlando West, Head of Chambers, appeared at the door of the clerks' room. 'Go easy on who? My protégé never goes easy on anyone! That's why he is the best junior in chambers.'

Anderson appreciated the compliment from his mentor. His old pupil-master was one of Manchester's top silks. Godfather to both of his children, Anderson worshipped the fifty-year-old QC. Another workaholic, chambers was West's life. People said he'd never married because he didn't want a family, that he hated kids, but many suspected he was gay, with a particular affection for John Anderson.

Anderson gave West a pat on the back as he left the clerks' room and joined his junior, Sam Connor, in the conference room, where he was studying a document. Connor's pupil, Tilly Henley-Smith, impeccably dressed in a black two-piece, was typing ferociously on a laptop. They both stopped what they were doing. 'Morning, John,' came the greeting, only from Tilly.

'How did you get on with the schedule, Sam?' Anderson asked.

'It's done.' Connor handed his leader a bundle of papers; columns with figures.

Ever the perfectionist, Anderson said: 'But you haven't numbered the rows?' He handed the pages back to Connor. 'It could be a problem, referring the jury to a particular entry.'

Connor's face turned red, a combination of anger and embarrassment.

Remembering Gary's words earlier, Anderson was anxious not to humiliate Connor, but winning the case was everything. 'I'm sorry, Sam, but you'll have to add a column. It's not a problem, just come across when it's done.'

'But what about the con with the CPS? How will it look if I'm not there?'

'Tilly can keep a note until you arrive if you like.' Anderson was already setting off for court with Tilly following obediently, hanging on his every word.

Sam Connor was fuming. He disliked Anderson. Rivals since pupillage, they were the same age, which had made Anderson's success even harder to come to terms with.

Anderson's parentage and powerful pupil-master had given him a head start; Connor had never caught up. And now, as the second biggest player in chambers, Anderson was leading him in the Crown versus Waqar Ahmed.

Connor had no choice but to live with it.

CHAPTER 6

Anderson and Tilly walked along the side of the huge 1960s concrete court building towards the entrance. Rectangular pillars spaced along its length with high glass windows between. Anderson knew every inch of it.

His opponent, Tahir Hussain, was already in the robing room – a grand name for a small, unimpressive, dusty space, crammed with boxes of paper exhibits from past cases, pink ribbons and rails of unclaimed coats. To Anderson it was home. He opened his wig tin, embossed in gold with the name B. Anderson – his late grandfather. He thought of his ancestry, of how he was living up to the expectations of his family, coping with the pressure of the big cases. It gave him more confidence, if any were needed, for the day to follow. 'I hope we're not going to have any more of your hackish defence antics today, Hussain?'

Sensing trouble, Tilly tried to blend into a coat stand.

Hussain was determined not to let this prosecutor get to him. In fact, he pitied him. Despite Anderson's success, he seemed lonely. Had an air of melancholy about him. 'What are you on about now, Anderson? I'm just doing my best to defend my client.'

'Do you have to try so hard?'

Hussain shook his head at his opponent. 'I can't believe you just asked that.'

'Don't you ever get fed up defending murderers and drug dealers?' Anderson loathed Hussain, convinced he suggested defences to his clients. It was the only explanation for his incredible win rate. 'All the lowlifes from Rusholme and Longsight do seem to come to you. I wonder why? Quite the Pied Piper of the Asian criminal community.'

'The reason all my clients are of Asian origin is because few white men in England want an Asian barrister and no Asian man in England trusts a white barrister. That says more about society than me, don't you think?'

Hussain had an answer for everything.

Several advocates came in and began unpacking their wigs and robes. Ignoring Hussain, they were all keen to congratulate Anderson on his award. Hussain on the other hand was an outsider, not a member of any chambers. A solicitor with a run-down office in Rusholme and a highly questionable reputation. Although there was no hard evidence of his dishonesty, there were plenty of rumours flying around various robing rooms about dodgy defences and backhanders.

The two men couldn't have been more different.

CHAPTER 7

Anderson strode along the concourse towards the courtroom. His entourage had grown: Connor's pupil, a CPS lawyer and the Officer In The Case. Last-minute instructions and titbits of information were fired at him.

Court Three, Manchester Crown Court, was heaving. A trial involving the criminal activities of a gangster like Waqar Ahmed always drew a crowd. A large, high-sided wooden dock surrounded by bulletproof glass dominated the back of the courtroom. Steps either side led down into the well of the court and counsels' rows, rising up again to the judge's bench. The jury box was situated to the judge's left so that they could see across to the witness box on the judge's right. A couple of journalists were still finding their seats in the press box towards the rear of the courtroom, next to the public gallery. Anderson took his place in counsels' row and began arranging his files. He noticed Hussain turn and nod to the defendant being brought up into the dock from the cells. A tall, overweight individual, Ahmed still had remnants of the physique needed to force a place in Manchester's villainous underworld. A white shirt and dark suit without a tie was the preferred uniform at court for organised criminals. Anderson had an uneasy feeling that there was more to their relationship than that of a lawyer and his lay client.

Anderson glanced around the courtroom. The buzz of anticipation.

'All rise!' called the usher as His Honour Judge Pounder came into court. He was a large man with a ruddy complexion to match his purple robes.

'Gentlemen, I decided to come in without the jury so that any outstanding issues relating to the next witness could be addressed.'

'I'm grateful, Your Honour,' Anderson replied before he was even on his feet. He had to take control before Hussain tried anything. 'As Your Honour is aware there are special measures in place for this witness.'

'Yes, screens I believe?'

'That's right. He will give his evidence behind a curtain which will be pulled partly around the witness box. Your Honour, counsel and the jury will be able to see him, but not the defendant, or the gallery.'

Hussain was on his feet. 'I object to the special measures, Your Honour.'

The judge sighed. 'This matter was argued at the pre-trial review, Mr Hussain. And I ruled against you, did I not?'

'I accept that, Your Honour, but I wish to renew my objection. The defendant knows what the witness looks like. His identity does not need protecting, and—'

'Mr Hussain,' interjected the judge.

Hussain ignored him. 'And the defendant is in a witness protection scheme, so could not be found, even if anybody wanted—'

'Mr Hussain!' barked the judge. 'You know the test. Will it improve the quality of his evidence if he can give it behind the screen? I have already ruled that it will. The jury are to be given the standard direction to counter any possibility of prejudice. Usher, bring them in, please.'

Hussain turned towards Ahmed in the dock as he retook his seat and shrugged.

Connor, clearly flustered, came into court and hurried to his seat carrying the amended documents for the jury. He passed them to his leader who gratefully acknowledged the supreme effort of being robed and ready before the witness was called.

The jury were brought in and after being given the appropriate direction about screens, Anderson announced: 'Your Honour, I call Martin Tredwell.'

Martin Tredwell cowered in the witness box behind a velvet curtain which screened off two sides. No hair on his head. Only skin, stretched and uneven as if chewing gum had been pulled across his face.

Anderson began: 'Would you give the Court your full name please?'

'Martin Tredwell.'

The answer was difficult to make out. Tredwell's horrific injuries prevented any facial animation.

'Would you be more comfortable seated, Mr Tredwell?' Anderson asked.

'No, I'll stand,' he replied, still defiant.

'Very well. I would like to start, if I may, with how you know the defendant, Waqar Ahmed?'

'I had a job at one of his takeaways. He used to come in at closing. About eleven.'

'Why would he come in?'

'Just to check on things. Collect the takings.'

'Where was that takeaway?'

'Wilmslow Road in Rusholme, on the Curry Mile.' Tredwell's voice became clearer as he got into his stride. 'The Kashmiri Palace.'

'And did you get to know Mr Ahmed?'

'Yes. He started asking me to run errands for him.'

'What sort of errands?'

'Collecting rent from tenants and shopkeepers, or dropping something off. Stuff like that.'

'So these people owed Ahmed money?'

'Maybe some did. Depends how you look at it.'

'How did you look at it?'

'I assumed it was protection money.'

Hussain shifted uneasily in his seat.

'Did people ever refuse to pay?'

'Yes.'

'What would happen?'

'I would tell Ahmed and he would send people round.'

'How do you know?'

'Stuff I would hear.'

'That's hearsay, Your Honour!' shouted Hussain.

The judge acknowledged the objection, but the damage was done.

'I see. How long did this go on for?'

'A few months, then he asked me to go places with him.'

'How would he get hold of you?'

'He'd come into the Palace or ring me on my mobile.'

'Could you please look at this, Mr Tredwell.' Anderson handed up his junior's schedule. 'We have copies for Your Honour and the jury.'

'This is most helpful, Mr Anderson,' said the judge, studying the document.

'Your Honour,' interrupted Hussain, before Anderson was able to openly credit Connor for his efforts. 'I would have been grateful for the courtesy of being shown this document before the witness was called.'

Anderson handed the document to his opponent.

'Well, now you have it, Mr Hussain,' said the judge. 'Now where were we, Mr Anderson?'

Anderson resumed: 'Can you just confirm that the two numbers at the top of the schedule are yours and Mr Ahmed's?'

'Yes.'

'We can see that throughout last year he would ring you several times a week?'

'Yes.'

'Thank you. If the jury would like to put that document behind divider four in their bundles. Now, where would Ahmed take you, Mr Tredwell?'

He held a cup of water up to his mouth and sipped. 'Bars, houses; he had some girls.'

'What do you mean? A brothel?'

'He had a couple. Sort of. Just houses where they lived. I would drive them out on jobs sometimes or deliver them to a house in Bradford.'

Anderson could see the jury were gripped by Tredwell's account.

'Just to be absolutely clear, were people paying them for sexual services?'

'Yes.'

'How do you know?'

'They gave me the money, after they'd been out on a job.'

'What did you do with it?'

'Gave it to the boss – Ahmed.'

'Mr Tredwell, so the jury understand, you have pleaded guilty to an offence of trafficking women within the UK for sexual exploitation.'

'Yes.'

'Do you know where the girls had come from?'

'All over. Mainly Asia and Eastern Europe.'

'How do you know?'

'They told me. I got to know them. I treated them right.'

'Were you involved in bringing them into this country?'

'No.'

'Do you know who was?'

'Waqar Ahmed. He had contacts abroad. They were his girls.'

'Did the women come willingly to the UK?'

'Hard to say. Some were confused. Some had been sold by their families. Some thought the UK would bring new opportunities. They were very young – eighteen, nineteen.'

Anderson moved on to count two – the GBH: 'I want to ask you about the events of August 23rd. The jury have already heard how police officers attended at the Kashmiri Palace. You were found in a very serious condition on the floor in a storage cupboard.'

Tredwell nodded.

'For the tape, Mr Tredwell.'

'Sorry – yes.'

'How did you come to be in that condition?'

'I got to know one of the girls – Naila.' His distorted face still managed to convey something of his emotions. 'I loved her and she loved me.'

'Did Waqar Ahmed know?'

31

'No. No one did. Not at first. I decided to speak to Ahmed about it. To say we wanted to live together. Get married.'

'Where did this conversation take place?'

'In the Kashmiri Palace. After we'd closed. He came in for the takings.'

'Was anyone else there?'

'Another worker called Bilal and a man that came in with Ahmed, don't know his name.'

'How did Ahmed react when you told him?'

'He lost it. Said I'd been helping myself to his property. That I was a thief. He told his pal to grip me.'

'And did he?'

'Yes.' Voice trembling. 'They both did.'

'Are you all right, Mr Tredwell?' asked his Honour. 'Would you like a break?'

Tredwell shook his head. 'It's fine. I can't cry. They melted my tear ducts.'   Anderson gave a moment's grace before continuing: 'What happened next?'

Tredwell held his head up for the first time and looked across at the jury. 'They pulled me through to the kitchen. Ahmed was screaming at me. Then he…' Tredwell's head dropped again. Quietly: 'He pushed my face into the fat fryer.'

The courtroom fell silent. Some of the jurors, deeply affected by Tredwell's account, were wiping away tears.

'I'll never forget the pain. Then I passed out.'

'Do you have much more, Mr Anderson?' asked the judge.

'No, Your Honour. Just a few more questions.'

'Very well. Then after that we'll have a break.'

It couldn't come soon enough for the defence.

'What is the next thing that you remember?'

'Coming round. I was out of it. In agony. I don't remember anything properly until the hospital.'

'Have you seen Bilal or the man with Mr Ahmed since it happened?'

'No.'

'Just in case the jury were wondering,' asked the judge, 'have they been traced?'

'No, Your Honour,' replied Anderson. 'The police have made every effort.'

'If they ever existed at all?' said Hussain.

His Honour ignored the comment. 'Mr Anderson, the jury could be told how the police came to be at the Kashmiri Palace, could they not?'

'Of course, Your Honour. They received an anonymous telephone call from a woman. The jury will hear a recording of that call. Giving the address where some illegal immigrants were staying and that they should go immediately to the Kashmiri Palace.'

Tredwell explained: 'It was Naila. She knew I was telling Ahmed about us. I told her if she hadn't heard from me by 2am she should leave the house – run.'

Hussain was on his feet in a flash. 'Your Honour, there is no evidence as to who made that call.'

'Yes, thank you, Mr Hussain,' was the judge's clipped response. He too found it impossible to disguise his dislike of defence counsel. He just wasn't one of *them*. Didn't have the polish of a traditional *English* advocate. 'Mr Anderson?' assisted the judge. 'Perhaps the 999 tape could be played to the jury now? Mr Tredwell may be able to identify the voice.'

The judge was definitely on Anderson's side. 'Yes, of course, Your Honour.' He handed the tape to the usher who put it in the machine. Within seconds the distressed voice of a young woman with an obviously Asian accent was captivating the courtroom in surround sound.

'Do you recognise that voice, Mr Tredwell?' asked Anderson.

The witness was distressed. Memories of another life. 'Yes, that was Naila.'

'Do you know where she is now?'

'No. I haven't seen or heard from her since that night. I don't know if she's alive or dead. Anyway, I wouldn't want her to see me like this.'

Anderson gave the witness a moment to compose himself. 'And finally, Mr Tredwell, your injuries? I know the jury can see them for themselves, but perhaps you could just list those that they can't?'

He nodded. 'I'm blind in my left eye and my sight's not great in my right. I can't smell. My hearing is badly affected too. I'm in constant pain. I just want to die – because of what that bastard did to me.'

'Let's be clear. Who?'

'Waqar Ahmed.'

Anderson remained on his feet long enough to let the final answer sink in.

The judge adjourned for lunch.

The prosecution team remained in the courtroom after the judge and jury had left to give Anderson pats on the back for his smooth examination of Tredwell. Connor reluctantly joined in, masking his jealousy – a skill mastered over many years.

34

Ahmed shouted across the courtroom: 'Oi, Hussain. I want to see you in the cells, now.'

Despite his embarrassment, Hussain acknowledged the order.

Anderson turned and had a good look at the man in the dock. Most striking of all were his deep-set eyes, radiating nothing but hate.

CHAPTER 8

Anderson joined Connor, Tilly and other members of chambers around one of the tables in the advocates' canteen. Tilly had saved him a seat, much to Connor's annoyance.

'John, couple of things I wanted to mention,' said Head of Chambers, Orlando West QC, across the table. 'One's a bit sensitive. In chambers, after court?' he asked with a wink.

'Of course,' Anderson agreed, remembering his commitment to Will's football match.

'And the other,' said West, raising his voice so everyone could hear, 'is that I've just got the Ted Harrison murder. Thought you might like the junior brief?'

Anderson didn't hesitate: 'I don't know what to say. Yes, please.'

Connor almost choked on his sandwich. He never ceased to be amazed by West's favouritism.

Drawing the rest of the table in with a knowing smile, West continued: 'We need to keep our future silks on the boil at Spinningfields Chambers.'

Anderson could feel Tilly's knee pushing against his. No doubt about it, she wanted him.

'I'll need a brief synopsis by morning,' said West. 'Got a con at eleven with the CPS. Don't worry, they know you're part heard.'

This time Anderson did hesitate, remembering his

commitment to Will. Then: 'No problem.' He glanced away to digest the betrayal. Trying to distract himself, he noticed Hussain sitting alone at another table, eating a packed lunch whilst engrossed in some notes, oblivious to the laughing and joking going on around him.

West's eyes followed Anderson's. 'You're not home yet, John. He might lack integrity, but he's not without ability.'

'I know,' Anderson replied.

CHAPTER 9

'All rise!' cried the usher.

His Honour Judge Pounder came into court.

Only Hussain remained on his feet. His nerves were fighting to show themselves. Understandable – a demanding client and a difficult cross-examination to conduct in front of a packed courtroom. All sympathies would lie with the witness. He took a deep breath and told himself that he was an advocate equal to the challenge. 'Mr Tredwell, firstly, I would like to offer my deepest sympathies.'

Tredwell gave an imperceptible nod, but wasn't fooled by Hussain's gesture; he knew not to let his guard down.

'And I make it clear that nothing I will suggest to you in my cross-examination seeks in any way to undermine the terrible injuries and the suffering which you have endured.'

Another nod.

'But I will speak plainly, Mr Tredwell.' A deep breath. 'You haven't told the truth to this jury, have you?'

'Yes, I have,' Tredwell replied, managing not to lose his cool.

'Let us assume for a moment that your account is true. The love of your life, who you say wanted to marry you, rang the police and gave them information which would inevitably start a chain of events that would culminate in your arrest for controlling prostitution.'

The witness considered the question. 'I've pleaded guilty to that offence.'

'We know, but that's not an answer to my question. Why would your fiancée want you to get caught?'

'She didn't. My safety was more important to her. She must have been worried that something had happened to me at the takeaway, when I told Ahmed about us.'

'Why didn't she tell the police that?'

'With the greatest of respect, Your Honour,' Anderson interjected, 'how can this witness answer as to what someone else was thinking during a telephone call at the making of which he was not present.'

'I agree, Mr Anderson.'

'Very well, I'll rephrase the question,' offered Hussain. 'Do you accept that there is nothing in that telephone call that makes any reference to you being in a relationship with the maker?'

'Yes.'

'It is equally consistent with the maker of the call giving information that would lead to your arrest?'

Anderson was up again. 'That is comment, Your Honour.'

Hussain asked another question before Anderson could slow him down: 'You see, none of the women from the house that made statements ever said anything about you being in a relationship with Naila.'

'That's because we kept it a secret. Too dangerous to tell anyone.'

'But they all remember you collecting money from them.'

'I've admitted to that.'

'None of them mention ever meeting or being aware of the defendant, Waqar Ahmed.'

'He kept his distance. That's what bosses do.'

'The only evidence that he is anything other than the legitimate owner of a takeaway called the Kashmiri Palace – is you.'

'I'm telling the truth!'

'You've made up Bilal, haven't you? No such person ever worked there.'

Tredwell shook his head.

'There are no employee records or any other documents to prove his existence.'

'Ahmed never kept records. All cash in hand.'

'I suggest that when the police arrested you at the Palace, you knew that you were off to prison for the large scale trafficking of prostitutes.'

Tredwell didn't bother to respond.

'So you decided to fit up my client?'

Again, Tredwell shook his head.

'Please answer the question, Mr Tredwell,' asked the judge. 'For the tape.'

'I didn't fit anyone up. I wasn't in any condition to be thinking like that when they found me.'

Hussain pressed on: 'You used the Palace as a base for your criminal activities – because you are a local gangster that can do what you like. Mr Ahmed paid you protection money because he was terrified of what you might do.'

Tredwell laughed at the suggestion. 'When did you think this up?'

'By pleading guilty and turning Queen's evidence against a co-defendant you knew it would keep you out of jail.'

'Rubbish.'

'Well, you did know turning QE would keep you out of jail. We can agree on that, can't we?'

'No promises were made.'

'But your lawyers must have advised you?'

'They said I had a chance of staying out. But that's not why I did it. It's for this,' he said, pointing at his face.

'My client has no idea how your injuries were sustained. A man in your line of business must have plenty of enemies, Mr Tredwell?'

'I don't know what you're talking about.'

'Whoever caused that also gave you the perfect foundation on which to blame my client and get yourself off the hook. Every cloud has a silver lining, does it not?'

'Mr Hussain!' exclaimed the judge. 'That really is a step too far.'

Without offering an apology, Hussain sat down.

Anderson got up to re-examine. It had to be good. The case hung in the balance.

Connor wanted his leader to make a mess of it, even if it meant losing the case. That was the depth of his jealousy and hatred of the man.

'Mr Tredwell, one thing on which the prosecution and defence agree is that you were given sums of money by the women. Monies they had earned for sexual services?'

'Yes.'

'Mr Hussain asserts that this was your criminal enterprise. Your operation. He also says people paid you protection money. So where is all the money?'

Tredwell understood the point. 'There isn't any.'

'Do you own a house?'

'I wish.'

'Where were you living when all this happened?'

'In a room above the Palace.'

'A room above the Palace.' Anderson glanced off to the jury. 'Do you own a car, Mr Tredwell?'

'No.'

'Do you have a bank or building society account of any sort?'

'No.'

'What do you own, Mr Tredwell?'

'Nothing.'

'Mr Anderson, have those enquiries been made by the Crown?' asked the judge.

'They have, Your Honour. Any evidence of wealth would have been disclosed to Mr Hussain. There's nothing. I have no further questions.'

'Yes, thank you,' replied the judge. 'Thank you, Mr Tredwell. Quite an ordeal for you I think. This Court is most grateful to you.'

'Your Honour,' said Anderson, now in full control of the trial. 'We now move on to the police interviews, which my junior, Mr Connor, will read to the jury.'

Connor begrudgingly got to his feet for the mundane task whilst his leader accepted the whispered congratulations of the rest of the team.

With a good closing speech Anderson felt sure he was home and dry.

CHAPTER 10

4.30pm. The judge rose. Anderson was shattered. The sustained adrenalin levels and nervous energy of a full day in court always took its toll on trial counsel.

Connor and Tilly followed Anderson out of the building on the short walk across Spinningfields back to chambers. He checked his watch. If he was going to make Will's football match he would have to leave *now*. But what about Orlando West? There was something West wanted to tell him. Maybe more good news? About his silk application? He couldn't let West down. He thought of Will standing there on the landing that morning. The sadness in his cherubic face, longing for attention. Anderson tried to block out the image. He was doing all this for them. To secure their future. 'Right, who wants a coffee before we go back to the ranch?' he asked, finally letting his appointment go.

'Not for me, I've got too much to do,' replied Connor, uninterested in anything vaguely social with his leader.

Tilly hesitated. 'Sorry, I've got to get off – if that's all right with you, Connor?'

'No problem,' replied her pupil-master, relieved that she had chosen to reject Anderson's offer. 'See you tomorrow, Tilly.'

Anderson hid his disappointment and headed off inside the coffee shop and ordered an Americano.

'Is that to go?' asked the barista.

'No, I'll have it here,' Anderson replied, catching sight of a discarded copy of the *Manchester Evening News* on one of the tables. He moved over to it and flicked through looking for a report on the case. Only a short column on page 16. Maybe tomorrow's reporting of Tredwell's evidence would do better, he thought. He retrieved his coffee and slumped wearily onto a sofa by the window, took out his iPhone and began to plough through the day's emails.

'I changed my mind.' Tilly dropped onto the seat beside him and bestowed an intimate smile.

Anderson could feel his heart beating. 'Great, what do you want?' he said, jumping up.

'Skinny chai tea latte, please.'

He watched her from the counter whilst he waited for the drink. A beautiful young woman, curves in all the right places. Clever too – hiding her disloyalty from Connor like that. Should he make a move on her? How? He wasn't good in personal situations. She would have to hand it to him on a plate.

He took her tea over.

'I thought you were superb in court today, John,' she began. 'I'm learning so much during this trial.'

'Pleased to hear it,' Anderson replied.

'I'd be so grateful for anything else you could teach me. Anything at all.' A rush of excitement – he was on the verge of suggesting they meet up later, after he'd seen West and done his synopsis. But what about Mia? Why was he even considering it? There had been problems for some time. They hadn't had sex for months. Or was it years? Deep down, he knew she didn't love him. Never had. Anderson's job and

44

parentage had just ticked the right boxes, nothing more.

Anderson craved a connection with someone and Tilly seemed prepared to fulfil that role. This was exactly what he needed. No one would ever know. 'Tilly, I've got to pop back to chambers for a bit, then perhaps we…'

Her eyes lit up. She leaned in to hear more.

Anderson could smell her perfume, glimpse her breasts nestled under her white blouse. Instinctively, he checked around himself for prying eyes. Something caught his attention, outside, across the road. Hussain, greeting a woman, probably his wife. And two young daughters. Hussain lifted one of them up onto his shoulders. All laughing. A happy family.

Hussain met Anderson's gaze, only for a split second, then they were away as Hussain steered them up the street.

Anderson suddenly felt a fool. Ridiculous. What was he doing? Thinking? He looked at his young companion, then stood up, knocking over the remains of his coffee in the process. 'I'm sorry, I've just remembered something,' he said. 'I've got to go. See you tomorrow,' he added on his way out.

Confused, Tilly had no time to react.

Outside in the cold winter air, Anderson felt a sense of relief. He took out his mobile and rang chambers: 'Gary, it's me. I've got an urgent appointment – a personal matter.'

'What about the Harrison papers? Mr West needs a synopsis.'

'Tell him not to worry. I'll be in at 5am. I'll have it done.'

Anderson found himself jogging to the car park, chastising himself for the time he'd wasted in the coffee shop. Lusting after a girl fifteen years his junior, when he had a wife and children waiting for him at home. What a bloody idiot he'd been lately. The whole silk thing had taken over his life. He'd lost his perspective. Maybe he'd take his foot off the gas, spend more time with the kids. Find a way to reach out to Mia. Maybe even fall in love.

He could still make it.

It wasn't too late. Anderson knew what he wanted – more than ever.

CHAPTER 11

Five Days Later

Detective Inspector Mark Taylor ran a team in the Force Major Incident Unit of Greater Manchester Police – murders. What he'd always wanted. A proper copper, investigating serious crime, not pushing a pen. And he was good at it. A quiet, unassuming man, he commanded respect and admiration from his colleagues. Always got the job done. He'd been summoned to the DCI's office – rarely a pleasant experience.

Unlike Taylor, Detective Chief Inspector Armstrong utilised a combination of condescension and insincere flattery to gain compliance from his subordinates.

With people skills like that, Taylor couldn't understand how he'd risen so high in the ranks. In fact, Armstrong was quite different towards his own superiors – an arse kisser.

Taylor knocked and waited for the customary, 'Come.'

'You wanted to see me, Chief?'

'Yes, come in, Mark. Take a seat.'

Using his first name? A bad sign, thought Taylor.

'How's the family?'

Even worse. 'I'm a bobby, Chief. Hardly see 'em.'

'Yes, well.' Armstrong didn't want to open up that sort of discussion. Far too intimate. 'Got a job for you. Death by dangerous.'

'Death by dangerous?' Taylor couldn't hide his outrage. 'In case you'd forgotten, Chief, I'm FMIT. We don't investigate driving offences.'

'I know, keep your hair on. This is a very serious case; two people died. A woman and a five-year-old girl.' Armstrong paused for effect. 'The suspect is a man called John Anderson. One of Manchester's most successful prosecution barristers.'

'Yeah, heard of 'im.'

'All very delicate, as you can imagine. We can't be seen to show any favouritism – quite the opposite. I want this wrapped up as quickly as possible.'

'But why me?'

'You were specifically requested by those in the corridors of power. Can't have any mistakes on this one – Anderson would be on it in a flash.'

'But I'm snowed under, Chief.'

'You should be flattered. You can have DC Waters for your leg work. That'll be all, Taylor.'

Taylor shut the door behind him and stood in the corridor, running a hand across his brow. When was he going to read the file? He checked his watch and sighed.

Another missed bath time.

CHAPTER 12

Mia opened the passenger door and handed Anderson his crutches. He manoeuvred his leg into position and hauled himself up. With her steadying hand he limped into the house. Felt good to be home.

Mia fussed around in the lounge, avoiding eye contact with her husband. 'I'll get you some water, then I've got to collect the boys.'

Anderson flopped onto a chair and watched her busying herself. He held out an arm as she passed. 'Mia?'

She ignored him.

'Mia. Please. Let's talk.'

'What about?'

'Everything.' Anderson's voice croaked. No one had told him anything yet. He was desperate for information about what happened. Who were they? How old? And he wanted to tell Mia that he was sorry. He'd been doing a lot of thinking in that hospital bed. Was it too late? Was he responsible for the deaths of two people? Could he live with that knowledge? Was that why he wanted to make it work with Mia? Fear of having to cope alone? He braced himself: 'Who were the people that died?'

Mia stopped and gave Anderson her full attention. 'One was a five-year-old girl. Molly Granger.'

Anderson winced, too much to bear.

'I thought you might know who the woman was?' She asked more as an accusation than a question.

'Why? What do you mean?' Anderson was confused.

'She was in *your* car.'

'What?' Anderson was stunned. 'Who told you that?'

'The police,' she replied. 'They wondered if I might know her.' A tear rolled down her cheek. 'I didn't.'

'What was her name?' Anderson demanded, unable to disguise his impatience.

'I can't remember.'

They held each other's gaze.

'John, I want you to move out.'

'What? Move out?'

'You can have a week or so to get back on your feet.'

'Mia, please!'

'I've already told the boys.'

'But I need you.' As the words came out he realised how rare it was for him to say it. To express his feelings in words.

'No, John. You didn't need me before the crash and you don't now.' She got up to go.

'I did,' Anderson protested. 'I just didn't know it,' he said, trying to get out of the chair. 'Mia, please?'

'It's too late. Why couldn't you have just gone to watch your son play football?' She was crying now. 'You'd rather have been with her. You bastard, John.' She left the room.

Her? Who did she mean? Tilly?

'Mia, wait, please!' By the time he was up she'd gone.

For the first time in his life he felt like sobbing. It was all too much to take in: Mia, the crash, his injuries. He balanced uncertainly on his good leg as he surveyed the room, appreciating it for the first time. The family home. Trying to

50

remember rolling around on the floor with the kids. Never seemed to be enough time. He tried to remember fun times with Mia. He couldn't. Not even in the early days. It had always been about money, material things. What she wanted.

He caught his reflection in the mirror above the fireplace. The first time he'd seen himself since the accident. A beard, with grey flecks in it. The left side of his face had a large rectangular bandage over it. He shuffled closer and rested one hand on the mantlepiece. With the other he slowly removed the bandage. Anderson gulped. A deep red scar snaked down the side of his face. The stitches gave it the appearance of a fishbone. It would serve as a reminder, a marker – not just to him but to everyone – of when his life had changed forever. He quickly covered it.

A knock on the front door. Anderson pulled himself together and hobbled into the hall. He was out of breath by the time he managed to open the door.

Orlando West. 'Hello, old chap.'

'Orlando! Come in.' West's visit couldn't have come at a better time. Just the lift he needed.

They made their way into the lounge.

'You look a lot better than when I last saw you,' said West.

'You came to the hospital? I didn't realise. I should've known you'd be there.'

'The whole of chambers has been really worried about you, John.'

Anderson took it all in.

'How's Mia coping?'

Anderson wasn't ready to tell him. Not yet. To announce her decision to separate would make it real. He shrugged.

'You know Mia.' Then he thought out loud: 'I think I need to get back to work as quickly as possible.' By way of explanation: 'I need the money.'

'First things first, old chap. You're recovering from a very serious accident. You need to take it easy for a while.'

'I need to read the papers in the Harrison murder.'

'All in good time,' West replied, chuckling at Anderson's enthusiasm.

'If only I'd gone back to chambers to collect the brief. And what was it you wanted to speak to me about?'

'Oh, I can't remember now. What do you remember about the accident?'

Anderson shook his head. 'Nothing. Just leaving court with Connor and his pupil.' He stopped. His heart beat faster. 'Orlando, do you know anything about the lady that died?'

They heard the front door opening. Will and Angus hurtled into the lounge and leapt onto their father. 'Daddy! Daddy!'

'Ouch! My leg.'

They both jumped off and apologised, devastated that they had caused their father more pain.

Anderson bit his lip. 'Boys, it's fine, come here,' he said, pulling the children to him. He held them tight, his eyes welling up. 'I'm sorry I didn't make the football match, Will. What happened?'

'We lost,' he replied. Then with more cheer: 'But I've got another game tonight! Can you come?'

Anderson smiled. 'I wouldn't miss it for the world. We'll be there, won't we, Angus?'

Both boys beamed.

West shot Mia a nervy smile.

Another knock at the door.

Mia showed two suited gents into the lounge.

Anderson thought he recognised them both.

The older man spoke: 'John Anderson, my name is Detective Inspector Taylor and this is DC Waters. I am arresting you for offences of causing death by dangerous driving. You do not have to say anything but it may harm your defence if you do not mention when questioned something which you later rely on in court. Anything you do say—'

'It's all right, gentlemen,' Anderson interrupted, once he was over the shock. 'I understand my rights.'

'I'm sure it's only routine,' West offered unconvincingly, more for the wider family's benefit. 'Where are you taking him, gentlemen?'

'Longsight police station, sir.' DI Taylor saw the distress on the children's faces. Sometimes he detested his job.

West quickly took control: 'Right, I'll have a solicitor there for the interview, John. I'll try and get Dewi Morgan.'

'Thanks, Orlando.' Anderson hugged his sons and kissed the tops of their heads. 'You might have to go to the match without me I'm afraid.'

They both nodded, understanding the solemnity of the moment.

Anderson thought he caught a flicker of empathy in Mia's face as the officers escorted him out to the squad car.

He'd never seen the criminal justice system from this side of the fence before.

An intense sense of foreboding took hold.

CHAPTER 13

Taylor took Anderson into the custody suite. After a few raised eyebrows the sergeant booked in the detainee.

'We're going to have to put you in a cell, Mr Anderson,' explained Taylor. 'Until we are ready for interview.'

Anderson said nothing.

'I'm sure it won't be long,' he added on sensing Anderson's apprehension. Taylor felt for the man. A few seconds of bad driving and his life was over. He'd seen it a hundred times before. Even if they survived the jail sentence, they never got over the guilt, especially when a child was involved. Still, Taylor had a job to do and he was sure Molly Granger's parents didn't see it like that.

The steel door clanged shut. Anderson stared blankly at the grey walls. He'd seen the inside of a cell as part of his training to be a recorder – a part-time circuit judge. But this was different. He sat down on the concrete bench and let his head fall into his hands, then flinched, having forgotten the injury to his face. Bereft, he tried to make sense of what was happening to his life. Was he being selfish? Two people had died. Was it his fault? Had he been rushing to get to Will's football match? With so much going on had he lost concentration? And who was his passenger?

The misery of his contemplation was broken by the sound of the hatch opening, and then the door.

He was joined in the cell by a short man with a ruddy face in a pinstriped suit, thrusting out a fat, nail-bitten hand. 'Dewi Morgan. Pleased to meet you. Big admirer of yours, you know.'

An encouraging start, thought Anderson.

A bloated-looking Welshman with a love of real ale, Morgan was also a highly respected solicitor, famed for his ruthless defence of his clients. He shot Anderson a mischievous smile. 'You've put a few of my clients behind bars over the years, I can tell you.'

'Well, let's see if you can keep this one out,' Anderson replied.

Morgan laughed. 'Right, down to business,' he said, taking out a pad and sitting down on the concrete bench. 'They've given me absolutely no pre-interview disclosure.'

'You're joking?'

'They're so paranoid about not appearing to do anything that could be seen as favouritism that they have gone completely the other way.'

Anderson shook his head in astonishment.

'Tell me everything you can remember of the accident?'

'I don't remember anything.'

'Nothing at all?'

'No.'

'Was drink involved?'

'No way. I'd never drink and drive.'

'On any medication?'

'No.'

'What's the last thing you remember?'

'Leaving court with my junior and his pupil. Stopping off for a coffee at Starbucks. That's about it.' Anderson didn't

55

see any point mentioning the flirting with Tilly. Was he already being economical with the truth? The realisation sent a shiver down his spine.

'Right, well. You'll have to go no comment.'

'No comment? I'm not doing that!' Anderson protested, appalled at the suggestion. 'How can I refuse to assist the police with their enquiries? I'm a prosecution barrister!'

'Right now, my friend, you're a suspect. If you tell them you can't remember anything, firstly they won't believe you, and secondly, when you do come up with a defence, a jury may wonder why you didn't mention it in interview.'

'A jury? You don't seriously think I'll be charged, do you?'

Morgan shrugged.

'I'm still not going no comment.'

'OK, it's your funeral.'

CHAPTER 14

'This interview is being tape recorded at Longsight police station. I am DI Taylor. I will be conducting the interview with my colleague, DC Waters. The suspect is John Anderson. Also present is his legal representative—'

'Dewi Morgan.'

The two officers sat facing Anderson across a table. No natural light in the small room. A dusty plastic palm tilted in the corner.

Anderson could feel his legs shaking.

'Thank you. The time now is 1903 hours. Mr Anderson, I need to remind you of the caution. You do not have to say anything but it may harm your defence if you fail to mention, when questioned, something which you later rely on in court. Anything you do say may be given in evidence.'

Things were moving so fast. Still adjusting, Anderson couldn't keep up.

'Right, Mr Anderson, you have been arrested in relation to a road traffic accident which happened on the westbound carriageway of the M56, just past junction five on the 24th of January this year. Do you have any recollection of that incident?'

'No, I don't.'

The officers exchanged glances. 'What is the last thing you remember, Mr Anderson?'

'Leaving court with my junior and his pupil. I was prosecuting in a trial – I'm a barrister. We went our separate ways. Then I went for a coffee at Starbucks on Quay Street.' Anderson thought hard about what he was going to say next. He swallowed. 'And that's it.' No mention of Tilly. What was the point of upsetting people, embarrassing her and himself? Causing further upset to Mia? Nothing happened anyway. But he'd just lied – on tape – during a police investigation. He'd just done an act *tending and intended to pervert the course of justice.*

No time to dwell on it, questions were coming thick and fast.

'What time was this?'

'About five.'

'Did you buy a drink?'

'Yes. An Americano.'

'That's a black coffee, right?'

'Yes.'

'Did you drink it?'

'Think so.'

'You don't sound very sure.'

Why hadn't Anderson thought about these things before? Furious with himself, he more than anyone knew how important it was to be decisive in a police interview. 'I drank most of it. I remember spilling some as I got up to leave. I was in a hurry.'

'In a hurry?' repeated DI Taylor, eyebrows raised. This was too easy. Not the usual cat and mouse when interviewing psychopathic murder suspects.

'Yes. To get to my son's football match. I wouldn't have driven like a madman or anything, you couldn't even if you wanted to at that time of day.' Anderson cringed as he heard himself say it. What was he thinking?

'You don't *know* how you drove – do you, Mr Anderson? I mean you say you can't remember?'

'Well – yes – but – I would never drive inappropriately for the conditions.'

'Oh, I see,' Taylor replied.

Anderson's solicitor decided to offer an explanation: 'It is perhaps worth noting at this juncture, officer, that Mr Anderson received a serious head injury during the accident. We of course consent to the police having access to those medical notes.'

'Is that what you are saying, Mr Anderson? You had a bump on the head which caused you to lose your memory?'

'He can't answer that, officer.' Morgan wasn't going to let Anderson get tied down to a defence at this stage. 'That is a matter for a medical expert.'

The interview continued in this vein for some time. The drip-feeding of information about the crash drove Anderson mad with curiosity. He couldn't wait any longer. 'Officer, I appreciate you are conducting this interview in your own way, but…' Anderson could hardly get the words out. 'I know a woman and a child died. No one has told me anything about them. Please, what happened?'

'I was just getting to that, Mr Anderson,' replied DI Taylor officiously. He wasn't going to let the suspect bully him, whoever he was. 'We have several eyewitnesses who describe your vehicle.' The officer glanced at his notes. 'A Volvo, registration BV52 EYS, drifting from the outside lane across the carriageway at speed and then colliding with another vehicle that had just entered the nearside lane from junction five.'

Anderson digested the information. He had no recollection of it at all. Had his brain erased the awful truth?

'The vehicle you collided with was driven by Mrs Granger. Her five-year-old daughter, Molly, was in the back. Had to cut her out of the vehicle. She died later in hospital from her injuries.'

Anderson wanted to blot out what he was hearing.

'Did you lose control of the vehicle in your hurry to get back?'

'No!'

'No you didn't, or no you can't remember?'

Dewi Morgan tried to rescue his client: 'Officer, Mr Anderson has already told you that he cannot remember the accident, but that he would never drive dangerously.'

'Your passenger was killed, Mr Anderson. A thirty-two-year-old woman, Heena Butt.' The officers waited for a reaction.

Anderson looked at his solicitor for some kind of explanation.

None came.

'Heena Butt?' repeated Anderson. 'I don't know that name. Who is…' He checked himself. 'Who *was* she?'

'We were hoping you could tell *us* that.'

'I'm sorry, I can't,' Anderson stuttered, struggling to take it all in. 'Do you have a photograph of her?'

Taylor nodded to DC Waters, who then removed an A4 brown envelope from a file and took out a photograph, which he then slid across the table towards Anderson.

Terrified at what or whom he might see, Anderson slowly cast his eyes down at the picture. Taken at the post-mortem, a lifeless body on a slab. The skull was impacted but he could make out the features of a woman. Asian, possibly Indian or Pakistani, with long brown hair. She'd been beautiful. Anderson gagged, then gave an involuntary sob. Was he really responsible for her death? He tried to compose himself. 'I don't recognise her, officer. I don't know this woman.'

'Mr Anderson, even if you can't remember the collision, surely you would remember how and when this woman came to be in your vehicle?'

'You would think so, officer, but I don't.'

'Do you often give complete strangers a lift in your car, Mr Anderson?'

All he could offer was: 'No, never.'

Taylor gathered up his notes. 'Right, that's all for now, Mr Anderson.'

'What, I can go?'

'For now, yes, but I'm sure we'll have some more questions for you when our collision investigator has completed his report.' Taylor checked his watch. 'I'm terminating this interview. The time now is 1933 hours.'

Anderson was relieved to feel the cold Manchester air nipping at his face as he balanced on the steps outside the police station. His solicitor wanted a quick debrief. 'You really don't remember, John?' he asked with the merest hint of a smile.

Anderson didn't hear him. Deep in thought – his old life; Mia, the children.

'John? Are you OK?'

'Yes, sorry, I was miles away.'

'You must be exhausted.' Morgan took Anderson by the arm and guided him towards the car park. 'I'll drive you home.' Morgan continued to moan about the police.

'Outrageous to pull you in like that, the day you get out of hospital.'

'Do you think it will go to trial, Dewi?' Anderson already knew the answer.

Morgan grimaced. 'It doesn't look good, does it?'

Anderson climbed into the passenger seat and tried to picture Heena Butt's face. Tried to remember if he knew her, or had seen her somewhere before. His head began to ache. He looked across at Morgan. 'We need to find out about that woman – Heena Butt. She must be the key to all this.'

'I'm not sure that's such a good idea, John. Might be better to let sleeping dogs lie.'

'What do you mean?' Anderson replied.

'We're both men of the world, John,' said Morgan, treading carefully with his client.

'Go on?'

'Well, acting on your instructions – which of course I do – you say you didn't know the deceased. If you met her that night and she was in your car…? What would a prosecution barrister think that meant?'

The penny dropped. 'You'd think I'd been kerb crawling.'

Morgan tiptoed on. 'And if you were distracted…'

Anderson shook his head in horror. 'You'd think I'd crashed the car because I was having sex with a prostitute whilst driving down the motorway?'

'As your lawyer, I have to tell you how it looks, don't I? What other explanation is there?'

Was this really happening? Was she a prostitute? Would he pay for sex? Could he be sure of anything? 'My DNA won't be inside her.'

'Maybe not. They haven't disclosed that yet, but it's not critical.'

Anderson was confused.

Morgan spelt it out: 'You know – blow job.'

Anderson looked skywards. 'Please, just get me home.'

CHAPTER 15

Anderson managed to dress himself and limp downstairs, using only one crutch.

The kitchen was standard for an upwardly mobile Wilmslow family. Large farmhouse table and chairs, central island with matching units, presided over by an Aga.

Mia ignored his entrance and continued to lay the table. Then: 'Did you find out who she was then?'

'Her name was Heena Butt. That's all I know.'

Mia scoffed, tossing a box of Shreddies onto the table.

They stood in silence, until the sound of her mobile phone vibrating on the worktop. She glanced over, then picked it up and slid it into her pocket.

'Who was it?'

'I want you out, John. Tonight. No, today.'

'What? Mia, please!'

She picked up a cereal bowl and threw it at the wall. Pieces cascaded over the table. 'Get out! Get the fuck out!'

Confused, Anderson got to his feet and moved clumsily into the hall. 'I don't understand, Mia! Why can't we talk about it? All of a sudden our marriage is over?'

Mia passed him and opened the front door. Will and Angus came running down the stairs almost crashing into him. He silently touched their heads as he left. Standing on the garden path, he took out his mobile and called a cab. He caught sight of the boys staring out of the window, tears rolling down their cheeks. Anderson forced a smile.

Inside, he was falling apart.

CHAPTER 16

The Grangers lived in Wythenshawe on a vast, sprawling housing estate just off the M56.

DI Taylor had no problem finding the address; he knew the estate well, having walked this beat as a wooden top. 'You wait in the car,' he said to DC Waters. 'Don't want to come back and find it sitting on bricks.'

Waters was glad to leave this job to Taylor. He pulled a Greggs sausage roll out of his pocket and took a bite.

'Bloody hell, Waters,' said Taylor, getting out. 'That's going to leave bits everywhere.'

'What? I'll be careful. Oh, and chuck us the keys, gov – for the heater. It's bloody freezing.'

Tutting, Taylor obliged then walked towards the house, a terraced two-up two-down.

Mr Granger opened the front door.

'Hello, Mr Granger? I'm DI Taylor.'

Tom Granger gave a languid nod. For him, life was moving in slow motion – still in shock.

Taylor followed him into the lounge where Mrs Granger was standing, wringing her hands. The house was immaculate. Taylor wasn't surprised; he'd come to learn how grief affected people differently. Some just gave up and dropped everything, while others clung to old routines like vacuuming, ironing or washing themselves. Trinkets on the mantelpiece and photos on the walls told a story of family life.

Taylor could see at a glance that these were hard working, modest people.

Mrs Granger's eyes followed Taylor's to a photograph of Molly on the coffee table. 'We only had the one. IVF. We got lucky,' she said, without any hint of irony.

'Beautiful little girl,' said Taylor, and he meant it. 'I'm sorry for your loss.'

She ignored the condolences. Must have heard them a thousand times. Nothing would bring Molly back. 'Would you like to see her room?'

Taylor was about to explain that it wasn't necessary, but Mr Granger got there first: 'Sandra, he don't need to.' Mr Granger turned to Taylor and said, 'She's been dusting it all morning, ever since you phoned to say you were coming.'

Taylor's heart went out to them. Showing a policeman her dead daughter's room was a way of keeping her memory alive, paying tribute. 'Yes, I would like to see it. Thank you.'

Taylor followed Sandra up the stairs to Molly's bedroom. Everything left just as it was, perhaps a little tidier. Crayon drawings on the walls. 'She was an artist?' Taylor observed.

Sandra didn't reply, but surveyed the scene as if seeing the room anew, noticing everything, marvelling at the wonder of it. Then: 'I don't know what I'll do now.'

Taylor had no answer. Seeing Molly's room hit home. He felt guilty for turning his nose up at the case. Whether their little girl was murdered by a serial killer or killed by a dangerous driver, the loss to the Grangers was the same. Either way, they wanted justice.

Back downstairs, without waiting for an invitation,

Taylor sat on the sofa. His hosts no longer considered such formalities.

Taylor began: 'I'm afraid I'm going to have to take witness statements from you, about what happened. I hope it won't take too long.'

'Is it true he fell asleep at the wheel?' asked Mr Granger.

'Who told you that?'

'A police officer at the hospital.'

'We don't know at this stage, still investigating.' Taylor was annoyed. He didn't like witnesses being given information before they had made statements. There was a way of doing things. He thought the Grangers should have been asked to give an account at the hospital but according to the officer in charge of the investigation at that time, they were in no fit state.

Mr Granger explained to Taylor that the impact was the first he knew about it, and that he was briefly knocked unconscious, remembering little after the crash. Sandra Granger had a much clearer recollection: 'I could see it, in my mirror, just gliding towards us.' The agony of remembering the critical moment was etched on her face. 'Then it smashed into the side, at the back. Molly were in 'er booster. After we stopped, I were afraid to turn around. Scared of what I might find. And when I did…' She broke down, sobbing into her husband's shoulder.

Taylor changed the subject: 'Just one more question, then we're done. Could you see into the vehicle at all, before the impact?'

'Yes. There were an Asian lady in the passenger seat and a man in t' driving seat. He were asleep?'

'You actually saw that?'

'Oh aye.'

'How could you tell he was asleep as opposed to being, say, unconscious?'

She paused. Eventually she answered: 'Cos he woke up. Saw him open his eyes, just before he hit us, but it were too late.'

'Are you absolutely sure, Mrs Granger?'

'Oh, I'm sure,' she replied.

Taylor now had an eyewitness to the crucial moments before impact.

A cast iron case.

CHAPTER 17

'Mr Anderson!' Gary got out of his chair. 'Welcome back, sir. We didn't expect to see you so soon.'

Anderson had missed the buzz of the clerks' room. 'You know me, Gary,' he replied, forcing a smile. 'Work is the best remedy and all that.'

'Yes of course, sir.' Gary didn't sound so sure.

'Where's the trial up to?'

'What trial?'

'You know what trial, Gary. The Crown versus Waqar Ahmed.'

'Mr Connor is in the middle of cross-examining the defendant.'

Connor appeared in the doorway, having heard the conversation. 'Glad to see you're up and about.'

Anderson noted the indifference in Connor's voice. 'Thanks for holding the fort, Sam. You finish the cross and I'll work on my speech.'

Connor stared at Anderson, open-mouthed. 'Are you insane?'

'Don't be silly, sir,' said Gary, trying to defuse the situation. 'You're in no fit state.'

'You're off the case, Anderson,' said Connor. 'Don't you get it? The CPS don't want you anywhere near that courtroom.' Connor had never spoken to his colleague like this before. Anderson was on the way down and Connor was enjoying being one of the first to make him see it.

Anderson looked to his clerk for an explanation.

'You understand, sir. They can't hand the defence any ammunition that Hussain could use against the prosecution. Once this driving business has been put to bed, everything will be fine.'

Anderson said nothing as he took in the further implications of the crash.

'Don't worry, sir. Things will soon be back to normal.'

Connor allowed a smirk to creep across his face.

Why hadn't Anderson ever realised the depth of this man's hatred of him? He was supposed to be perceptive – a canny advocate – yet he'd missed the glaringly obvious.

'Mr West is in his room, sir. I know he'd like to see you. Been very worried about you,' said Gary, trying to break up the meeting.

'OK,' Anderson replied with an air of resignation. 'Good luck then,' he said to Connor. Anderson had surprised himself. He'd never normally be so gracious to someone who had just crossed him. Had the accident mellowed him a little?

Connor ignored the gesture and disappeared off down the corridor.

On seeing Anderson stagger into his room, West got to his feet with the spring of a much younger man. 'John! Sit down. How did it go last night?'

'Not great,' he sighed, taking the weight off his stronger leg. 'It doesn't look good.'

'Chin up, old chap. You will get through this.'

'Mia's thrown me out.'

'I know, she phoned me. She's worried about you.'

'Really? I'm not so sure.'

'Why don't you borrow my flat, just until you get back on your feet? I'm always at the house in Alderley Edge. I never use it. You'll be near chambers. No need for taxis.'

'That's really kind but I need to be near the kids.'

'Mia will drive them over. So will I. We'll sort something out. Don't worry.'

In truth, Anderson couldn't afford to rent anywhere. 'Thanks, Orlando. I don't know what I'd do without you.'

'Forget it,' he said, tossing Anderson a set of keys. 'Go to the flat, get plenty of rest and come back when you're ready for action.'

Orlando West's pep talk lifted Anderson's spirits. He was going to fight this. John Anderson wasn't beaten that easily. He had friends. People who cared. He put his head through the doorway of the clerks' room on his way out. 'I'm off, Gary. Going to recharge the batteries for a few days.'

'That's the ticket, sir,' he shouted above the noise from his chair at the other end of the room.

'Where are the papers in the Harrison murder?' he asked, casting an eye over the sea of briefs wrapped in pink ribbon on the table next to Gary. 'Might as well use the time productively.'

Silence suddenly descended over the room.

The junior clerks all turned towards Gary, then to Anderson.

Gary got up and gently ushered him out to save his blushes. 'I'm sorry, sir. The CPS can't use you whilst the driving matter is hanging over you.'

'I haven't been charged yet!'

'I know, but the Harrison trial is a long way off. If you

were charged, you'd have to return it. They need to be guaranteed continuity of counsel. It's out of my hands, sir.'

'So who got the brief?'

Gary paused before replying: 'Sam Connor.'

Another crushing blow. He tried not to let it show. 'Oh well, at least we kept the brief in chambers.'

There was nothing else to say as Gary watched the former star hobbling towards the exit.

Anderson stopped and turned. 'Gary, my wig and gown, and my laptop? Are they in chambers?'

'Er, no, sir,' Gary replied, embarrassed that he had already cut the service to one of his former stars. 'They must still be in the robing room. I'll send someone over for them right away.'

'No, it's OK, I'll get them.' He limped out of chambers; once a sanctuary, now just a reminder of his downfall.

Anderson stopped outside Starbucks and tried to peek through the window, hampered by the condensation, reminding passersby of the warmth inside. He examined the baristas behind the counter, the customers, and then the sofa where he'd been with Tilly. Hoping for something to jog his memory, he went in and ordered an Americano, then sat by the window, racking his brain for a trace of something. Anything.

Nothing.

He looked out at the Mancunian morning passing him by. Commuters scurrying past. All with somewhere to be. A job to do. How he envied them. Head throbbing, after an hour of trying to remember, Anderson could take no more. He pulled himself up and set off for the crown court.

He acknowledged a few nervous 'how-are-yous' from the

security guards at the entrance. No one quite knew what to say. Should they mention the crash? Was it a taboo subject? News certainly travelled fast in the Manchester legal world.

To his relief, the robing room was empty: everyone was already in court. Anderson put his things into his red bag and made his way back down to the concourse on the first floor. He stopped to rest outside Court Three. What was going on in there? He longed to know how the cross-examination of Ahmed was going. He wanted to see justice done, above all else, even if it meant Connor getting the glory.

'Hello, John.' It was Tilly. Impeccably dressed, as always, in a pinstriped two-piece under her gown. Nails perfectly manicured on slender hands. A few rogue blond locks poked out from under her new white wig, softening her formal attire.

Anderson clocked the shocked expression at the state of his face, so quickly rummaged for something to say as a diversion: 'Hello, running late?' He immediately realised how it sounded – a poor attempt at a joke.

She saw it as a dig. Anderson wasn't even in the case anymore. In fact he'd nearly derailed it. 'How are you feeling?' she asked.

'So so,' he replied, putting up the usual barriers when anything vaguely personal was to be discussed. 'I'm on police bail.' He considered asking if the police had been in touch but decided against it.

'No one's asked me for a statement yet.'

He was grateful for the unprompted disclosure. Then he worried that she'd worked out he hadn't mentioned her being in Starbucks in interview.

She studied his face. 'Who was the woman that died?'

What a question from a pupil he hardly knew. She had a boldness that hadn't existed before. Or at least, that he'd never noticed. The power had shifted.

Now that she was completely out of reach, he found her even more attractive. 'I don't know.'

She didn't seem surprised by the answer. 'They are saying your career is hanging in the balance.'

Anderson thought he caught a flicker of excitement in her eyes. The rush of adrenalin at being the one to tell him how bad things were. He didn't respond.

'Good luck, John Anderson. You'll need it.' She gave him a deliberately pitiful smile then disappeared into Court Three.

Was that it? Gone already? Just like that? She used to hang on his every word. Everyone did. Now he was nothing. A nobody.

Anderson hobbled over to the door and held it open a few inches. No one could see him. The wooden, high-sided dock at the back of court blocked any view of the entrance. He could hear the buzz of the courtroom. For the first time in his career, it felt foreign to him. Now he was an outsider, on the wrong side of the law.

Connor was coming to the end of his cross-examination of the defendant. 'Mr Ahmed, not only were you trafficking women for prostitution, you were running a protection racket?'

Anderson cringed – two questions in one.

Ahmed didn't answer.

The judge helped Connor out. 'Mr Ahmed, were you trafficking women for prostitution?'

'No I wasn't, Your Honour.'

Connor tried to regain control of the cross-examination, hiding his embarrassment. 'Were you running a protection racket?'

'No I wasn't. Where's your evidence?'

A question – Connor was thrown – lacking the sharpness of mind to bat it away.

The judge came to the rescue again: 'It is prosecution counsel's task to ask the questions, Mr Ahmed, not to answer them.'

Ahmed wasn't going to let it go. 'But where are the records? There'd be books, ledgers, wouldn't there, Mr Connor? I couldn't have known the police were coming to arrest me. Did they find anything? The jury should be told.'

The judge peeked over his glasses at Connor as if to say: what have you started?

Connor made the mistake of ploughing on with his questions.

Ahmed took advantage: 'Why are you ignoring the question, Mr Connor? Don't you want the jury to know that nothing was found?'

Prosecution counsel had completely lost control of the defendant. He cut it short and sat down with Ahmed riding high. A total disaster.

Hussain hardly re-examined. Why ruin a great finish for the defence?

Connor didn't have the courtroom presence to prosecute a case like this. Anderson wondered what the rest of his cross had been like.

The jangle of keys signalled that the prison officer was leading the defendant from the witness box back into the dock. As he was about to take his seat, Ahmed looked down and caught Anderson peeping through the door below. They held each other's gaze for a split second. Ahmed's mouth widened into a demonic grin, then he winked. Despite his predicament, it was he who held the power. Was it the power of knowing something that Anderson didn't?

Anderson jolted, felt a shiver. He shut the door, almost falling back.

Did Ahmed have something to do with the crash?

CHAPTER 18

Anderson took refuge in West's flat, glad of the opportunity to hide away from the world. He couldn't get Waqar Ahmed's face out of his mind.

He eyed up West's drinks tray then checked his watch – only eleven o'clock. What the hell? He poured himself a large brandy, gulped it down, then another.

Why couldn't he remember?

Now he wanted to forget.

6pm. The buzzer woke him. Someone at the door. He picked himself up, straightened his tie and peeked through the spyhole. A man clutching a holdall. Anderson opened the door.

'Evening, sir. Aces couriers.' He handed over a bag. 'From a Mrs Anderson.'

Anderson thanked him and went to shut the door.

'Payment on delivery, sir. £28, please?'

He had just enough to cover it. He retreated back inside to examine the contents. Maybe there was a letter, something to give him hope? Only clothes and the clean dressings the hospital had given him. If he'd been in any doubt before, he knew now that the separation was final.

He turned on his iPad and listlessly began to google a few words. His own name brought up previous cases and a few newspaper reports of the accident – his job and being released on police bail. Then he tried Heena Butt. No match.

In despair, he poured himself another drink, making a mental note that he would need to buy his friend another bottle. He took out his mobile and dialled home. 'Hi, Will, it's me – Dad.'

'Hi, Dad. I miss you.'

A choked reply: 'I miss you too. How's Angus?'

'Fine. When are we going to see you?'

'Soon. I'll speak to your mum. We'll arrange something, OK?'

'OK. Love you, Dad.'

'Love you too. Will?'

Will had already hung up. Anderson poured another drink.

Then another.

CHAPTER 19

The next few days passed in much the same way. A haze of booze, a few painful meetings at the flat with his boys and unfocused searches for a defence. At least he could limp around unaided and he was getting used to leaving his facial scar uncovered, but the more time went on, the weaker he felt mentally. The thought of going back into the courtroom terrified him.

Anderson only ever went out to buy drink and the odd ready meal from the Waitrose on Bridge Street, fast becoming a familiar figure, shuffling across Spinningfields with a plastic bag full of clunking bottles. The subject of much discussion, he'd become a morality tale about how quickly one can fall from grace in the legal profession. Of the cruel unpredictability of life.

Only alcohol could numb the pain of his humiliation.

He'd heard nothing from chambers for two weeks. Desperate for money, it had finally dawned that chambers didn't want him back until the case was over – his name cleared. If he wanted a brief, he would have to call Gary and demand one.

The nudge he needed came when the cashpoint would only dispense £10. Out of food and, more importantly, brandy, he staggered back to the flat with a few meagre supplies and made the decision to ring in. 'Hello, Gary, it's me.'

A pause. Then: 'You sound different. How are you, sir?'

'I'm fine. Any cheques?'

''Fraid not, sir.'

'Well, I'm back now. Raring to go.'

'OK, sir, I'll bear that in mind.'

Anderson was irritated by the lukewarm response. He'd spent seventeen years giving everything for this chambers. 'I don't think you understand, Gary. I need a brief. Now. Anything.'

After a deafening silence: 'All right, sir, I've got a return. A sentence in a burg at Crown Square. Defending.'

'Burglary?'

'You did say anything.'

Anderson swallowed his pride. 'Yes, thanks. Can you get one of the lads to send the brief round to West's flat?'

'Of course, sir,' Gary replied.

'Oh and Gary, what happened in Ahmed?'

'Not guilty, sir.'

'Oh no! And Tredwell?'

'Bender.'

'Suspended sentence? So both walked. Shit, poor Connor.'

'I wouldn't worry about him, sir. The CPS are blaming *you*.'

Anderson's head couldn't accommodate any more bad news.

His life had been destroyed and yet Waqar Ahmed was now a free man. Anderson raged at the injustice.

He reached for his glass and gulped down the contents.

CHAPTER 20

The comforting damp of recent rain hung in the air.

He'd noticed her hours ago. So clean and innocent. Following at a distance from bar to club. He worried she was cold in that slinky little dress. So much bare flesh.

Laughing with friends. Celebrating her eighteenth birthday.

He wanted her so badly. He would give her something to remember, forever.

It had been far too long. Years. Desperate to hold a woman in his arms. See the terror on her face. Have a bond that would last a lifetime.

At last, goodbyes from her friends. Only two of them left now, stumbling across Spinningfields. Flicking their hair, giggling, arm in arm.

He hid in the shadows of a doorway as they passed. So close he could almost smell her, but for the odour of roasting doners wafting out of the takeaways on Deansgate. He put his hand in his coat pocket and felt the knife, waiting to do its work. He pulled it out, lifted his top and pressed the blade against his stomach. Drawing it upwards, he left a dripping red line. He grinned. A marker to help remember this night.

A taxi pulled up. Only one got in. Not her. It was meant to be.

Time to meet her destiny.

CHAPTER 21

Defence advocate, Tahir Hussain, woke up after another hard night, lying there in the dark, remembering all the heartache. Reliving every moment, each one worse than the last. He went into the bathroom and splashed his face. There were good days and bad days. Today was definitely going to be one of the latter. A feeling of emptiness, of hopelessness, overwhelmed him. Why had his family been chosen? They never saw it coming. Hussain's life had been predictable, happy, until then. Encouraged to study hard by his immigrant parents, he'd exceeded all their expectations. First a degree, then qualifying as a solicitor. After twenty years of hard graft in small firms around south Manchester, he set up his own office. Everything had been going so well, until the recession hit. That was the beginning. When their luck changed.

His wife, Safa, came up behind and put her arms around his waist. How would he have got through this without her? He loved her so much. He thanked Allah that he could still feel love. He'd known it since the day they met. Made for each other. This was their biggest test. He turned to face her, like a lost child, wide-eyed and frightened. He ran his finger over the gold braiding on her sari, draped over her shoulder. Worn with such pride. A Muslim woman born in Manchester, Hussain's wife often chose to wear traditionally

Hindu garments. She'd always had a mind of her own.

She hugged Hussain. 'Come on, Taz, you should be pleased, Ahmed was acquitted. You won.'

He was unable to shake the melancholy: 'Nothing seems to matter any more.'

She understood.

'I can't face it today. Dealing with all the psychos.'

'Do you mean the criminals or the lawyers?' she asked, trying to raise a smile.

He forced one. 'Both.'

She hugged him again. 'One day at a time.'

CHAPTER 22

Despite his nerves, Anderson's physical improvement was such that he was able to walk into Manchester Crown Court with some purpose. The security guards fixed on his scar as he negotiated the metal detector. By the time he reached the door to the robing room his heart was pounding. He stopped outside and listened to the familiar clattering of wig tins and the chattering of advocates. A deep breath, then into the lion's den.

A sudden cessation of all noise. Everyone stared at Anderson, his scar. They offered nothing, even barristers from his own chambers. Anderson wasn't welcome.

How could they have turned on him so quickly? He hadn't even been charged, let alone convicted. Or was it that they'd never really liked him? Just waiting for an excuse to reveal their true feelings?

Then a voice from the other end of the room. 'Anderson!'

His heart soared, but he couldn't see who it was. Someone pushing his way to the front, against the wall of silence. 'How are you? Great to have you back.' A hand reached out to take Anderson's.

No! Not him. Not Tahir Hussain, of all people. Anderson avoided eye contact, then shrunk away. Was it because he didn't trust the man? No, he knew the reason: years of conditioning, learnt from his father, to shun 'non-

85

establishment' figures at the Bar. Instilled in him from an early age. Only at that moment was Anderson aware of it, of his prejudices. He saw the disappointment in Hussain's eyes. The feeling of rejection. Anderson had turned away from the only person who had been prepared to reach out with the hand of friendship, despite all their history in court.

He felt sick to the stomach.

Hussain recovered swiftly and said more quietly, 'Welcome back,' before adjusting his wig and exiting the room.

Anderson's eyes followed him. He wished he could turn the clock back thirty seconds; he would have hugged Hussain, but it was too late, the moment had passed. Anderson unpacked his wig and gown, noticing a few surreptitious grins. He knew what they were thinking – Anderson ostracised, Hussain his only friend; how the mighty had fallen.

Hugh Coleman, a newly qualified barrister, put his head around the door. 'Anyone defending a burg called Simpson?' he called out, unaware of what had gone before.

'Yes, I am,' Anderson replied.

Coleman's surprise at the seniority of his opponent triggered muted laughter around the room.

Anderson took the opportunity to usher Coleman out.

'We're first on,' said Coleman. 'Got everything you need?'

'Apart from a copy of his antecedents?'

'No problem.' Coleman rifled through his brief and pulled out a copy of the defendant's previous convictions. 'Here you go.'

Anderson thanked his opponent and set off for the cells.

It wasn't until he saw the cell visiting room that he realised how long it had been since he'd defended anyone – years. It had become unfamiliar to him.

A twenty-something heroin addict with a yellow pallor sloped into the room, handcuffed at the front. The prison officer took off the cuffs and left the defendant alone with his barrister.

'Kyle Simpson? I'm defending you today. My name is John Anderson.'

Simpson was immediately unimpressed. 'Where's the barrister I had last time?'

'I'm sorry, he's tied up in another matter,' replied Anderson, looking at the name of instructed counsel on the brief – a far more junior member of chambers.

'So, what am I lookin' at?' Simpson asked, getting straight to the point.

'Well, it's a domestic burglary, at night whilst the occupiers were in bed, so there are quite a few aggravating features. And you've got a previous conviction for the same thing, but you pleaded guilty so you'll get a third off.' Anderson paused to show he was giving the question a great deal of consideration. 'Ball park, about eighteen months, maybe a bit more.'

Simpson nodded, apparently satisfied with the answer. 'I'll serve half, less my remand time. I'll be out in six months.' Kyle Simpson was a career criminal. He had no problem paying the price for his crime, as long as it was legal and fair.

'What about all the jewellery?' Anderson asked. 'If we could assist in its recovery that might bring the sentence down a bit.'

'It's gone. Sold it to buy brown.'

'OK. Why this particular house?'

'Between us, I like easy targets. Gnomes in the garden – had to be old people.'

Anderson made a mental note not to mention that to the judge. 'Have you done anything to address your drug problem whilst on remand?'

Bored of the questions, Simpson replied: 'Just keep it as short as you can.' 'OK, I'll see you after.'

Counsels' rows were full of advocates waiting to get on. Her Honour Judge Kent had a full list, mainly pleas and sentences.

The usher called on Simpson's case. The elegant, businesslike judge was already on the bench. Simpson was led up the steps into the dock.

Anderson looked around him at the familiar faces. He noticed his colleagues in a way that he hadn't a few weeks ago. His confidence was shot to pieces – worrying about his impending performance in a poxy burglary sentence that would pay less than £100, even before chambers took its cut.

Coleman opened the case with an effortless fluency that surprised Anderson. He'd forgotten how competitive the Bar was at the bottom end, how good one had to be to survive. The young prosecutor read out well-chosen extracts from the victim impact statement to the Court.

Her Honour Judge Kent harrumphed on hearing the details.

Coleman finished by confirming that the judge had a copy of Simpson's previous convictions.

Anderson got to his feet. 'There is no pre-sentence report, Your Honour. The defendant is realistic. He expects a custodial sentence, the only issue is length.'

The judge nodded. Anderson tried to read the judge's expression. Did she know about the crash? Was she against Anderson? She'd always been very kind to him in the past, respectful even.

The judge remained poker-faced.

'Your Honour, the defendant pleaded guilty at the first opportunity and is extremely remorseful…' Anderson soon got into the flow. Felt good to be back in the courtroom. 'If I can refer Your Honour to the sentencing guidelines…' Anderson was building to the main thrust of his submission. 'Taking into account the guilty plea, it is my submission that the appropriate sentence is not more than eighteen months' imprisonment.'

The judge stared at him. Was she thinking about the submission? Impressed by it? No, Anderson's instincts told him otherwise. He looked across at Coleman, whose eyes were trying to tell him something, but what?

Other counsel could smell blood – Anderson's.

'Mr Anderson,' said the judge in a tone that indicated her disappointment. 'The defendant has two previous convictions for dwelling-house burglaries.' Anderson   felt faint. How could he have missed that?

'The *minimum* sentence is three years' imprisonment. The statute allows a maximum discount of twenty per cent for a guilty plea on a three-strike burglary. I am prohibited, in law, from imposing anything less than twenty-eight months.'

Shaken, Anderson tried to repair the damage: 'Of course, Your Honour. I do apologise. I can only argue for a sentence of twenty-eight—'

'Hang on, Your Honour!' Simpson was on his feet in the

dock. 'My barrister told me eighteen months. That ain't right, that.'

Humiliated, Anderson could say and do nothing.

'Sit down, Mr Simpson,' ordered the judge. 'I'm not interested in what was discussed between you and your counsel. My discretion is fettered by law. It's as simple as that.' She proceeded to sentence the defendant to twenty-eight months' imprisonment.

Simpson continued to protest as he was taken down.

Anderson had created a sense of injustice in his client that was entirely unfounded – all because he hadn't read the brief properly – and within hours, if not minutes, the whole of the Manchester Bar would know it. Head bowed, he left the courtroom, still reeling from the indignity of his error.

'I'm sorry, John.' Coleman was waiting outside court. 'I should have said in opening that he was a three-striker.'

Anderson shook his head. 'No, Hugh. It was obvious. You assumed I'd notice it in the antecedents. It was my fault.' It had been a long time since Anderson had made a mistake like that in court, if ever. His focus just hadn't been there. Pulling his gown tight around him for protection, he began the long walk to the cells.

Simpson ranted and raved at Anderson for half an hour, getting vast reserves of anger out of his system. He couldn't comprehend that Anderson's mistake had no effect on the sentence, the judge having imposed the minimum term allowed. It also meant a complaint to the Bar Standards Board wouldn't have any real legs, to Anderson's relief. He was in enough trouble as it was.

Once Simpson had finished his tirade of abuse, Anderson headed back to the flat. He couldn't face chambers after the morning's events. Everyone would know.

The bottle of brandy on the lounge table caught his eye. He guzzled a large tumbler full, then poured another. His phone rang.

'John?' Dewi Morgan. 'They want to re-interview, at two o'clock. You ready?'

His heart sank. 'As I'll ever be.'

CHAPTER 23

Anderson took the train to Levenshulme, the nearest stop to Longsight police station. The car was a write-off and so he hadn't driven since the crash. It was the first time in his life he'd been late for anything. The simple knack of planning his day, of being ready, was lost. He turned up the collar of his coat to protect his ears from the biting wind.

Dewi Morgan was already waiting outside for his client, shifting his weight from one leg to the other to keep warm. On seeing Anderson he gave an enthusiastic wave. 'Good to see you, John – how've you been?' He gripped Anderson's hand. 'Have you been drinking?'

'No, of course not. Just a glass with lunch,' Anderson replied, shamefaced.

'Jesus Christ, man, you smell like a brewery. If you're not fit to be interviewed…?' Anderson's decline since Morgan had last seen him was shocking. He was beginning to look haggard. A far cry from the confident barrister he'd seen strutting around the courts of the northwest.

'I'm fine. I need to get on with this, Dewi.'

Morgan was not convinced.

'The waiting has been unbearable.'

Morgan softened a little and took some mints out of his pocket. 'Here, have a few of these.'

Anderson stuffed a couple in his mouth, deeply conscious of his lawyer studying him.

'Have you been able to remember anything else, John?'

He shook his head.

CHAPTER 24

The same officers, Taylor and Waters, conducted the interview. Their approach began in a slightly more conciliatory manner than before. Anderson prayed that it meant they weren't going to charge him.

Once the caution had been given, the interview got underway with DI Taylor taking the lead. 'Mr Anderson, our expert collision investigator, PC Henbury, has finished his report into the crash, as a result of which we need to ask you some more questions.'

'Of course. I want to assist the investigation in any way I can.'

'Thank you, Mr Anderson. Some good news. We've had the toxicology back. Clear for drink and drugs.'

'That's no surprise, officer,' Dewi replied. 'Mr Anderson told you he hadn't been drinking and he doesn't do drugs. He's a highly respected prosecution barrister, as I'm sure you know?'

Unmoved by Morgan's interjection, Taylor continued: 'I can also tell you that the impact damage and post-impact movement of the vehicles have been examined. PC Henbury has been able to calculate the speed, or at least a range, of your vehicle prior to impact.'

Anderson waited with baited breath.

'In short, even at the top end of the range, you were not exceeding the speed limit.'

He let out an audible sigh. 'That's good to know, officer. Thank you.'

Dewi Morgan couldn't resist adding: 'So the assertion you made last time – that my client was in a rush to get home – appears to be unfounded?'

Taylor ignored the comment. He had something better. 'Having looked at the marks left on the road, the angle and distance travelled by you, as described by witnesses, prior to the collision, it appears that you fell asleep at the wheel.'

'What? That's not possible!'

'Well, that is the opinion of our collision investigator and also Professor Hawthorn, an expert on sleep.'

'But I wasn't tired!'

'But you can't remember the crash, can you? And Professor Hawthorn says that is typical of sleepy drivers. You went into a micro-sleep shortly before the impact. That's why you can't remember it.'

Anderson was becoming more agitated. 'This is ridiculous. It was five in the afternoon.'

'Actually, Professor Hawthorn says that statistically, twilight is the most common time of day for people to nod off whilst driving. Don't ask me why.'

'I wouldn't just drop off like that. I had a passenger for God's sake! Someone I could only have just met. Why can't I remember her – who she was?'

Morgan put a hand on Anderson's arm, to avoid the tape picking up the advice. He shot him a look that told him to calm down. Morgan then tried a more measured approach. 'The passenger, whom Mr Anderson did not know, she could have been distracting him, attacking him, robbing him? It could have been a carjacking?'

Anderson nodded his agreement. There must be another explanation, he thought. Not sleep. Not at that time of day.

The officers grinned at Morgan. Normally such a clever lawyer, offering such a ludicrous explanation. 'We can rule out that possibility, Mr Morgan.'

'How so?' he asked.

'The movement of Mr Anderson's vehicle prior to impact. It was in an arc. And no skid marks were left on the road. If he'd been awake there would have been some evasive action – steering or braking. Professor Hawthorn says the movement of the vehicle in this way is typical of the driver having a micro-sleep.'

Anderson and his lawyer stared at the officers, open-mouthed. They had no answer. No explanation.

Taylor wasn't done. 'We also have an eyewitness account. Sandra Granger was in the vehicle you impacted with. She saw you wake just before the impact.'

'What?' Anderson was dumbstruck. 'She must be mistaken.'

'Mr Anderson, we know you were prosecuting in a very difficult trial. It must have been exhausting?'

'Yes it was, but that's my job. It's always exhausting.'

'Were you working late the night before?'

'Until tennish, but that's not unusual.'

'Then an awards ceremony, I think?' asked Taylor, looking at his notes.

'I was in bed by one.'

'And what time did you get up the next morning?'

'About six. I know what you're getting at, but that's my daily routine. Like it or not, that's the life of a criminal barrister,' Anderson protested. 'Officer, I didn't feel tired.'

'But you say you don't remember the car journey? Any of it?'

Anderson could see how it looked.

'Do you, Mr Anderson?' Taylor persisted.

Anderson shook his head.

'For the benefit of the tape?'

Eventually, Anderson answered: 'No, I don't. But I know my own character. I would *not* have driven that tired.'

'I see,' said Taylor, making it obvious by his tone that he didn't believe a word. 'Can I just clarify, Mr Anderson? What is the last thing that you *do* remember? I think you said during the last interview…' He checked his notes again. 'It was leaving the coffee shop?'

'Yes… that's right.' Anderson's response sounded uncertain. What was coming next?

'You see, we have a statement from a colleague of yours.'

Anderson's heart sank – Hussain? One minute he was greeting Anderson like a long-lost friend, the next he was stabbing him in the back.

'He said he walked past Starbucks.' Reading from the statement: 'At about ten to five.' Taylor paused for a reaction from the suspect.

Anderson could hear his heart thumping.

Taylor scrutinised the detainee. 'And he saw you through the window with… Tilly Henley-Smith?'

Anderson could feel the sweat break out on his forehead. Why had he lied before? What an idiot he'd been. Now he was stuck with it.

Taylor continued reading out loud: 'He was drinking and chatting…' Taylor looked up at Anderson and waited for a response.

97

Anderson tried to think how best to deal with it. Confess his earlier white lie? He couldn't, it would look awful: a self-confessed liar. 'Oh yes, Tilly. That's right. It must have slipped my mind. We did have a coffee.'

'So you remember that now, do you?' asked DI Taylor.

'Yes, I do.'

'When did you first remember her being there?'

Anderson's stomach was churning. Could they see that he was panicking? 'Now, when you mentioned it.' Another lie.

'Quite a busy afternoon for you wasn't it, as far as young women were concerned?'

'What's that supposed to mean, officer?' interjected Morgan. 'If you've got something to say, just say it.'

Taylor ignored Morgan's rebuke. 'Maybe you can remember Miss Butt as well?'

'No, I can't. I'm sorry.'

'You do see how it might come across to a jury, don't you, Mr Anderson?'

'What do you mean?' he replied, understanding exactly where the officer was going.

'As soon as a witness turns up – someone whose character is beyond reproach – says he saw you with a woman, you accept it, because you have to. Because you remember everything. Are you being selective, Mr Anderson? Selecting what you can remember?'

Anderson couldn't take any more. He put his head in his hands.

'Would you like a break, Mr Anderson? Time to consult with your solicitor?' Maybe he was about to confess all, thought Taylor.

Anderson shook his head. 'I can't explain it, officer. Something has gone on here that we don't know about. Please, you've got to find out what happened!'

'Like what?' Taylor replied, unable to hide his cynicism.

'I don't know. That's your job. Waqar Ahmed, the man I was prosecuting when this happened would be a good start. Maybe he set me up?'

'Set you up?' repeated Taylor.

Waters couldn't help but laugh. 'You fell asleep, Mr Anderson. He wasn't even in the car.'

Anderson gave up on the interview. A complete disaster. 'That's it. I'm not answering any more questions. I've told you all I can. From now on I'm going no comment.'

Taylor wasn't surprised by the suspect's change of tack, but it was too late. They had him. 'Don't worry, I think we're done here. This interview is being terminated. The time now is 1436 hours.'

Anderson was taken to the custody suite with his solicitor in tow.

'John Anderson, I am charging you with causing the deaths of Heena Butt and Molly Granger by your dangerous driving.'

The hairs on the back of his neck stood up.

This was going to be the most important trial of his life.

CHAPTER 25

Anderson caught the train out to Wilmslow. He missed Mia; not just for a shoulder to cry on, he wanted another chance. Desperate to cling on to his old life in some way. Salvage something. Maybe he could go with her to collect the kids from school, surprise them.

'Jesus! You look like shit, John!' Mia exclaimed on opening the door.

'It's been a tough few weeks.'

Mia wasn't interested in prolonging his visit. It took a great deal of negotiation just to be invited inside. They stood in the kitchen exchanging pleasantries, almost as strangers. She rejected his suggestion of collecting the children. 'Let's just stick to the pre-arranged visits. You can't just turn up like this.'

Mia's open hostility towards him over the last few weeks had been replaced by indifference. She seemed distant. Even the prospect of his conviction didn't seem to concern her. How did she think he was going to pay the mortgage from a jail cell?

'Mia, I promise you I don't know who that woman was. I have never been unfaithful to you. You know me. Let's talk about this.'

'John, I don't want to talk about it. Just go, will you?'

He couldn't understand how things had changed so

quickly. She'd never really given him a chance to try and explain. He brooded over it during the walk back to the station. Was he missing something? Had something else happened?

He cut through the woods on Lindow Common and stopped. Something made him turn around. He listened. Only the distant mooing of a cow. A curious sensation. That someone was watching him. Was he losing his mind on top of everything else?

CHAPTER 26

6pm. Anderson went to the Alchemist Bar in Spinningfields to meet Dewi Morgan and Orlando West, who had arranged a crisis meeting to discuss the next stage. Anderson was buoyed by the thought that at least West cared about him.

The bar was full of suits – the after-court crowd. Anderson realised his Head of Chambers had chosen this place as a public statement: he was standing by his barrister. He was a good friend.

'John, some great news! Gary said there are a couple of cheques in your pigeon hole, for cases you did months ago, apparently.'

For once Anderson was grateful that the CPS took forever to pay for work done. 'Orlando, before we start, I would just like to say...' Anderson hesitated before making his big request. 'I can't think of a better friend or a better barrister in England than you. Will you represent me in this matter?'

West gave his friend a warm smile and patted his shoulder. 'I'm flattered, John. I want to more than anything, but I can't.' West sighed. 'I thought you might ask, so I rang the Bar Council. They told me not to. Said it was inappropriate, as your old pupil-master, head of chambers, godfather to your children, etc... the relationship is too close.'

Anderson's head dropped. 'Of course. That makes sense.'

'But I'm happy to be a character witness?'

Anderson accepted the offer. That was something, at least. He put aside his disappointment and launched into a list of tasks for Dewi Morgan, starting with an investigation into Heena Butt. He could see that West and Morgan were observing him as if he were mad – totally disconnected from his analysis of the case. 'What?' he asked. 'What is it?'

West went first: 'Obviously we haven't seen any papers yet, but the prosecution case sounds compelling. Dewi has explained what the reconstruction expert says, and the eyewitness. There's no defence to falling asleep at the wheel, is there?'

'But what about my passenger? I've no idea how she came to be there, or who she was.'

'I understand that,' West replied. 'But that seems to me to be something of a red herring.'

'And as I've said,' added Morgan, 'if we poke around too much in that area, it could be very embarrassing for you. And for Mia and the boys.'

Anderson felt betrayed. 'You got me here to talk me into pleading guilty?' He made to get up.

West gestured for him to sit back down. 'Look, John. This isn't easy for me. To tell it how it is. I'm your friend. You know you will only get full credit if you plead guilty at the prelim.'

Anderson fixed his eyes on West. 'Orlando, two dead. This is at least four years, even on a guilty plea.'

'I know, but it's six after a trial.'

'I can't plead guilty. Not just because Strangeways is full of people I put in there, but because I need answers. And what about my career?' It hurt Anderson that West could give up on it so easily, after all the years they'd spent nurturing it.

'You're a clever bloke, John. You can turn your hand to anything.' He patted Anderson's arm. 'But I understand. As long as you appreciate what you're getting into?'

'I do,' Anderson replied.

'All right then. I just don't want this to turn into a media circus. Promise me you'll think about it properly, John? Objectively?'

Anderson agreed to the request.

Once the meeting had broken up he walked across to chambers to collect his cheques. Still shell-shocked from the conversation, reality began to dawn. Maybe he should plead guilty? Face facts. Get it over with. One thing was for sure, whatever the plea, he needed a barrister to defend him. He wanted someone he knew. Someone with whom he could talk things through properly.

Chambers was quiet. The clerks' room was empty. He collected his cheques and had a quick look down the corridor. A light was on in one of the rooms: Connor, working at his desk. Anderson felt bad about the way their relationship had deteriorated. He'd known him a long time, since Bar School. Although Connor wasn't the best advocate in the world, he was thorough and always gave one hundred per cent. Anderson wanted to make amends. 'Hi, Sam, burning the midnight oil I see?'

Without looking up: 'What do you want?'

'Sam, I'm sorry we haven't always seen eye to eye. I just want you to know that I'm sorry if I've ever offended you. I consider you a friend.'

Connor didn't respond.

'Sam, I was wondering. I need a top barrister to defend me. Would you consider it?'

Connor held Anderson's gaze now. 'I'm sorry, I can't.'

'Why not?'

'I wouldn't be able to remain objective.' Connor paused a moment before adding: 'I dislike you too much.' He stared Anderson right in the eye, then turned his attention back to his brief.

Anderson was crestfallen.

He made his way back to the flat and drank himself into oblivion.

CHAPTER 27

Solicitors' firm, Hussain & Co., in the heart of the Curry Mile, Rusholme, shared a building with a textile wholesalers. Hussain occupied the ground floor, consisting of a tiny reception area with a few mismatched desks and a conference room. Based outside the city centre, away from the larger firms, he was a community lawyer through and through.

The office felt icy cold. They were trying to reduce costs to adjust to the huge cuts in fees for legal aid work. Heating was one of the first luxuries to be hit.

Hussain greeted his only employee, Adey Tuur. Still with her coat on to keep warm, she was already at her desk. Adey, in Somali, meant fair-skinned. Tall and slender, with a swanlike neck and light brown skin, her soft features and grace of movement were incongruous with her unruly afro. Bristling with attitude, she had no idea of her effect on the opposite sex. What would Hussain have done without her over the last year? She had kept the practice together. Adey had watched him falling apart, but without passing comment and without complaint had taken it upon herself to deal with the daily bureaucracy that was required to run a solicitor's office, on top of all her own case preparation.

'I've just made some coffee,' Adey offered, getting up to pour her boss a cup.

Hussain didn't answer, already engrossed in the pile of post on his desk.

Adey's long delicate fingers placed the drink on his desk in the only free space amongst the piles of letters and papers. 'Have you seen it? Full article on page ten.'

'Seen what?' muttered Hussain, hardly registering the question.

She tossed a copy of the *Manchester Evening News* onto his lap. 'They've charged John Anderson – death by dangerous.'

Hussain read the headline and sat back in his chair. He shook his head. 'Poor man.'

'What do you care? I thought he always treated you like a piece of shit?'

'He does – did,' replied Hussain with a half-smile at the clarity of her language. 'But he is a truly great advocate.' He opened the paper. 'Fell asleep at the wheel? No, I don't believe it. Not John Anderson.'

'Do you know something that I don't?' Adey asked.

'No, I just mean he's too organised to let something like that happen.' Suddenly concerned: 'Why, do you?'

'No.' She sat back down at her desk, on the other side of the room. After a few minutes she broke the silence. 'I know what you're thinking.' Adey had come to know how Hussain's legal brain worked better than anyone.

'What?' Hussain replied without looking up.

'Waqar Ahmed had something to do with it?'

'No, of course not!' He paused. 'All right, maybe.' Another pause. 'He's certainly vindictive enough, but do you think he's got the expertise to set someone up like that?'

'Yes, possibly. He's one sick bastard, but he's also clever. Manipulative.'

Hussain agreed. 'The moment I heard about the crash I had a bad feeling about it.'

'Well,' said Adey, 'if Ahmed did set Anderson up, it worked. He's destroyed his career and got himself acquitted.'

'I know – that's what worries me. We'd never have won it with Anderson still on the case. Ahmed knew that.' Hussain got up and started pacing the office.

Adey could see how it was going to eat away at Hussain. It didn't surprise her that he was so concerned about a barrister who had shown Hussain only disrespect.

Hussain stopped pacing. 'Maybe I should ask him?'

'Who, Ahmed?'

'Why not?'

Adey considered the suggestion. 'But what if he admits it? You're not currently acting for him in any matter, so—'

'So it wouldn't be privileged.'

'As a witness to his confession you'd have to tell the police. You'd have to give evidence at the trial.'

'Yes.'

'Forget about it, Tahir. I'm sure he had nothing to do with it.'

But Tahir Hussain couldn't forget about it.

CHAPTER 28

Anderson walked down Deansgate towards San Carlo's, his father's favourite Italian restaurant. He hugged the sides of the shopfronts to avoid the worst of the beating rain. He'd decided to wear a suit, even though he hadn't been in court that day, or any other day recently, but it was lunchtime and Anderson wanted to look as if he had somewhere to be. A sick feeling gnawed at his stomach. Nothing new when seeing his parents. Even as a boy, when they came to visit him at boarding school.

His father, His Honour Judge Howard Anderson, had arranged to meet up, obviously to discuss the case. Anderson was dreading it. Even he was surprised at how long it had taken his mother and father to make contact after the crash. Hardly the actions of doting parents. Too painful, he pushed such thoughts to the back of his mind and stopped to check out the window of Kendals department store. Anything to delay the inevitable. The *Manchester Evening News* stand caught his eye. It was on the front page. He bought a copy and opened it to read the full article. A photo of Molly Granger jumped out at him. A beautiful little girl. Smiling, happy. Was he really responsible for her death? He prayed to God that he wasn't.

Bracing himself, Anderson crossed the road and into the restaurant.

His coat was soaked. As he waited for the maître d' to relieve him of it he saw his parents sitting in one of the booths. Someone else was with them.

He handed over his coat and joined them at the table.

His father stood up to shake his hand. 'Hello, John.'

Anderson's mother, Mary, shot her husband a nervous glance, seeking his permission to give her son a hug, which she did. Forty years of marriage to a cold, insensitive man had taken its toll on Mary Anderson. Dulled by decades of anti-depressants, she did nothing without Howard Anderson's approval. A tired, washed-out face on a petite frame. Mary had learnt how to blend into the background to survive the endless rounds of social engagements. Always careful not to irritate her husband, or steal his thunder. Now she had no energy left for anything. Disguising her unhappy marriage for so long had drained her of all zest. She noticed her son's scar, then put a hand over her mouth. 'Oh, John.'

The third member of the group, Stephen, John's older brother, gave Anderson a lopsided, knowing grin, in the way brothers do. They had never been close. Childhood arguments and fights had developed into jealous rivalry, particularly on Stephen's part. He'd watched his little brother's successful legal career for over a decade, whilst as a Tory MP he'd languished in opposition.

John took a seat and reached for the bottle of Chardonnay nestled in an ice bucket and poured himself a large glass, then braced himself for the inquisition to follow.

His father was never one to mince his words. 'What the bloody hell were you thinking, John? Who was she?'

Mary placed a hand on her husband's sleeve and said, 'At least let him have a drink first, Howard.'

Howard flinched and moved his arm away.

'I don't know who she was,' Anderson replied, tired of giving people the same answer. 'Anyway, how did you know about her?'

'Don't be so naive, John,' barked his father. 'I'm a judge. I hear things. In fact everyone is talking about it. I don't know how I'll get through it. It's all very embarrassing.'

'How *you'll* get through it?' replied Anderson, aghast at his father's selfishness. 'Dad, I could lose everything.'

Howard Anderson didn't see the irony in his remark. He leaned forward and spoke with less volume: 'Look, John…'

Anderson could tell that a mandate was about to be issued.

'I know it's the preliminary hearing tomorrow. You're going to have to plead guilty.'

'What?' John reeled back in horror. 'Not you as well, Dad! That would mean prison. And the end of my career.' His eyes searched his father's face for a reaction.

The judge sat motionless, waiting for his words to sink in.

Anderson felt the same emptiness he had the day his father told him he had to go away to school. Remembering how Howard Anderson hadn't been able to connect with his eight-year-old son's fear and anxiety at the news. He'd almost wallowed in it.

Still that lost little boy, Anderson pleaded: 'Dad, don't you want to know my side of things?'

Howard was unmoved.

Anderson turned to Stephen for support, who remained tight-lipped.

Howard Anderson continued to abandon his son:

111

'Stephen's career is at a crucial time, to say nothing of my own hopes for elevation to the High Court Bench. He's now a junior minister. There's talk of a place in the cabinet.'

'Still just talk at the moment,' Stephen stressed, delighted to confirm the truth of their father's account of his recent success.

Howard said, 'We need to bury this with as little fuss as possible.'

John was stunned. To his own family he was nothing more than an embarrassing news story. For the first time in his life he felt rage rising up in him. Unadulterated anger at his predicament, his parents, everyone. 'I don't think I can do that, Dad. I could've been set up. I need to know.'

His father still wasn't interested. Raising his voice: 'You can and you will, John.' Then he added, 'I've heard about the split by the way. I'm prepared to carry on paying the school fees, but not if you persist in this madness.'

Anderson sat back in his seat, then slowly shook his head. 'Oh, Dad, was that your ace card? Were you saving it until the end? To use my children's education to blackmail me?'

Howard Anderson avoided eye contact. Even he could see the indignity in it.

The waiter broke the silence. 'Are you ready to order?'

John replied, 'I've just lost my appetite. My coat please.' He stood up, but before leaving, said to his father, 'You break my heart.'

John Anderson walked out of the restaurant without looking back.

CHAPTER 29

John Anderson spent the rest of the afternoon perched on a bar stool in Mulligan's, off Deansgate, downing pints of bitter and thinking about his plea, and his family. He was deeply wounded by their abandonment of him, their selfishness, yet strangely, he was not surprised.

He noticed the other drinkers, men sitting alone in darkened corners. His own loneliness had rendered them visible to him. A common bond. Lost souls with nothing better to do than drink away the daylight hours. Everything had changed. The foundations on which he thought he had built a life were turning out to be an illusion. Not just his parents, everyone. His thoughts turned to Will and Angus. He missed them so much. Remembering all the wasted weekends spent working in chambers. And now it could be too late to make amends. To be the father he should have been. He took out his phone and rang Mia. Maybe she'd allow an impromptu visit. No answer. He left a garbled voicemail.

Obsessively, his mind inevitably returned to the crash. He couldn't have been that tired, could he? To fall asleep with a passenger he didn't know? It didn't make sense. Was it possible that someone else had made this happen? If so, Waqar Ahmed had to be the prime suspect. He more than anyone had something to gain from Anderson being out of the way. And as a result, he was acquitted. But how could he

113

have been involved? Maybe Anderson was being paranoid, starting to lose his mind. All these thoughts made his head ache. And what about Hussain? Would he stoop that low? At the very least he might know something.

With a renewed alcohol-fuelled determination, he stood up, knocking the bar stool over in the process.

He staggered out to find some answers.

It was after five o'clock by the time Anderson had walked into Rusholme from town. His leg throbbed, but the journey had given him time to think. Wet through, he was oblivious to the rods of sideways rain illuminated in the neon signs on the shops and restaurants along the Curry Mile.

At last he reached Hussain & Co. A tiny ramshackle frontage, squeezed between an Indian takeaway and a shop selling saris. The Kashmiri Palace was directly opposite.

He could see Hussain through the window, at his desk, shuffling papers. Anderson burst in and stumbled into a filing cabinet.

'John Anderson!' Hussain exclaimed. 'You're soaking. Give me your coat.'

Anderson steadied himself, then waved a finger at his old adversary. 'Thanks for going to the police and making a statement,' he slurred.

'What are you talking about?'

'About seeing me in Starbucks.' Anderson didn't wait for a reply. 'Did Waqar Ahmed set me up?'

Hussain moved towards Anderson and looked him straight in the eye. 'I don't know, John. I really don't know.'

Anderson was taken aback by Hussain's refusal to defend his old client with more fervour.

Adey came out of the back, having heard the commotion. 'What's going on?'

Anderson was instantly distracted. Mesmerised.

Hussain seized the opportunity to change the subject. 'John Anderson, meet my trainee, Adey Tuur.'

'So you're the famous Anderson?' He was much better looking than she had imagined, despite the angry scar that snaked down the side of his face. His eyes were sad, lost. She moved across the room towards him with a serenity that was instantly calming and ran a finger down his scar. 'Does it hurt?'

He was lost for words. It felt wonderful. He couldn't remember the last time someone had touched him, displayed any tenderness. He wanted to cry, wail, until there was no pain left.

In fact, he did and said nothing, suddenly feeling a fool for turning up like that; ranting, drunk.

He turned on his heel, pushed open the door, and disappeared into the streaming rain.

Hussain puffed out his cheeks and exhaled. Neither he nor Adey said anything.

CHAPTER 30

Anderson watched the Bentley pull up in a side road, next to the Kashmiri Palace. He checked his watch: 11pm, just as Tredwell had described in his evidence. Waiting outside in the winter cold and rain had been gruelling. Shivering, Anderson was soaked to the skin; his leg throbbed, but nothing would stop him now. Not knowing was destroying him.

From across Wilmslow Road, he could see a young, muscular Asian man get out of the driver's side, and walk round to the passenger door whilst opening an umbrella. With his free hand he reached for the handle. Waqar Ahmed, wearing a black cashmere coat, stepped out of the vehicle, careful to avoid the gutter.

Anderson's eyes locked onto him, fury rushing through his veins.

Uninterested in anything else, the minder's attention was focused on keeping the umbrella over Ahmed's head on the short walk into the Palace.

Anderson could see them through the front window, Ahmed giving a few orders, pointing, and then stuffing what looked like a wad of notes into his coat pocket. Within minutes they were back outside, walking towards the car.

Once they were off the main drag and back into the side road, Anderson seized his opportunity. Clumsily dodging a few cars, he crossed the main road. 'Waqar Ahmed, I want a word with you.'

About to climb into the passenger seat, Ahmed looked up. At first he didn't recognise the bedraggled figure approaching, fists clenched by his side.

'John Anderson? The barrister?' Ahmed grinned at the realisation.

'What did you do?' Anderson demanded.

Ahmed laughed.

Anderson carried on towards Ahmed, now only feet away. The minder stepped between them but Ahmed waved him back. 'Come on, Johnny boy, let's see what you got.'

Anderson swung a punch with his right hand. Ahmed casually tilted back, preventing contact. The momentum caused Anderson to lurch to the left. He felt a blow to the top of the head, then a fist in his face. Crashing to the ground. Kicks to the stomach, legs. Again and again.

No resistance. Pain.

Ahmed used his foot to roll Anderson into the gutter, diverting a channel of rainwater around his body. Just enough strength to turn his submerged head, allowing him a breath.

The bottom of Ahmed's shoe sunk into Anderson's cheek, pinning him down.

Agony.

'Look, Omar,' said Ahmed. 'I'm above the law.'

They both chuckled.

Ahmed removed his foot and crouched down over the lawyer. 'This is where you belong now. It's where I started, and where you'll finish.' He grabbed Anderson's hair and lifted his head to make sure he could hear. 'And if I get pulled in over this little beating, I'll cut up your family.'

Ahmed released his grip, letting Anderson's head flop back onto the road.

Car doors shutting, then the noise of the Bentley pulling away.

Alone, only the sound of rain glugging down the drains.

Anderson lost consciousness.

CHAPTER 31

Anderson opened his eyes. A familiar feeling. Everything ached, especially his ribs. He'd been here before. Where was he? He sat up. In hospital, on a ward full of patients.

A young female nurse saw him and came over. Hair tied back in a ponytail, a picture of efficiency. 'Feeling better, Mr Anderson?'

'What happened?'

'You were unconscious when they found you. Looks like you'd been attacked. In Rusholme. Can you remember?'

Anderson gathered his thoughts. 'What time is it?'

'Just after six-thirty in the morning.'

'I need to go.' He drew back the covers. 'I need to go home and change. I'm in court this morning.'

'Yes, admissions said you're a barrister, but you're in no fit state to work today.'

'No, I'm not working, I'm...' He paused, then rubbed his forehead, hoping the headache would stop. 'Doesn't matter,' he said, sliding off the mattress onto his feet. Feeling giddy he reached for the bed frame and steadied himself.

'Mr Anderson, please, get back into bed, you need to rest.'

Anderson reached for the pile of damp clothes, folded neatly over the back of a magnolia metal chair.

'At least wait for Doctor Nesbitt. He wants to see you.'

Anderson remembered him – from his stay after the crash. 'OK, if he's quick, I'll wait.'

The nurse pulled the curtain along the rail to give Anderson some privacy then hurried off.

Anderson took off the hospital gown and began to dress himself. After the effort of bending down to get his trousers on he sat back on the bed, catching sight of himself in the circular mirror on top of an MDF cabinet. His face was a mess. Red and swollen. The cheek laceration from the crash had been re-stitched.

'Mr Anderson? You decent?' He was already pulling back the curtain. 'Do you remember me?'

'Yes, of course, Dr Nesbitt?' he replied, getting to his feet.

'That's right. I hear you are adamant that you're leaving? Well I won't try to stop you. They've cleaned you up as best they could but I thought I ought to come across and see how your memory was?'

'What do you mean?'

Nesbitt put a hand under Anderson's chin and scrutinised his face in a way only a doctor can. 'Do you know how you got these injuries?'

Anderson hesitated. A thought flickered across his mind, only for a moment; to lie, pretend he'd had another blackout. He dismissed it. 'I remember.'

An awkward silence.

'But you'd prefer not to say?' asked the doctor.

Anderson nodded.

'You really aren't having the best of luck lately, are you, Mr Anderson?'

'You could say that,' he replied.

'What about the car accident? Anything? Sometimes a

head injury can jog the memory.'

It hadn't even occurred to Anderson. He strained to think. Closed his eyes. A fleeting image. Heena Butt's face. In conversation. A feeling of fear. Was it real? Or had his mind constructed something from the post-mortem photo? Anderson sighed. He thought about Ahmed. How he'd admitted nothing. If he'd had something to do with the crash wouldn't he have enjoyed telling Anderson? Wallowed in it?

'No, nothing, doctor. Maybe it's because I was asleep at the time?'

Dr Nesbitt didn't reply. Only a sympathetic nod. Then: 'Good luck, Mr Anderson.'

CHAPTER 32

The preliminary hearing was at Bradford Crown Court on the north-eastern circuit. A barrister could not be tried for a criminal offence on his own circuit. The train journey across the Pennines from Manchester Victoria only took an hour. In any other circumstances Anderson would have enjoyed taking in the snow-covered mountains as the train chugged over the top. Today his stomach was in knots.

The courts were across the road from Bradford Interchange, behind The Great Victoria Hotel. Morgan found Anderson sitting in the public canteen. He immediately noticed his bruised and swollen face. 'Jesus Christ! What happened to you?'

Anderson ignored the question. 'Have you got any papers yet?'

Dewi handed his client the advanced disclosure he had just received from the prosecution. 'Are you all right, John? What's going on?'

'Where's the rest?'

Realising Anderson wasn't going to divulge anything, he replied, 'That's all they've given me. It's only a prelim, remember. I think we've got two eyewitness accounts there, and the experts on sleep and the reconstruction.'

'I would have liked to see all the witness statements, and a transcript of my interview.'

'It was awful – trust me.' He regarded Anderson, who was still turning the pages of the Advance Disclosure. Morgan put his hand over the papers. 'Stop, John. You need to tell me what we're doing. As far as credit is concerned, the clock starts ticking today. Are we going to indicate a guilty plea?'

'Morning, gentlemen.' A tall forty-something barrister, wigged and gowned, was standing over the table.

Dewi jumped to his feet to make the introductions. 'John Anderson, meet your barrister, Michael Forster.'

Anderson recognised him vaguely but hadn't known him to speak to.

'Michael is from the Bradford Bar. I thought it was important to have someone local, who knows the judges.'

Anderson tentatively nodded his approval, hiding his embarrassment at being the defendant in a client/barrister relationship. 'Michael, who's prosecuting?'

'A silk. Hannah Stapleton from Leeds. A right ball-crusher. What happened to your face? Is that from the crash? It looks recent.'

'I fell. A silk? A death by dangerous wouldn't normally justify Queen's Counsel.'

'It would if you're prosecuting one of your own. To show you're not getting any special treatment,' Forster replied, still wondering about his lay client's explanation.

'But I am,' Anderson protested. 'Harsher.'

Forster shrugged and sat down, clutching his own copy of the AD. 'I've had a look at the papers, John. My sympathies go out to you, they really do. It's damage limitation, isn't it? A trial would be suicide. We're in front of His Honour Judge Cranston. He's no softie, especially after

123

a trial. We need to have you arraigned today to get full credit – early guilty plea scheme and all that.'

Anderson looked at Dewi. 'But what about Heena Butt? Did you manage to find out anything?'

'Afraid not, but you know my views on that. There's nothing there that could help you. The driving is what it is.'

Out of options, Anderson agreed to plead guilty. No one believed in him, not even himself anymore. 'What about bail?'

'He won't remand you in custody until the sentence, when probation have done their report. You've got three weeks or so to put your affairs in order,' replied Forster, before stopping to listen to the tannoy.

'Would all parties in the case of Anderson go to Court One immediately.'

They made their way up the stairs to the circular landing, a central hub where interested parties could wait outside the courtrooms. Anderson kept his head down to avoid eye contact with the various counsel and solicitors who obviously recognised him.

The usher greeted Forster at the door of the courtroom. 'You're first on. The judge wants to get this one out of the way – press interest. He's coming in in two minutes.' She then turned to the defendant. 'Mr Anderson?'

'Yes.'

'If you'd like to go into the dock please.'

He followed the usher and his legal team into court.

Hannah Stapleton, QC was already in counsels' row. Just on the right side of fifty, she'd once been the belle of the Leeds Bar. Still with a twinkle in her eye, she now had the maturity and presence of an elite performer. She acknowledged Forster but ignored Anderson, who made his way into the dock. He looked across at the press box, full of reporters scribbling on their pads. The public gallery was also bursting, not with his friends and family, but strangers.

This was officially the end of John Anderson, yet those who mattered most to him didn't seem to care.

'All rise!' cried the usher as His Honour Judge Cranston came into court. A fat, self-important, no-nonsense Yorkshireman. Cranston said what he meant and gave significant discounts for a guilty plea. He had no time for those who chose to play the system, especially at a cost to the public purse. Once seated, he surveyed the packed courtroom, then rested an eye on Anderson.

The clerk identified the defendant: 'Are you John Anderson?'

'Yes.'

Stapleton was on her feet. 'Your Honour, I appear to prosecute, my learned friend, Mr Forster, defends. I have drafted an indictment, as I understand from Mr Forster that the defendant is content to be arraigned today.'

His Honour gave a solemn nod, then gave Anderson a double-take, but decided not to make reference to his condition. 'Very well, let the indictment be put.'

The clerk stood up and signalled for the defendant to do the same. 'John Anderson, you are charged with two counts. On count one you are charged with an offence of causing death by dangerous driving in that...'

All eyes were on Anderson. A bruised and broken man. He just wanted it to be over. Not just the hearing, the prison sentence – everything. All fight was gone and with it, all hope.

'...on the 24th day of January 2012, you drove a mechanically propelled vehicle, namely—'

'Wait!'

Everyone switched their attention towards the door of the courtroom. Who was the source of this interruption?

'Who is that?' erupted the judge. 'What is the meaning of this?' He peered over his half-moon spectacles, searching for a clearer view of the man in a grey suit. 'Come forward.'

'Profuse apologies, Your Honour. I know it's highly irregular but I must speak with the defendant before he's arraigned.'

Hussain? Anderson was astounded. What the hell was he doing?

'Who are you?' His Honour Judge Cranston persisted.

'Tahir Hussain, Your Honour. I'm a solicitor from Manchester. I was involved in a case with the defendant at the time of the alleged offence. I must speak to him.'

The judge let out a sigh. 'This isn't how we do things on this side of the Pennines, but very well. I'll stand the matter down for five minutes – and no more. Bail as before.'

'I'm grateful, Your Honour.' Hussain bowed and left court to wait in a conference room just outside.

A furious Forster stormed in, followed by Morgan and then Anderson. 'This had better be good,' said Forster.

'John,' said Hussain, still catching his breath and ignoring Forster. 'Can we have a couple of minutes alone?'

Morgan didn't give his client time to answer. 'No chance. You're just here to poach a brief. Have you no shame?'

Hussain ignored the insult. 'Look, John,' he said, then saw Anderson's face properly. 'Who did this to you?'

Wearily, Anderson replied, 'What do you want, Hussain?'

Refocusing, he began. 'I don't know you on a personal level, but you don't strike me as the kind of man who would fall asleep driving home to Wilmslow at five in the evening. I just don't believe it. Judging by what you were saying last night, neither do you?'

Anderson was confused. This person who he'd spent years trying to humiliate in court, who he loathed, who he slagged off behind his back at any opportunity, was seemingly the only person in England who actually believed he might be innocent. He must know something. 'Do you know what happened?'

Hussain gulped in some air. 'No I don't. Like yours, my instincts tell me maybe Waqar Ahmed was involved, but I've got no evidence. But more importantly, if you say you're innocent of this, I believe you.'

Morgan sneered at Hussain. 'I thought so. He's got nothing.'

'I don't understand,' said Anderson. 'Why would you come all the way over to Bradford just to tell me that?'

'Because you're a bloody good advocate. The best. I don't want to see you throw everything away just because you think it's the right thing to do. Where's the fight in you?'

Anderson considered the advice, could feel himself welling up.

Hussain wasn't finished: 'It's too early to plead guilty. Once you do, that's it. There's no going back.' He pointed at Morgan. 'John, what's he actually done? Has he explored all avenues? Maybe you had a seizure. Have you had a brain scan?'

Morgan was outraged. 'How dare you question my judgement!'

'He's right, Dewi. You haven't done anything, apart from tell me how strong the Crown's case is. What's the rush?' Hussain was only saying what Anderson had thought since the police station.

'You listen to this reckless lawyer and you're doubling the sentence,' warned Morgan.

The usher knocked, then poked her head around the door. 'The judge wants you in court – now.'

Morgan and Forster attempted to steer their client out of the conference room.

Hussain stopped him. 'Just so you know, John, if you need a lawyer prepared to defend this, I will gladly do it.'

Anderson's head was in a whirl. 'But you're a witness. You've made a statement about seeing me at Starbucks. You can't defend me.'

'I don't know what you're talking about,' Hussain protested. 'I did see you there, but I haven't spoken to the police about it. It's not my style to kick a man when he's down.'

Anderson was beginning to realise that he'd made a grave error of judgement as far as Tahir Hussain was concerned. He looked at Morgan and Forster then back at Hussain.

Hussain offered Anderson his hand – for the second time since the crash. 'Guilty or not guilty?'

'Don't do this, John,' said Morgan.

Anderson wasn't going to make the same mistake twice. This time he shook it firmly. 'Not guilty.'

PART II

CHAPTER 33

The door flew open. 'Have you heard?' shouted Detective Chief Inspector Armstrong, directing his question to DI Taylor, sitting at his desk.

Instinctively, Taylor glanced over at Waters, who was equally bemused and replied: 'No, Chief, heard what?'

'Anderson, he's gone not guilty.'

'You're joking?'

'Do I look like I'm joking? Thought you said the evidence was overwhelming. Got experts coming out our ears, you said.'

'It is. We have.'

'You can hardly blame 'im, Chief,' Waters chipped in. 'Got a lot to lose. Worth having a punt on a trial.'

'Did I ask your opinion?' Armstrong snapped.

'Sorry, Chief.'

Taylor didn't appreciate his officers being spoken to like that, but decided to let it pass this time. 'All we can do is prepare the case, Chief. How he pleads is out of our hands.'

'I suppose so,' Armstrong replied, calming down. 'Is it watertight? That's all I want to know.'

'Yes,' Taylor replied firmly. Unable to resist winding up his boss, he added: 'But you know what lawyers say? There's no such thing as bang to rights.'

'What the fuck is that supposed to mean?'

'Well, we haven't been able to bottom the identity of his passenger.'

'Thought you had some Indian name?'

'That's from a library card found in her handbag. There's no other ID. It doesn't matter technically, as long as we can prove the death, and we've got a body, but it might give the defence something to play with.'

'And who do you think she was?'

'Dunno, Chief, but if I was a betting man I'd say she was a prostitute. We may never know.'

'And the five-year-old girl in the other vehicle? I take it you know *her* identity?' Armstrong asked.

'Yes, obviously,' Taylor replied.

'Good, because I want you to go and tell her parents there's going to be a trial. It's the least you can do.'

'Yes, Chief.' His stomach churned.

CHAPTER 34

Tom and Sandra Granger had aged in the few weeks since DI Taylor last saw them. The house was the same – spotless. Even the magazines on the coffee table were arranged in a perfect fan.

Taylor sat on the settee, noticing the freshly ironed arm-caps. A way of life, deeply ingrained – great pride in their tiny home – as they must have had in their beloved daughter.

Still in his overcoat, Taylor refused the offer of a cup of tea, not wishing to prolong matters. 'As you know, the plea hearing was today. I wanted to tell you in person that—' He paused. There was no way to make this easy. 'The defendant is denying it. He's pleaded not guilty.'

It took a while for the information to compute. Then: 'Denying it?' Tom Granger couldn't understand. 'How can he deny it? Our Molly's dead.'

'I know,' Taylor sighed. 'So there's going to be a trial.'

'Does that mean we'll have to give evidence?' Sandra asked, fiddling with a tissue in her sleeve.

'Yes, you will.'

'Good. I want to, if it helps. For Molly.'

'Of course. Is there anything else you've remembered about what happened?'

'No.'

Something made him ask, 'Or anything you think you could have got wrong in your statement?'

'Like what?' asked Sandra.

'Oh, I don't know. Anything?'

'No, I don't think so.'

'OK, just checking,' Taylor replied.

'I've heard he's an important man,' said Tom Granger. 'The bloke who did it?'

'No more important than you, Mr Granger.'

'A barrister, isn't he? If he knows the law, might he wriggle out of it?'

'Not if I can help it,' Taylor replied. He got up to leave. 'If there's anything you want to ask, please, feel free to call me anytime.'

'I just can't understand it,' said Mr Granger.

'Understand what?'

'Why it couldn't have been me.' His face broke up. Sandra held him. They held each other.

'It should've been me,' he said. 'It should've been me.'

Taylor showed himself out.

CHAPTER 35

Hussain left a set of papers in *R v Anderson* with Adey. He'd managed to scrounge a full bundle of depositions as well as transcripts of the interviews. They were only missing the unused material.

Adey couldn't wait to get to work. She didn't believe a word of Anderson's account to the police. To her it was obvious – he'd messed up. Probably had a fight with a hooker over money and crashed the car. If anyone knew how to get out of a situation like that, it was a prosecution barrister. He might be able to take Hussain for a ride, but not Adey Tuur. She'd been around the block too many times. She'd uncover the truth soon enough. But there was something about John Anderson that drew her. An austere man, yet such a commanding presence. His quiet charisma was almost magnetic. She remembered him bursting into the office full of anger. Adey had never met anyone remotely like him before. Like her, he seemed so lost, yet their lives to date couldn't have been more different.

Born in Somalia during the civil war, Adey knew little about her father, only what her mother told her, and that was almost nothing. A white Englishman, he'd said he was an aid worker, but was more probably a gun-runner. Adey had never got to the bottom of whether her mother had had a one-night stand on the evening of her conception or whether she'd been raped. She would often look into Adey's eyes before she died, and comment on the miracle of how someone so beautiful had come out of something so terrible. Her uncle, who lived with them in Mogadishu when she was young, had been involved in politics. She still had nightmares about the men who came to their home during the night. Tattooed on her memory, peeping out from the bedroom door with her brother, Bahdoon. She remembered the torchlights glistening off the machetes, raining down on her uncle. The sound of flesh being chopped – blood-spattered walls. Her mother sobbing as she surveyed the dismembered corpse, confused as to which body part to cling to.

After the withdrawal of UN forces in March 1995 her mother had fled, taking Adey and Bahdoon to the UK as political refugees, eventually settling in Moss Side, Manchester.

Unable to come to terms with the traumatic events in her life, Adey's mother committed suicide when Adey was fourteen, leaving her and a sixteen-year-old brother to fend for themselves.

With Hussain out at court she treated herself to an extra notch on the electric heater, then set about trying to find out something on Heena Butt.

She started with the basics: Facebook and Twitter. Nothing. Maybe she'd made a mistake with the spelling. She flicked through the brief. To her surprise, there was a hole in the prosecution case – no death certificate and no evidence to prove the identity of the deceased. Paramedics described finding a body in Anderson's vehicle, pronounced dead on arrival by doctors at the hospital, but no one had confirmed her name. The only reference to the name Heena Butt was from the police officers in Anderson's interview, but she couldn't work out where they got it from.

Even basic searches of the electoral role were hopeless without a date of birth or address. And with no details to go on, other searches were pointless. She was stumped, unable to progress this aspect of her preparation until the prosecution disclosed the schedule of unused material. She could only hope that would turn up something. Fortunately for the client, it meant a stay of execution.

CHAPTER 36

Anderson caught the bus from town. He wiped away the condensation on the window and took in the bright lights of the Curry Mile. His senses revelled in the different sights and smells as he alighted in the centre of Rusholme, a welcome respite from the monotony of sitting in West's flat. The swelling to his face had reduced and his movement was less restricted.

Surviving on what remained of a £1200 cheque for a trial he'd prosecuted six months before, he was now formally suspended from practice by the Bar Standards Board – not that the clerks had been giving him anything anyway. At least Mia wasn't pressurising him for maintenance. She seemed to understand his predicament. That was something to be thankful for. God knows what she and the children were living on.

Anderson's spirits had been lifted. He still couldn't quite believe how Hussain had driven all the way to Bradford to persuade him not to plead guilty. A man Anderson had despised more than anyone else in the legal profession. He'd thought he had good judgement about people, a sixth sense. How could he have got things so wrong? Anderson found himself actually looking forward to seeing Hussain, being able to talk about the case to someone who wanted to hear his take on things. He hurried along the icy pavement, only the grit keeping him upright.

Before going into Hussain's office, Anderson stopped and stared across the road at the Kashmiri Palace. Remembering the beating, he shuddered. Was that where the answer lay? Or was he closing his eyes to the obvious – that he, John Anderson, was responsible for the death of two people?

The office was freezing but Hussain's greeting was warm. He stood in the reception area, holding a kettle. 'Fancy a brew?'

'Yes, please. Black, no sugar,' Anderson replied, undoing the buttons on his overcoat.

'I hardly recognised you,' said Hussain, grinning.

Anderson didn't get it.

'In your civvies. You look almost relaxed – almost.'

For some reason he had chosen to dress down for the conference: sports jacket, white shirt, jeans and Italian loafers. This uniform was usually only reserved for weekends.

Hussain had taken off his day collar and tie. His suit jacket was replaced by a thick woollen jumper with holes in the elbows. 'Sorry about the temperature. We put the heating on in the boardroom especially for you!' he said, gesturing towards a closed door. 'We've never had such an important client.'

Anderson was flattered.

'I've got every lawyer and trainee in the firm working on your case, waiting in the conference room. Come through.'

Anderson followed Hussain into the back room. Peeling, white wallpaper and a dirty red carpet in the centre of which was an oval-shaped wooden dining table with six mismatched chairs. Only one seat was taken – by Adey Tuur.

'Hi, only me I'm afraid,' she said, expecting disappointment.

Her instincts were wrong. He'd hoped she would be at the conference.

'Take a seat, John. You remember Adey, don't you? She will be doing the day-to-day case prep as well as some digging.'

Anderson was sure he blushed as he gave her an appreciative smile.

Wasting no time on pleasantries, she asked, 'Who did that to your face?'

'It's nothing. I was drunk.' Anderson was embarrassed by his pathetic explanation.

Adey tutted. She didn't like being lied to.

Hussain changed the subject. 'Right, let's get started. You'll be pleased to hear that I stayed behind at court and managed to beg a full bundle of deps and transcripts of both interviews. It's not paginated and I haven't got the unused material, but it's a start. I've only skimmed it, but Adey's had a proper read.'

Adey handed Anderson a copy of the bundle. 'You'll see that they haven't been able to formally identify the deceased yet. It's clear from your interview that the police are assuming it's someone called Heena Butt. So we'll work on that basis for now.'

Hussain agreed. 'There were probably some documents on her. They'll be in the unused material. We'll let you know when the schedule is served.'

'OK. Initial thoughts?' Anderson asked.

'A very compelling case compounded by two terrible interviews.' Hussain saw Anderson's disappointment at the analysis, then added: 'I won't lie to you.'

Anderson agreed with the approach.

'The Crown's case is that you drove knowingly tired, fell asleep, veered across the carriageway into a vehicle travelling in the nearside lane, causing the death of rear seat passenger Molly Granger, and your own passenger, Heena Butt.'

Anderson winced every time he heard the enormity of the allegations against him.

'John, before we start going down the road of potential defences, is there anything that you didn't tell the police that we should know?' Hussain paused. 'Or any lies you told?'

Anderson hadn't expected this so soon. It was a critical moment. If he didn't come clean with his legal team, his whole case would be based on a false premise. And if it came out later, all trust between them would be lost. He dreaded having to admit it.

No choice, he had to grasp the nettle: 'There was a lie in my interview.'

'OK, which was?'

To Anderson's relief, Hussain seemed unsurprised by the admission. 'I didn't mention Tilly in the first interview. I always remembered going for a coffee with her. The last thing I remember, always remembered, was leaving Starbucks.'

'Why lie?'

'I didn't want anyone to know I'd been having a quiet drink with a twenty-five-year-old woman. People might have thought…' He checked himself. 'Mia might have thought that I was having an affair.'

'And were you?'

'No.'

'Were you hoping to?'

'Maybe. Yes,' Anderson replied. 'But I changed my mind and left.'

'Got cold feet, did you?' Adey asked, grinning. 'If you'd shagged her you might not be in this mess.'

'That thought hadn't escaped me,' he replied. Adey's frankness, as well as his own, was curiously liberating.

'Anything else?' asked Hussain.

'No that's it.'

'OK, do you have any medical conditions?'

'Not that I am aware of.'

'All right, so there are three potential defences here. The first is medical. Something happened, beyond your control, that caused you to lose consciousness; some kind of seizure, or neurological event. Or possibly a pre-existing medical condition of which you were unaware, such as sleep apnoea.'

'Which would raise the defence of non-insane automatism?'

'Yes. We'll have you examined over the next week or so by various medical experts.'

'OK,' replied Anderson, pleased with the way his lawyers were attacking the case. 'And the other two defences?'

'That Butt was in some way responsible. Whether it was a robbery, a fight or whatever. And the third,' he said, getting up and going over to a white board fixed to the wall, 'is that somehow you were set up.' He picked up a marker pen and wrote at the top: 'Suspects'. 'Adey is going to see what she can turn up. It's a massive job, so let's try and narrow down the field for her?' Hussain wrote the name Heena Butt.

Anderson was in no doubt about the next name on the list. 'You can add Waqar Ahmed to that list.'

Hussain wrote the name, then said, 'The third name is my own.' He wrote 'Tahir Hussain'.

'Don't be ridiculous,' said Anderson. 'I know you didn't have anything to do with it.'

'Do you? You think I'm a bent lawyer, too close to my clients. Acquittal for Ahmed was acquittal for me. Don't tell me it didn't cross your mind that I was involved?'

Anderson was embarrassed. 'OK, it did briefly, but now I know better. Know you better. Cross it out.'

'There's no room for sentiment here, John. Only an unanswerable argument will remove any name from the list.'

Anderson felt ashamed. Out of practice, he racked his brain for an argument. Eventually: 'All right then, you're not mentally unstable, so your motive could only have been ambition or money. Not being caught would be crucial. My pleading guilty would have ensured that, buried the truth, and yet you came to court and persuaded me to change my plea. That would risk exposing you in the trial process. Doesn't make sense.'

Hussain smiled. 'Very good.' He crossed out his name.

Anderson was impressed. Right at the start, Hussain had smoked out any nagging doubts Anderson had about his lawyer and then cleared the air. 'Following that through, a lot of people advised me to plead guilty: Dewi Morgan, Forster, my head of chambers, and even my father.' It pained him to reveal his lack of support from elsewhere.

'I think we need more than just negative advice on plea at this stage to make them a suspect. After all, the evidence is, on the face of it, overwhelming.'

Anderson was relieved, particularly about his father; not that he thought for a moment he could be responsible.

'What about your wife?' suggested Adey, again with a cheeky grin.

'Mia? Why?'

'I heard she's thrown you out. This is one way to get you out of the picture.'

'Who told you that? It was *because* of the crash that we separated, and besides, she'd be destroying her only form of income.'

'What's she living on now?' she asked.

Anderson paused before answering: 'I don't know.'

'I don't think we can eliminate her yet,' said Hussain. He wrote the name Mia Anderson.

Adey didn't hide her amusement.

Anderson couldn't figure her out at all.

'Anyone with opportunity?' asked Hussain.

Anderson considered the question. 'I don't know what that means? I suppose you would have to say Tilly Henley-Smith. She was the last person to see me before the crash. But opportunity to do what? Hit me over the head? Drug me? When you say set me up, does that include trying to kill me?'

'We'll work that one out later. For now she goes on the list.'

Anderson typed the names on his iPad, as did Adey.

Hussain continued: 'Does anyone hate you enough to do this to you?'

Anderson scoffed. 'Of course not.' On reflection, in jest, he offered, 'Unless you count Sam Connor? He told me the other day how much he dislikes me.'

'And he got to take over for the prosecution in Ahmed,' said Hussain.

'And he saw you cosying up to his pupil in Starbucks,' said Adey.

'What?' asked Anderson in surprise.

'His statement is in the full bundle. He saw you there with Tilly. The statement you thought Tahir gave to the police – it was actually Connor.'

Anderson leaned back in his chair and took in the information. 'Connor? Why would he come back? He said he was going back to chambers, and his car was in the opposite direction. He thought Tilly had gone home. They both turned down my offer of a coffee. Then Tilly came back.'

'To avoid her pupil-master finding out she wanted a servicing from you?' observed Adey. She had an uncanny insight into human nature.

'Probably,' replied Anderson.

'Maybe Connor changed his mind? Felt bad, came back to join you?'

'No chance,' said Anderson.

Hussain added Sam Connor to the list. 'Anyone else?'

'Yes,' said Adey. 'Everyone Anderson has ever prosecuted to conviction.'

'Everyone?' Anderson replied. His head was full of the worst kind of memories. It came with the job. He'd seen the photos, heard the testimony of countless victims, parents. So much depravity had been pushed into his head over the years, he even felt uncomfortable bathing his own kids.

Hussain considered Adey's suggestion. 'Let's limit it to everyone that got sent down. I know it will be lengthy, John, but you've got the time to do it. Write on the list the sentence they got so that we can know if they were still serving on the date of the crash.'

Anderson agreed to undertake the task.

'John, Adey will take a full proof from you in due course, but is there anything else we need to know now?'

'No, I don't think so.' Anderson was encouraged by the methodology of their preparation, compared to that of Dewi Morgan, who seemed to have done absolutely nothing.

'There's something else,' said Adey.

'Go on,' replied Hussain.

'The central feature of this case is the mystery of Heena Butt. Who was she and why you don't know who she was.'

'Yes, I agree,' said Anderson, pleased that someone was getting to the heart of the matter.

'It may be suggested that she was a prostitute you'd just picked up. You know, kerb crawling, and maybe you lost your memory of that due to the head injury?'

'I'm glad you asked me that,' he replied, looking deep into Adey's eyes. 'Dewi Morgan was of the same view. There's just no way. I was going home to watch my son play football, but also, I don't use prostitutes. Why would I suddenly change the habit of a lifetime?'

'Everyone has a dark side, you know? Secrets? You can tell us.'

'There's nothing more to tell, I swear to you.'

Adey appeared to accept his answer.

They all agreed to have another meeting the following week to monitor progress.

Anderson expressed his heartfelt thanks to both of them.

Things were finally moving.

Anderson caught the bus back to town. He sat down on the top deck and phoned Mia. He wanted to speak to the boys before bed. As usual she fobbed him off. Lately, they were always out, asleep or busy doing something important. He offered an apology about his inability to give her any maintenance. Maybe that was why she was making contact with the boys so difficult, but she seemed so relaxed about it. She had to be getting money from somewhere.

He listened to his voicemail. Only a message from Orlando West saying that he'd heard about the plea, that he understood Anderson's decision and that he was there to help in any way he could. It was a relief to know someone from chambers was still in his corner.

He opened his iPad and read the list of suspects:

Heena Butt

Waqar Ahmed

~~Tahir Hussain~~

Mia Anderson

Tilly Henley-Smith

Sam Connor

Everyone I ever prosecuted to conviction – and went to prison.

The conference with Hussain had given Anderson's paranoia some credence. Was it really possible he'd been set up? Worse still, had someone tried to murder him?

And if so, was that person on the list?

CHAPTER 37

Tahir Hussain made a detour on his way home. Waqar Ahmed had asked for a meeting. The Little Taj, a sit-down restaurant on the Curry Mile was another of Ahmed's businesses. A much bigger concern than the Kashmiri Palace; Ahmed used a relative as a dummy director.

The waiters greeted Hussain with much pomp and ceremony. He was something of a celebrity as far as Ahmed's crew were concerned.

'I'm not here to eat. I need to see Mr Ahmed.'

'Of course, Mr Hussain,' replied one of the waiters in Punjabi, showing the solicitor to a stool at the bar.

A waiter handed him a bottle of Cobra. 'Please, on house.'

Hussain left the drink but reached into some mints on the bar, then thought better of it, remembering he'd read in some magazine that they were always covered in different people's piss – customers who hadn't washed their hands.

Several minutes later Ahmed appeared with outstretched arms. 'Tahir Hussain, the best lawyer in Manchester. I'm honoured by your visit. Come, my friend, sit down.'

Hussain followed him to a table in a secluded corner. A waiter quickly removed the cutlery, leaving only a fraying red table cloth and two paper napkins folded into swans. Hussain sat down opposite his best client. He loathed having to

148

associate with the man. Ahmed was like a cancer: once he had a hold over someone, he would gradually spread into every aspect of their life. Hussain wasted no more time on formalities: 'You wanted to see me, Waqar?'

'Yes, to see how it's going and to congratulate you.'

'Congratulate me?'

Ahmed sniggered. 'On getting him to accept you as his brief. Can't have been easy.'

Ashamed of his duplicity, Hussain forgot himself. 'Someone beat the crap out of him. Was that you?'

Ahmed didn't give an answer. 'Does he have a defence to killing those people?'

Hussain ignored the question but posed one of his own: 'Did you have something to do with what happened in that car?'

Ahmed's expression twisted into one of anger, then contempt. 'You dare to come into my restaurant and ask me that?'

No going back now: 'Well, did you?'

Ahmed leaned across the table. 'Just make sure you lose.'

'What?' Hussain's mouth went dry. 'That wasn't part of the deal. You said just get the brief. Tell you what's going on. Nothing bent. I won't lose it on purpose. I can't do that to him.'

'Then I think it's time for you to pay back my money.'

'You know I haven't got it.'

'You've got two choices: get my money, or lose the trial. Understood?'

There was nothing else to say.

Hussain got up to leave.

What the hell was he going to do?

CHAPTER 38

Standing in front of total strangers in a pair of pyjamas was extremely difficult for John Anderson, but he had to go through with it.

Professor Cutler didn't notice his patient's blushes. His own attire was entirely functional. Reading glasses hanging on string so as to prevent misplacement, over a white coat; all pockets stuffed with pens, a thermometer and a ruler. Having studied some apparatus and twiddled a few knobs, he instructed Anderson to lie on the bed, then placed some belts across Anderson's abdomen and chest. 'This procedure is called a polysomnography. Please try and relax.'

A nurse attached electrodes to Anderson's face and scalp whilst the doctor continued to explain. 'We are testing you for a condition called sleep apnoea. You need to try and sleep until morning.'

'What are the symptoms?' Anderson asked, trying to take his mind off his predicament.

'Well, it's a sleep disorder characterized by abnormal pauses in breathing. Each pause can last as long as a few minutes.'

'I'm sure I'd know if I had it.'

'You'd be surprised. The sufferer is often unaware. He becomes conditioned over time to daytime sleepiness and fatigue. Becomes the norm, you see.'

'So, if I've got it I could have fallen asleep whilst driving, without realising I was tired?'

'Exactly! Giving you a defence which you lawyers call non-insane automatism.'

'How likely is it that I've got it?'

The doctor smiled. 'We'll have to wait for the results but it's more common than you might think. Studies have shown that one in six of Britain's 100,000 lorry drivers are undiagnosed sufferers. A terrifying thought, don't you think?' He finished attaching the last few electrodes. 'Sweet dreams, Mr Anderson.'

Anderson stared up at the ceiling, afraid to move. It reminded him of when he woke up in hospital after the crash. The memory of it made him anxious; Mia crying. Were her tears for him, or the life she was losing? Thoughts whirring around; his head was crammed.

John Anderson prayed for sleep.

CHAPTER 39

Adey lit another cigarette to break the monotony and jiggled about to stop the frozen night from settling in her bones. She had a good view of Anderson's house from her vantage point at the end of the garden. A Victorian semi. She'd expected something even grander for a barrister. She'd been amazed to hear how little Anderson had actually been earning over the last few years, unaware that the cuts in legal aid had hit barristers so hard. And the size of the mortgage. Perhaps Mia had been disappointed? Adey had to stop herself feeling sorry for Anderson. But the case was drawing her in. Why had Sam Connor gone back to Starbucks? Why was there no evidence about Heena Butt and who she was?

Her mind wandered. Thoughts of her brother, Bahdoon. It made her sad. She'd seen him that morning, as she did every month. Anything more was too painful, watching his life waste away. Each visit, he seemed a little more detached, his eyes a little more lifeless. She'd preferred the rage and resentment of the early years of his sentence. Now there was only resignation.

A light came on in the upstairs bedroom. The man who had arrived in a taxi an hour earlier clearly wasn't going anywhere. Adey couldn't wait all night, she was freezing. Time to make a move.

She slipped silently through the hedge and across the

lawn. Effortlessly, she shinned up a drainpipe and onto the garage roof, then padded over to the window and peeked through the gap allowed by the curtains.

Adey wanted to giggle – a woman on all fours, on a bed. Velvet-covered handcuffs attached her to the bedposts. Mia Anderson was a handsome woman, with a firm body. At thirty-five she definitely still had it.

'Fuck me,' she snarled repeatedly to the man kneeling behind her, thrusting with all his might.

Only able to see part of his face, Adey didn't recognise him. She couldn't risk a photo – the flash might reveal her presence.

Did Anderson fuck Mia like that? She quickly dismissed the thought. No man had managed to get close to Adey Tuur, and John Anderson certainly wasn't going to be the exception.

CHAPTER 40

Anderson had been looking forward to this day all week. Even Mia's indifference couldn't dampen his spirits. Their conversation on the doorstep went no further than a succession of orders concerning the boys' care and return.

They took the train from Wilmslow, changing at Crewe for Chester. He'd never spent a full day alone with his children before. It seemed crazy to him now. How did he let that happen?

Today Anderson felt alive – even happy. For a few hours he forgot about the case. Will and Angus were giddy with excitement. Their first visit to the zoo.

The reticence of the larger animals to come out of their cosy retreats into the chill of the open air didn't spoil the fun, it became a source of amusement. Anderson hadn't enjoyed himself so much in years. He'd missed out on all this, and for what? Bigger cases and longer hours. Why had it all been so important to him? Was it just his father's expectations, drilled into him from an early age? A poor substitute for love?

Angus was mesmerised by the chimpanzees. 'Mum says that'll be you soon.'

'What do you mean?' Anderson asked, studying his son's pained expression.

'In a cage, locked up.'

No point denying it. For the first time, he considered it

as a real possibility. His children had to prepare for the worst. 'I don't know yet, Angus, but if I do get locked up, I will think about you every day until they let me out.'

'Have you done something very bad? Is that why they want to lock you up?'

Will watched his father intently. The boys needed answers just as much as Anderson.

'I can't remember what happened. I really can't.' He put his hand on his chest. 'But I know in here, in my heart, that I didn't do anything wrong.'

'I believe you, Dad,' Will whispered.

'So do I,' said Angus.

What a fool he'd been. Priorities all wrong. He knelt down and hugged them. Was it too late to make things right?

They decided to finish the outing with a ride on the monorail that weaved its way around the zoo above the enclosures. Angus pointed out the black rhinos and lions below, once they'd set off from monkey island. 'Who's that, Daddy?'

Anderson's eyes searched the path below where Will was pointing. A man in a woolly hat waving up at them. Anderson tried to make out the face – disfigured. Tredwell!

Tredwell pointed directly at them with his hand shaped into a gun, then moved his arm as if firing it.

Angus laughed and fired back.

Will sensed something wasn't right. 'I don't like that man, Dad. I want to go home.'

Anderson quickly shepherded the children out of the zoo, checking around them on their journey back. Will kept asking about the man with the strange face. Anderson made light of it, saying he was just a crazy old fool. What was he doing there? Was it a coincidence or had he been following them? And what could he have against the barrister who prosecuted the man that caused his horrendous injuries?

He decided not to mention it to Mia. Why worry her? No point overreacting. The kids couldn't be in any danger. He'd wait until he knew more.

Once he'd dropped them off he rang Hussain, who told him to come to his house in Longsight after he'd reported the matter to the police. A record had to be made.

Anderson called in at the police station and asked for DI Taylor, who couldn't have been more disinterested. Only after a great deal of persuasion did he formally record the matter. The detective inspector tried to convince him it had been an unfortunate coincidence and a bad joke.

Privately, Taylor wondered whether this was a clever ruse by Anderson to blame everything on Tredwell, and to prove to the jury threats had been made, but he agreed to investigate. A part of him couldn't help but feel sorry for Anderson. He took no pleasure in destroying the life and career of a decent family man over a few seconds of bad driving. That wasn't why he'd joined the force all those years ago.

It was after nine o'clock by the time Anderson arrived at Hussain's house. An end terrace on three floors, extended at the back, it had a warm, lived-in feel. Hussain's wife insisted on preparing some food.

Anderson didn't protest.

Hussain showed him into the lounge where they sat down and analysed Tredwell's actions. Anderson was at a loss to understand them.

'Maybe he blames you for Ahmed's acquittal?' suggested

Hussain. 'If you hadn't crashed your car, Ahmed would be inside.'

Anderson wasn't convinced. 'He'd have to be crazy to think like that.'

'He is.'

'What do you mean?'

'He's been in and out of psychiatric institutions all his life. Got a history of schizophrenia.'

'How do you know that? Don't tell me you accessed his medical records?'

Hussain scoffed. 'Never mind that. You should've disclosed it!'

'I didn't know!'

'I'm sure the police did. They probably didn't tell you because you would've disclosed.'

'What else didn't I know?' asked Anderson.

'Quite a lot actually. Tredwell was a very manipulative and mysterious figure. The whole Naila story was bullshit.'

'Really? What about the 999 call?'

'Who knows? One of the girls probably saw what was going on at the Kashmiri Palace, or overheard what was going to happen and saw an opportunity to get her captors arrested. Whoever she was, she disappeared because we couldn't trace her. And anyway, Martin Tredwell isn't into women.'

'How do you know?'

'Adey hacked into his email account.'

'What? You didn't! That's an outrageous breach of data protection legislation!'

'Yeah,' Hussain replied matter-of-factly. 'That's why we couldn't use it in the trial.' He decided not to divulge anything else until Anderson asked. He didn't have to wait long.

'Well go on then, what did she find out?'

'Tredwell is into boys. A paedophile. Grooming and file sharing with other sickos.'

Anderson took a moment to digest the latest revelations. 'So, are you saying Waqar Ahmed is innocent?'

'No, I'm sure he shoved Tredwell's face in that fryer, but it was more likely an argument between business partners. Tredwell wasn't a joey, he was much more involved in the trafficking than he let on.'

'So we add him to our list of suspects?'

'Yes. Trouble is, he's in witness protection. Not even Adey would be able to locate him.'

Safa came in and guided Anderson to the kitchen table where she had placed an assortment of Indian dishes. Anderson helped himself to some lamb keema and a roti. The first decent meal he'd eaten for a long time.

Hussain sat in silence, watching him devour the feast. Once he'd finished, Hussain broke the bad news. 'I've got the experts' reports, John. They found nothing. No sleep disorder. No evidence of a seizure or anything medical.'

Anderson took it in. 'And the accident investigator?'

'Not good. Everything is consistent with sleep. The drifting, no braking, et cetera. I can't serve any of our reports. They're all damning. I'll just have to cross-examine the prosecution experts, see what I can turn up.'

Anderson felt deflated. They still didn't have the slightest foundation for a defence.

'We've also got the problem of Sandra Granger,' Hussain added. 'I'm going to have to put it to her that she's either lying or mistaken.'

Anderson puffed out his cheeks. 'The jury won't like that.'

'What else can I do?' Hussain's mobile rang. 'Excuse me, a client.' He left the room to take the call.

Anderson and Safa exchanged nervous smiles in the way people do when virtual strangers are left alone in a room together. Despite her generosity, Anderson sensed resentment. A feeling she didn't want him there. Perhaps something needed saying?

'I'm so grateful to Tahir for defending me. I was never very nice to him, you know?' Anderson's sense of shame was obvious. 'I can't understand why he is doing so much to help me. He's a good man.' Anderson noticed a photo on the dresser. The whole family: Mum, Dad, two girls and a boy. He remembered seeing the girls with Hussain on the day of the crash. 'I didn't know you had a son too?'

The question caught her by surprise.

Hussain's reappearance diverted their attention.

'There's something you need to know, John,' said Hussain. 'It's a bit delicate.'

Safa took her cue to leave the room.

Anderson was intrigued.

'It's about Mia,' Hussain said gently.

'Go on.'

'She's seeing someone.'

'What? Who?'

'I don't know. Adey saw her with someone. She didn't recognise him.'

'How does she know they are actually *seeing* each other?'

'They were having sex.'

Anderson stared at Hussain in disbelief.

'Adey was on your garage roof, looking through the window.'

Anderson placed a hand on his forehead. 'Why was Adey there?'

'As part of her investigations. Whoever this man is, he has to be considered a suspect.'

Anderson's mouth was dry. Mia with another man? So soon after the split? 'What did he look like?'

'Couldn't say. Her view wasn't great. We'll find out soon enough, John. I'm sorry.'

Anderson was shell-shocked. In no mood for further discourse, he left.

He didn't know his wife at all.

CHAPTER 41

DC Waters parked up outside Taylor's house. He knew better than to knock on the front door. Taylor emerged with a Yorkshire pudding held between his teeth. Struggling against the wind to pull his coat on, he hurried down the path.

Waters leaned across and opened the car door. 'Sorry, gov.'

Taylor got in, took a bite, then cupped the remaining half, careful not to let the gravy drip onto his clothes. 'This better be good, Waters. First time the kids have seen me for a week.'

'It's Martin Tredwell, he's gone AWOL.'

'Not this again.'

'Witness protection haven't had any contact for five days. They went round to the Stockport safe house after I called in Anderson's complaint about the zoo. He's gone. Packed a bag.'

'Bloody marvellous. That's all I need. More time-wasting. He's got nowt to do with the death by dangerous. Not our problem.'

'I know but they say there's stuff at the house you ought to see.'

Taylor huffed. 'All right, let's go.'

Waters started the engine and used the back of his hand to make a cursory wipe of the condensation on the windscreen.

Once Taylor had swallowed the last bite: 'What else do we know?'

'Very little, gov. Witness protection are concerned that the bloke he grassed on in the trial has caught up with him.'

'What's his name? Ahmed?'

'Yeah, Waqar Ahmed. But they've got nothing on him.'

'What do we know about Tredwell?'

'Some mental health issues – clever though. NCIS say he likes kids. Sexual violence but never been caught for it. Even though he got a suspended sentence in the Ahmed trial, apparently he took the defendant's acquittal very badly. As always happens, he blamed the lawyers.'

The safe house was in fact a flat on the fifteenth floor of a council block minutes from the centre of Stockport.

'Surprised he was prepared to be so near home,' said Taylor as they came out of the lift.

'He insisted apparently.'

A middle-aged man wearing a cheap grey suit answered the door. 'Hello, gents, thanks for coming. Bob Smith, witness protection. I would shake hands, but…' He raised his arms to show a pair of yellow marigolds. He went into the lounge, tied up a black bin bag, tossed it in the corner, then took off the rubber gloves. 'Just cleaning up for the next unfortunate.'

'Already?' said Taylor.

'Resources, you know the score. A lot of witnesses and very few properties. He broke the rules so someone else gets it. Thought you'd better see this, before I take 'em down.' He opened the bedroom door.

Taylor and Waters stepped inside. Photographs covered every inch of wall space, ceiling included. All of children.

'We think he printed them off on that,' said Smith, pointing to a PC and printer.

Taylor took a closer look at the walls. Some of the pictures made him wretch. Mutilated bodies, in the throes of an agonising death. 'Jesus, are these mocked up?'

'Dunno yet. I bloody hope so.'

Taylor exchanged glances with Waters, conveying a mutual understanding that there was always something new to chill the bones of even the most experienced police officers. Waters picked up a pile of photos by the computer. 'Did Tredwell take them himself?'

'Well, we know most of them are just files other nonces trade and share on the net. The paedophile unit had a quick look. They recognised half of them, but not those,' he said, pointing to the bundle in Waters' hand.

Taylor took them and sifted through. Unsuspecting children outside a school, some in a park. 'Do we know who any of these kids are?'

Smith shook his head. 'Potential victims? Who knows? With all the level 5's on the wall, he's high priority.'

Taylor nodded.

'All right,' said Taylor. 'If the paedophile unit catch up with him, let us know, but he's not actually part of our enquiry.' Forcing himself to take one last look at the walls, Taylor said, 'Which means my chief would go ape if I spent any time on this.'

'Understood,' Smith replied. 'Will do.'

CHAPTER 42

Taylor met Adey Tuur at the front desk. He was taken aback by her beauty. A real stunner. He wasn't fooled by her unconventional appearance. A legally trained defendant was bound to have clever lawyers, even if she did wear jeans and baseball boots to work.

'You're late,' she said. 'I've been waiting for nearly an hour.'

Preoccupied with his mobile, Taylor replied, 'I'm sorry. Something came up.'

Adey scoffed. She noticed his tie had gravy stains and didn't match the shirt. A contented family man who'd long since given up on making an effort, she thought.

Taylor took her back through the secure entrance and down a corridor and left her in a room with a chair and a desk. He returned a few minutes later carrying a cardboard box. 'All the unused is in here. Put anything you want to one side and I'll photocopy it for you. Just text me when you're done.'

Adey rummaged through the pile of documents and other items, which were in sealed bags. She found nothing of interest: custody record, transcripts of 999 calls, medical notes from the hospital in relation to Anderson's treatment and Ms Butt's death, and a few witness statements of people who arrived on the scene after the crash and so saw nothing of relevance. She put a few irrelevant documents to one side for copying so that Taylor would be none the wiser as to what she had really come to see. At last she found it – a plastic exhibit bag containing the possessions of the deceased. A leather handbag, purse, mobile phone, lipstick, Manchester Central Library card in the name of Heena Butt with date of birth, and a key. She took a compact out of her own bag and opened the lid. She pressed the key hard into the putty inside, creating an imprint, then replaced the key. She checked the purse: £450 in cash, nothing else. It didn't add up. She could have been a prostitute – a lot of cash, no credit cards – but it was all too sterile. None of the usual crap: receipts, bits of paper, tissues. The bag only contained the bare essentials, as if it had just been bought or someone had deliberately tried to avoid leaving any trail. Nobody travelled without proper ID, unless for good reason. Had the prosecution based the deceased's identity purely on a library card?

Amongst the documents in the box was a Technocel report – an analysis of the contents of the phone. Only four numbers in the contacts. A history of traffic but only sporadically and only for the six weeks preceding the crash. It didn't fit a typical usage pattern. Adey was intrigued. Who was this woman? She picked up the handbag again and ran her hands around the inside. Her fingers felt a bump in the lining. She turned the bag inside out. A tiny hidden pocket. She could only fit two fingers in. She pulled out a piece of paper, folded over several times. The police had clearly missed it. She unfolded the paper. Blank. She turned it over. Scrawled handwriting. Her heart skipped a beat. Someone had scribbled:

John Anderson, Spinningfields Chambers – 05man.

The part she couldn't fathom was '05man'. It had to mean 5am, Manchester. But the deceased was in the car at around 5pm. One thing was for sure, she had planned to meet Anderson. Had he been aware of that meeting? Adey cursed. Rather than finding the evidence that proved Anderson's guilt, the mystery had only deepened.

Once she'd finished, Adey handed Taylor a wad for copying. The thought of taking the piece of paper without revealing its existence to Taylor had occurred to her, but that would forgo the ability to prove where it was recovered. 'You missed this; I'll take a copy,' she said, thrusting the note under Taylor's nose.

He scrutinized the contents, then Adey's face.

'You're not going to suggest I put it there?' she asked, reading his mind.

Taylor took the bundle of documents for copying. 'Of course not.' He'd dismissed the possibility of a plant, only because he couldn't see how it could help Anderson's case, and he wasn't in the least bit surprised that traffic had missed it.

Once he came back Adey pressed Taylor for more information: 'Have you tried to cell-site the numbers in the deceased's phone?'

'You are joking?' scoffed Taylor. 'Do you know how much an expert charges for that?' But it was a reasonable request. He'd already asked Armstrong to authorise it. He'd refused on the basis that it couldn't assist the prosecution and the cost couldn't be justified. Taylor was more interested in doing right by the deceased. After all, she was someone's daughter, or even mother. Her family could be wondering where she was. It wasn't in his nature to just leave things hanging like this.

Adey persisted: 'We need to know who she was. It's a proper line of enquiry.'

'Tell it to the CPS,' Taylor replied, seemingly unmoved.

Adey made to leave.

'Just a minute.' Taylor had a thought. 'Look, why don't you try and get the judge to order us to do it. Or make a third party application. We both want to know who she was.'

Adey hadn't expected that. This copper seemed all right.

'Don't go telling anyone I suggested that,' he said.

CHAPTER 43

The car park was deserted, other than Ahmed sitting in his Bentley. He flashed his headlights.

Hussain weaved his way around the potholes full of rainwater towards the vehicle. He opened the passenger door and climbed in. He could smell the leather seats. 'What do you want?'

'Just an update on the case, my friend.'

Hussain studied Ahmed's face. 'Why do you care so much?'

'I don't like prosecutors. Especially good ones.'

'Or you had something to do with the crash? People died.'

'Be careful what you say to me, Tahir.'

Hussain stared out through the windscreen, unable to bear the sight of the man next to him.

'A little bird tells me you've listed the case for a *mention* hearing tomorrow. Trying to get disclosure?'

Hussain wasn't surprised that Ahmed knew. He had informants everywhere, even in the police. 'Yes, I have.'

'Make sure you don't try too hard. You will remember to lose?'

Hussain cringed on hearing his part of the bargain repeated. 'I've got to make it convincing.'

'Look at me,' Ahmed demanded.

Hussain turned his head and held Ahmed's gaze. He could see the evil in his eyes.

'Just remember how unlucky you are with children, Tahir.' He grinned. 'I'm not sure your wife could cope with losing another.'

Hussain made to grab Ahmed's collar, then stopped, only just managing to control himself. He thrust the door open and got out. Before Hussain was able to slam the door shut, Ahmed said, 'I'll be watching you.'

CHAPTER 44

'Third party application by the defence in the case of Anderson, Your Honour.' The court clerk handed the file up to the judge.

His Honour Judge Cranston looked at Hussain, who was already on his feet. 'Yes, I've read the application, Mr Khan.'

'It's *Hussain*, Your Honour.'

The judge ignored the correction.

'Your Honour will have seen from the defence statement that our case focuses on the mystery surrounding Heena Butt, one of the deceased, and the issue of why she was in the vehicle at the time of the crash. By investigating the provenance of the telephone numbers in the deceased's contacts, and cell-siting the phones at least on the day of the crash, we may be able to ascertain not only who she was, but also her movements on that fateful day.'

'Miss Stapleton, what do you say?'

Hannah Stapleton rose to her feet with all the gravitas of a successful silk. 'Well, it's very vague, Your Honour. Firstly, how does any of this deal with the real issue in the case, whether or not the defendant fell asleep whilst driving? We haven't been served with any defence expert report dealing with that. Secondly, as I am sure Your Honour knows, we are a week from trial and it could take months for the network providers to find and disclose the information. It would inevitably mean vacating the trial date.'

'Yes, I agree, this is a hopeless application, nothing more than a fishing expedition.'

Hussain was back on his feet. 'But, Your Honour—'

'Mr Hussain! I've made my ruling. Call on the next case.'

Hussain called Adey from the robing room with the bad news. She was now on the case full-time, which was killing the practice. 'Another brick wall. You got anything?' he asked, in hope rather than expectation.

''Fraid not. Been following Connor's pupil all morning. Total waste of time.'

'Tilly?'

'Yeah. Back where it all began, believe it or not – Starbucks. She's just bought a coffee.'

'Leave it now, Adey. We can't afford to waste any more time on her. Let's take stock at my house this evening.'

Adey was disappointed. Her instincts told her there was something here to know. 'All right,' she said, giving up her place in the queue. 'Oh, hang on!'

'What is it?'

'She's got her laptop out.'

'All right, ten minutes.'

Adey had already hung up. She sat down and got her own laptop out and waited. Bingo. Tilly had logged into the coffee shop Wi-Fi – an insecure network. It took Adey all of ten seconds to hack in and see what Tilly was doing. Writing emails in her personal account. Perfect. Adey was soon reading emails, sent and received. A few sickly exchanges with a boyfriend – Josh. She got the impression he was working abroad, possibly in the armed forces. Also a few emails from Connor. Strange they weren't on the chambers email address. 'Oh my!' Adey said out loud as she read the contents. The exchanges started as a bit of flirty fun, but became increasingly explicit. No doubt about it, Connor was sleeping with Tilly, and had been at the time of the crash. Why the hell had she been sidling up to Anderson in Starbucks?

Perhaps the day hadn't been completely wasted.

CHAPTER 45

Despite his leg, Anderson's step quickened down Water Lane.

The walk from the station to what had been the marital home was only fifteen minutes, but his desperation for answers made it seem like an eternity.

Hussain's revelation about Mia's infidelity was eating him up. He wasn't sure why. He didn't even know if he still loved her – ever really loved her. Perhaps it was the humiliation – the rejection – the not knowing that he couldn't stand. He was going to get the truth. It had to be face-to-face, while the kids were at school.

He hurried up the garden path, despite his injury. The place seemed different, alien almost. Anderson knocked and waited, fidgeting nervously.

The door was flung open, then a flicker of disappointment crept across Mia's face. 'Oh, it's you. What do you want?'

'Were you expecting someone else?' His jealousy had revealed his hand in the first question.

Mia held the door firmly, preparing for battle. 'I think you'd better go. You know the children aren't here.'

Such coldness. He'd looked after her all these years and this was his reward. Tossed out like an old pair of shoes. 'Can I come in?'

Mia remained resolute.

'Please? Just for a few minutes? I don't want to do this on the doorstep.'

Sighing, she relented. She led him into the kitchen. 'Make it quick.'

This time he disguised his emotions. 'I was worried about you, Mia. Whether you had enough money?'

'You know, I get by. I have some savings, but there was no point asking you. You haven't got any.'

A bleep from a mobile on the worktop – a text – pulling Mia's eyes. Anderson's followed. They both froze for a moment, then Anderson moved towards the handset. Mia lunged, clumsily grabbing hold of it. Anderson gripped her arm. 'Who was it?'

'None of your business.' Mia jutted out her chin, her eyes wide with mockery, enjoying her husband's pain and her power over him.

Anderson tried to wrestle the phone from her grasp.

'What are you going to do, hit me?'

Anderson stopped, surprised by the question. 'Hit you? I've never hit you.'

Mia pulled away victorious. 'I think you'd better leave. Go on, get out.'

Anderson could see her contempt for him. 'I know you're seeing someone. I have a right to be told who. Is it someone I know?'

'My personal life is none of your concern, now piss off, John.'

He opened his mouth to protest but there was no point. And he didn't have the strength. Silently he turned and shambled out into the garden. The slam of the front door made him flinch. His legs buckled. Something from deep within stopped him falling. He straightened up, and limping slightly, headed back towards the station.

His phone rang. His first thought was Mia. Maybe she wanted to apologise? He checked the screen: 'unknown'.

'Hello?' All he could hear was laughter. Male.

'Hello? Who is this?'

'You're a—'

The obscenity took his breath away.

'You're going down.' More laughter.

'Who is this?'

The call ended.

Anderson was stunned. He didn't recognise the voice. It could've been Tredwell's. He seemed to have so many enemies. So few friends.

The platform at Wilmslow station was empty. Anderson stood, contemplating his life. Why couldn't he just give up, throw himself under a train? They'd all be better off without him. Even the boys.

The crackle from the tracks signalled an approaching train. He took a step forward to the platform's edge. Then…

The train arrived. Anderson had missed his opportunity. What was that blasted thing inside that made him carry on?

Hope.

Anderson alighted at Piccadilly, still shaken by his earlier thoughts. He trudged back to the flat.

On entering he heard a voice call out a greeting. It startled him.

Orlando West appeared in the hallway, still wearing his coat. 'Hello, old chap. Didn't want to scare you. Wanted a chat.' West went on nervously: 'Hope you don't mind me letting myself in?'

After an uncomfortable silence, Anderson replied, 'No, of course not, it's your flat after all. What's up?' Anderson had never seen West so unsure of himself.

'It's the apartment. You know, with the trial on Monday.' West held out his hands, palms up in a gesture of resignation.

Anderson was slow to catch on. 'I don't get what you mean, Orlando?'

'Chambers had a vote. They think it's inappropriate for you to stay here during the trial. We must be seen to take a neutral stance.'

'But… it's *your* flat.'

'I know, but I can't run roughshod over the will of chambers. I am the head, after all. You understand, old chap. But I'll still be giving character evidence.'

Anderson watched West reach for the front door, desperate to avoid any further discussion. Anderson could only mutter, 'Right, OK.' Then: 'And thanks for the use of it. I'm really grateful.'

'Not a word of it,' replied Anderson's old pupil-master as he disappeared out of the door. Then, over his shoulder: 'Need you out by Sunday. There's a good fellow.'

Anderson closed the door.

He prayed for the end.

CHAPTER 46

'Can you stand still for five minutes, Tahir?'

Safa's husband didn't hear her, but kept striding up and down the kitchen. The smell of saffron filled the air. Anderson and Adey were coming to the house for a final con before the trial on Monday.

Hussain felt he'd achieved nothing since getting involved. But that wasn't why he was pacing like a caged animal.

'I knew you shouldn't have got involved. You couldn't walk away, could you?' chided Safa. 'What's Anderson ever done for you anyway?'

'Hush woman. Stop your nagging.'

'You stopped him. He was going to plead guilty. What if Ahmed finds out?'

'He won't.'

'Tell me exactly what he said?'

'I've already told you a hundred times.'

A knock at the door stopped the argument from escalating. 'You'd better not let Anderson know anything about this,' Hussain warned his wife.

It was Adey who had arrived first. She took one look at Hussain's face and knew something was up.

'Don't ask!' he snapped, leading Adey into the kitchen.

She exchanged concerned glances with Safa.

Anderson's arrival seconds later prevented any discussion

between the two most important women in Hussain's life, much to his relief.

Adey noticed Anderson's appearance had deteriorated further in the short time that she'd not seen him. He'd lost more weight and looked exhausted. An unexpected rush of affection overcame her.

'Are you OK, John?' asked Hussain, having made the same observations as Adey.

'Yeah, I'm fine,' he replied wearily. 'I've just seen Orlando West. He's told me I've got to leave the flat.'

'You're kidding?'

'No. He doesn't want me staying there during the trial.' Anderson slumped into a chair at the kitchen table. The abandonment of his only real friend had taken its toll. 'Says it's unfair on chambers to be associated with me when we don't know which way it will go. He was very apologetic.'

'Bullshit,' Adey replied. 'He's punishing you for not pleading guilty.'

'And for instructing me,' added Hussain, shooting his wife a look that only a spouse could read. She imperceptibly shook her head. Anderson would have to find somewhere else to stay.

Anderson shrugged. 'Oh, and someone rung me up to tell me I'm a – well – the "c" word – that I'm going to prison. Excuse my French.'

'Give me your phone,' demanded Adey. 'Have you got a number?'

'Unknown caller,' replied Anderson, handing it over.

Adey pressed a few buttons and started making notes.

'Do you think it was Tredwell? Should I report it to Taylor?'

'What's the point?' replied Adey. 'Half of Manchester thinks you're a—'

'Thank you, Adey,' interjected Hussain in a tone of mild rebuke. He could see Anderson wasn't in any state to receive more knocks right now. 'Of course it could be Tredwell. But it could also be a random nutcase. That line is going nowhere for us, John.'

'So what line of enquiry *is* going somewhere?' Anderson asked. 'It's Friday night, the trial is on Monday. From where I'm sitting, we've got absolutely nothing – no defence.'

Nobody spoke.

Eventually, Adey offered all she had: 'Connor and Tilly are an item and were at the time of the crash.'

'And?' replied Anderson, only mildly interested.

'And nothing,' said Adey. She wasn't going to dress it up.

'More importantly, have you found out who's sleeping with my wife yet?'

'No, not yet.'

Anderson sighed and let his head fall into his hands.

'You can stay with me if you want?'

Anderson looked up. Had Adey said that?

'It's a shithole in Hulme, but I've got a spare room.' She winked. 'As long as you don't try anything.'

Everyone laughed apart from Anderson, who turned crimson. Once he'd composed himself he said: 'I don't know what to say. Thank you.'

'Don't say anything, just focus, because we do have a lead that we need to discuss.'

Anderson perked up and paid full attention whilst Adey explained in detail the contents of Heena Butt's handbag, including her phone and the handwritten note concealed inside.

Anderson kept repeating '05 man'.

'What does it mean?'

Adey shrugged.

Hussain took a seat at the table in front of Anderson. 'We can't work it out.'

'Maybe it's a flight number?' Safa suggested.

'Possibly, I'll check it out,' Adey replied.

Anderson acknowledged the contribution with a grateful nod. 'Do you still think she's a prostitute?' he asked outright.

Adey thought for a moment. 'I don't know. It all seemed so—'

'So what?'

'Clinical. No clutter. Who would have a bag like that?'

'Not a hooker,' replied Anderson. 'What about condoms?'

Such an obvious point. Why hadn't it occurred to her? 'None.' She'd been blinkered by the assumption of Anderson's guilt – a dangerous state of mind for a criminal defence lawyer. She wouldn't make that mistake again.

'I did a case once,' said Hussain. 'The deceased was a man, but he too had almost nothing to identify him.'

'And did you find out who he was?' asked Anderson.

'Yes.' Then tentatively: 'He was an assassin.'

Nobody offered a reply.

Anderson broke the silence. 'So who employed Heena Butt? Waqar Ahmed?'

Nobody had an answer. It was all speculation – no hard evidence to go on. Every enquiry seemed to lead to more unanswered questions.

The final conference before trial and as usual, no further forward.

CHAPTER 47

A young wooden top lifted the cordon marking out the crime scene to allow DI Taylor through. Nice touch. He felt like a celebrity under the gaze of the gathering crowd.

'Body's upstairs, sir.'

Taylor didn't react. Important to show the new recruits that he'd seen it all before. Privately, he was delighted to be back on a proper homicide, not nannying some poxy death by dangerous as a favour for the DCI just because the suspect was a big cheese in the legal world. He had better things to do.

The terraced house was in a Rusholme side street, just off the main drag. It stank of untreated damp. Rancid carpets and rubbish everywhere. Unlived in, the property had the feel of a crack house, or was at least used for some nefarious purpose; certainly not a bog-standard dwelling. The SOCO photographer's flash blinded Taylor momentarily as he walked into the upstairs bedroom. The emerging vision was of a naked man – Asian – on his back with both hands tied to the bedposts. His stomach and chest were punctured with numerous stab wounds.

'Another bloody sex crime,' Taylor muttered, almost in a groan.

'I doubt it very much,' offered a cheery female voice. A plump woman in her fifties, wearing a white paper suit, took off her glove and offered a hand. 'Maggie Blunt, forensic pathologist.'

Taylor shook it enthusiastically. He'd been in the job long enough to know these experts invariably pushed a murder enquiry forward at breakneck speed. 'Why do you say that?'

'No marks on the wrists. He would have struggled. And look here.' Blunt pointed to a couple of cuts to the right forearm. 'Classic defensive injuries. This man was tied up after he was dead.'

'Oh yes,' Taylor replied, marvelling at her analysis. 'Ritual?' he suggested, without thinking it through.

'Doesn't have that feel. It's only tying him up. My instincts tell me it was a rather muddled attempt to throw you off the scent. I can't decide if the number of stab wounds was part of a frenzied attack or just to confuse.'

'You're saying it could be a professional hit?'

Blunt turned her attention from Taylor, back to the corpse. Pensively: 'Yes, probably. Or at the very least, with a motive other than sexual gratification.'

'Do we have a name for him?'

'Yes, gov,' replied DC Waters, flicking through a small notebook recovered from the deceased's jacket pocket. Like Blunt he was in a white paper suit, though unlike her, Taylor thought he looked ridiculous. 'Waqar Ahmed.'

Taylor recognised the name immediately. 'Not the fella Anderson was prosecuting?'

'The very same, gov. You'd better have a look at this too.' Waters showed the notebook to Taylor with a plastic gloved hand, holding a page open.

'What am I looking at?' Taylor asked impatiently.

'Looks like a dealer list. It's certainly a debtors list. Look at that entry. It's a lot of money, gov.'

Taylor went down the list of names and figures until he came to the one by Waters' thumb. '20k – Tahir Hussain.' Taylor looked up at Waters, catching up. 'Hussain was his brief? Dodgy fucker.'

Waters nodded. 'Definitely makes him a suspect. We're going to have to pull him in, aren't we?'

Taylor took a deep breath then exhaled. 'Yes, but it's going to cause mayhem – Anderson's trial starts Monday and Hussain is supposed to be defending him.'

CHAPTER 48

The tower blocks in Hulme were only a ten-minute walk from Orlando West's city centre apartment, yet they couldn't have been more different locations.

Anderson's anxiety at entering this alien place subsided on realising that the groups of hoodies milling around on the estate ignored him entirely. A dishevelled man with a limp and a scarred face carrying his worldly possessions in a holdall didn't even trigger the raising of an eyebrow.

Adey's flat was on the twelfth floor. Striped black and yellow tape blocked the entrance to the lift. A makeshift sign read: OUT OF ORDER. Anderson let out a sigh before locating the stairwell and beginning his ascent. A group of youths ran past on their way down. A straggler slowed as he passed, taking in Anderson's face. A flicker of recognition. Had Anderson prosecuted this person? Possibly. Avoiding eye contact, he pulled himself on, using the iron bannister for support. At last, Adey's floor. The graffiti on the walls and ceiling provided an intimidating backdrop, but that wasn't why Anderson felt so nervous – he was going to be alone with *her*. Stay in her flat.

Adey opened the door and looked Anderson up and down, then without any greeting gestured for him to enter.

He stopped in the doorway. He couldn't believe his eyes.

Adey's flat was exquisite. Contemporary art on white

walls, clean lines, and all open-plan with a hi-tech kitchen. The sun cascaded through the windows, bouncing off the black granite worktops and glass units.

Such a contrast with the desolation outside the front door. 'Wow!' was all Anderson could think of to say. He walked through to the lounge area and saw the view of Manchester open up to him through the window that ran the length of the apartment. Far better than West's view, he thought.

'Great for entertaining,' Anderson said, wanting to fill the silence. 'I had no idea Hussain paid so well.'

'He doesn't. I have nothing else to spend it on. It's a council flat.' She watched for a reaction in Anderson's face then said defensively, 'All bought legitimately.' Then, with a glint in her eye, 'Well, almost.'

'What about going out? Having a good time? Holidays?' Anderson couldn't figure her out at all.

Adey shrugged off the question, then posed one of her own: 'Are you guilty?'

Anderson was getting used to her directness in all matters. He found it a very unusual and attractive quality. He held her gaze and answered, 'No, I'm innocent.' He qualified it: 'I believe I'm innocent.'

'You really don't know what happened in that car. Do you?'

'I thought I had a flicker of something a while ago, but maybe not. So no, I don't know what happened.'

'The neurologist said your injury could explain why you don't remember anything, why Heena Butt was in your car.' She regarded him harshly. 'But you'd still be guilty.'

Anderson was distracted by a piece of paper stuck on the

window. There were several. All over the flat in fact. He walked up close to one. It read:

John Anderson, Spinningfields Chambers – 05man.

Adey offered an explanation: 'I hate not being able to solve puzzles. Since I was a kid.'

Anderson turned to face her, seeing her anew. First, the offer of a place to stay. Then, all this effort for his case – for him. And yet he hardly knew her. He smiled. 'Me too.'

She pretended not to notice the tear in his eye. 'I don't think it's a flight number. Not a full one anyway.'

Neither spoke for a moment too long. Was the attraction mutual or was Anderson imagining it? Had he lost his judgement along with everything else?

Adey's mobile broke the spell. She took the call.

Anderson saw an expression on Adey's face that he hadn't seen before: concern.

'That was Safa. She's on her way round. Tahir's been arrested.'

'What? What for?'

'Murder.'

CHAPTER 49

Safa could barely speak – shock. Adey guided her into the lounge and sat her down. Safa's red *shalwar kameez* stood out against the white sofa.

Adey wasted no time. 'What happened? What do you know?'

Hussain's wife looked blank.

Adey held Safa's upper arms and gave her a gentle shake, which seemed to bring her back at least enough to point at Anderson. 'It's all his fault.'

'What do you mean?' Adey asked.

'I can't say. Taz made me promise not to tell anyone, even you.'

They both stared at Anderson.

Adey pressed her: 'Please, Safa. Why is it Anderson's fault?'

No response.

Adey switched to more immediate concerns: 'Who's representing him at the police station?'

'No one, he doesn't want anyone there. He says he knows what to do.'

'Well, who's been murdered?'

'Waqar Ahmed. I hope he rots in hell.'

Adey looked at Anderson for a reaction.

He could sense she was unsure of him again. The moment of shared intimacy, of trust, was lost.

Safa took a folder out of her bag and tossed it onto the glass coffee table. 'This is why I came.' She sneered at Anderson. 'Taz told me to give it to you. It's your case papers.'

The consequences for him of this development finally dawned on Anderson – he would have to represent himself. Why hadn't he listened to West and everyone else? They had all warned him about Hussain. Now Anderson would pay the price for his lack of judgement.

Once Safa had gone, Adey was not in the mood for further discussion. She showed Anderson his room. She wanted to be alone to try and make sense of things.

Anderson had to say something. 'Adey, I've no idea what's going on here. You can trust me.'

She turned away. 'Not now.'

Anderson tried to read through the papers. He struggled to take anything in, though a picture gradually emerged – damning prosecution statements and useless defence expert reports. He contemplated his predicament. He was in no state, physically or mentally, to defend this. He laid back on the bed, exhausted. At least it would be his final sleepless night before the trial. His mind raced. Hussain a murderer? Surely not. And what if Ahmed had somehow caused the crash? Had the answers Anderson so desperately needed been lost forever? He thought about the day to come. The humiliation. All those people – barristers, the judge and jury. Reporters. Prison.

Broken sleep.

Cold sweat. The sound of screaming. A woman. Anderson sat bolt upright. Had he been dreaming? He took a moment to adjust. No, it was real. Coming from Adey's room. Panic. He leapt out of bed and ran to her bedroom. What was it? He opened her door and called out into the darkness. 'Adey?' The screaming stopped. A bedside light came on. Anderson could see her sitting up in bed. The beads of sweat on her forehead glistened in the lamplight. 'Adey, what is it? Are you all right?'

Staring straight ahead, almost in a trance, she said, 'I see it every night. Lived it a thousand times.'

'See what?' whispered Anderson as he perched on the side of the bed.

'My uncle's murder. It will never leave me.' She lay down, her back to Anderson. 'I'm sorry I woke you. Goodnight.'

Anderson gently touched her bare shoulder. He yearned to take her in his arms. To comfort her. Kiss her.

He got up and left the room.

CHAPTER 50

DI Mark Taylor couldn't wait to get stuck into this interview. There'd been rumours about Tahir Hussain for years, but nothing concrete. Unlike many of his colleagues, he'd been reluctant to pass judgement. Good defence solicitors were easy targets for canteen gossip, but now it seemed obvious to Taylor that Hussain was up to his neck in some kind of criminality, possibly even murder.

After the formalities had been complied with, Taylor got straight to it. 'Your lawyer–client relationship with Waqar Ahmed is well known. How far back does it go?'

'No comment.'

Taylor shrugged at DC Waters. Unbelievable. Hussain was going to block the enquiry. Refuse to answer questions. 'You represented Waqar Ahmed in a recent trial, didn't you?'

'No comment.'

'And he was acquitted?'

'No comment.'

'We know that he was legally aided. You are aware that it's a very serious offence to take money as payment for services from a legally aided client?'

'No comment.'

'I'm sure you know it's called topping up?'

'No comment.'

'Similarly, it's illegal to accept money from a client for

winning a criminal case. You know that, don't you?'

'No comment.' It was agony not saying anything, but Hussain had no choice. He could only gamble that they didn't have enough to charge.

'We have a notebook here, a ledger, found at the crime scene, in Mr Ahmed's coat.'

DC Waters passed his boss the exhibit.

'There's a list of names here with amounts written next to them.' Taylor opened it and showed a page to Hussain. 'It looks to us like a tick list. You know what that is, don't you?'

'No comment.'

'For the benefit of the tape, that's a list drug dealers use. They have to keep a note of who they've supplied with drugs, on tick, and how much they are owed. Why is your name on that list?'

'No comment.'

Taylor could see Hussain was becoming more agitated. Keeping his mouth shut was really getting to him. 'Is it to do with drugs?'

'No comment.'

'Did you owe him money?'

'No comment.'

'Or is it money he owed you for your services?'

'No comment.' Was Taylor just fishing? Did he know anything?

'Did you have something to do with Waqar Ahmed's murder?'

'No comment.'

'Were you trying to wipe out a debt?'

'No comment.'

'Or did he have some black on you?'

'No comment.'

'As a solicitor I'm sure you know this already, but I have a duty to warn you that a jury may draw an adverse inference from your refusal to give an explanation for why your name appears in that ledger.'

'No comment.'

'Don't worry, Mr Hussain.' Taylor stared intently at the suspect. 'We will get to the bottom of it. You mark my words.'

Hussain's mouth was dry. How was he going to get out of this?

CHAPTER 51

The Bradford train rattled over the Pennines. Anderson distracted himself with the view of undulating hills and snow-capped, stony crags. How he longed to walk these mountains without a care in the world. All the old ambitions that had consumed him seemed so unimportant now. He craved simple pleasures.

Adey hadn't said a word since they left the flat. She wasn't quite sure why she had come along – Hussain & Co. were no longer representing Anderson. It seemed like the right thing to do, but her head was in turmoil as a result of Safa's revelations.

The photographers were waiting for Anderson outside the courthouse. He'd become immune to such humiliations. Once they were past the metal detectors Anderson suggested to Adey that they go up to court and wait for the prosecutor. His eyes scanned the landing for a friendly face, for his supporters. He expected his parents to show up or at least his brother. Would Mia be here, he wondered, and a representative from chambers?

There was no one.

Adey sensed his disappointment but said nothing.

'John Anderson?' The voice came from behind him.

'Yes, that's me.'

A small, unremarkable woman in her late forties. 'You don't know me. You killed my daughter.'

Sandra Granger.

Anderson reeled back. 'Mrs Granger?' He saw the loss etched into her face. 'I'm so sorry about what happened to Molly.' Anderson felt the blood rushing to his head. Dizzy.

'Sorry? Sorry?' she hissed. 'When they told me you weren't man enough to admit you'd done wrong, I knew you weren't just a liar. You're a coward 'n' all.' She spat in his face.

Stunned, Anderson didn't know what to say. Nothing he could say or do but watch her walk off towards the witness waiting room. A woman eaten up by anger and bitterness towards one person – him. And for good reason. He turned to Adey, who wiped away the spittle with a tissue.

She wanted to say something reassuring, but there was no point. Neither of them knew what lay ahead.

With only a minute to spare before the trial was due to start, Hannah Stapleton came up the stairs followed by an entourage of CPS lawyers. Her silk gown marked her out as someone special, and she knew it.

Anderson approached her and was about to explain his lack of representation but she raised a hand to stop him. 'I know you were a barrister, Mr Anderson, but I'm sure you understand that I can't speak to you. That's what your advocate is for.'

'Yes I know, that's what I wanted to discuss. It looks like I'm now a litigant in person – my advocate has withdrawn.'

Her face dropped. No barrister wanted the additional work and complications of prosecuting a litigant in person. 'Why?'

They were interrupted by the usher calling the case on.

Anderson took one last look around the landing for a

friendly face, then, feeling sick to his stomach, made the long walk into the dock of Court One.

His Honour Judge Cranston was already on the bench. 'Good morning, Miss Stapleton. No defence counsel this morning?'

Stapleton got to her feet as instructions were being whispered in her ear. 'No, Your Honour, I am being told Mr Hussain, the instructed advocate, has been…' She paused, unsure she'd heard correctly. 'Arrested?'

The judge raised his eyebrows and said with a leer, 'Well, that is a surprise. Such a nice fellow.' He turned his attention towards the dock. 'Going to represent yourself, Mr Anderson?'

Anderson stood up. It felt strange addressing the judge, not from counsels' row but the dock. 'As much as I would like to get on with matters, Your Honour, I must apply for an adjournment so that I can secure new representation.'

'Secure new representation?' Cranston scoffed. 'And how long is that going to take?' Without waiting for an answer: 'Justice delayed is justice denied, Mr Anderson. We will continue. Jury panel please, madam usher.'

'But, Your Honour,' Anderson persisted. 'I'm not ready to—'

'Mr Anderson, I've ruled, and anyway, as I understand it, you are a qualified barrister. So, as I said, jury panel.'

Still on his feet: 'Your Honour.'

'If you do not sit down, Mr Anderson, I will hold you in contempt. Do I make myself clear?'

Anderson slumped back into his seat, head in hands. How could this get any worse?

CHAPTER 52

Morning break. Tredwell watched the children running in all directions. The sounds of laughter. Innocence. Without a care in the world. All so full of life. It made his heart soar.

He moved closer to the railings, yards from a group of boys chucking sticks into a puddle. Tredwell was interested in one particular child, slightly away from the group. 'Come here,' he called out with an air of authority that demanded obedience.

'Me?' the boy mouthed in surprise, pointing to his own chest.

Tredwell nodded.

After a few seconds, hypnotised by the grotesqueness of the stranger's disfigurement, the boy moved slowly closer.

So engrossed in their splashing game, the others didn't notice.

Once there was only the fence between them, Tredwell asked: 'What's your name?'

In a terrified whisper: 'Angus.'

'Do you want anything bad to happen to your daddy, Angus?'

Angus moved his head slowly from side to side.

'Then you mustn't tell anyone you saw me and you must always do what I say. Do you understand?'

A nod.

'There's a good boy. I think we are going to be very good friends.'

Tredwell produced a small digital camera from his pocket and put his eye to the lens. 'Smile, Angus.'

Bewildered, he didn't.

'That's all for today, Angus.' He reached through the fence and brushed two fingers across the boy's hand. 'See you soon.'

CHAPTER 53

Before the usher could move, the door burst open and a panting Hussain almost fell into the courtroom. Catching his breath as he moved towards counsels' row, he offered: 'A thousand apologies for my tardiness, Your Honour.'

Showing only contempt for the spectacle, the judge said, 'Late again? We thought you'd chosen a new career, Mr Khan?'

Hussain ignored the jibe and the incorrect address, grabbed the case file out of Anderson's hand as he passed the dock and collapsed into his seat.

The reporters in the press box exchanged bemused grins. What story had they missed?

Anderson had questions for Hussain but now wasn't the time – this judge wasn't in the mood for more delays. At the short adjournment Anderson would demand answers, and he resolved that if he wasn't satisfied he would sack Hussain there and then. Being defended by a murderer was not an option.

Adey was relieved the firm were back on the case. It didn't feel right leaving Anderson without any representation. And besides, to her chagrin, she was developing feelings for him. She handed forward a note to Hussain asking what had been going on.

He ignored it and focussed on the job in hand – the

swearing of the jury. Hussain was happy with the look of them. A good racial mix, as one would expect in Bradford. He made a mental note of those he could definitely connect with. His concern lay in the nature of the defendant: could this collection of twelve apparently working-class Yorkshire men and women relate to, or at least sympathise with, an ex-public school barrister? Probably not, but there was nothing Hussain could do about that.

As expected, Hannah Stapleton's opening speech was polished. Interesting, yet beautifully simplistic in exposition of all matters expert and technical. In short, damning. It was easy to see why she had taken silk. All those in court wondered why on earth Anderson was contesting the case.

Hussain felt the weight of responsibility as he noticed the steely glares of the jurors towards the defendant in the dock.

Stapleton called her first witness to set the scene, a motorist who saw the whole incident play out in front of her on the carriageway. A mother with two children in the back, her evidence would be beyond question. 'All of a sudden the car just veered off to the left.'

'Had the vehicle impacted with another vehicle?'

'No.'

'Was there an obstruction in the road?'

'No,' she replied without hesitation, eager to share her evidence with the court. 'It just veered off for no reason. Then crashed sideways into another car and spun off onto the hard shoulder.'

'I see,' said Stapleton. 'And then what happened?'

'We all slowed down and stopped. Me and some other drivers. We went up to the vehicle. Two people were slumped in the front, still in their seat belts, covered in blood. A man and a woman. I thought they were both dead.'

'Can you describe exactly what injuries you saw, Mrs Hodges?' asked Stapleton.

Hussain rose to protest: 'Is this really necessary, Your Honour? There is no dispute that Miss Butt died as a result of the crash.'

The judge thought for a moment, searching for a basis to justify the admission of such prejudicial evidence. To his dismay, he couldn't. 'He has a point, does he not, Miss Stapleton?'

The QC nodded. 'As Your Honour pleases. I have no further questions. Please wait there, Mrs Hodges.'

Hussain wasn't going to get anything from this witness. It needed to be short and sweet. 'So when the car veered off the road, before the impact, could you see inside the vehicle?'

'No, it was too far in front.'

'So you were unable to assess the condition of the driver?'

'What do you mean – the condition?'

'Well, whether he was unconscious for example?'

'Oh, I see.' She thought for a moment. 'No, I suppose not.'

The prosecution-minded judge saw his opportunity to expose the defence: 'So is that your case, Mr Hussain? The defendant was unconscious? So the jury can understand what they are being asked to decide.'

'It's one possibility, Your Honour, but the defendant has no recollection of the crash.'

'Oh, I see,' replied the judge with a flicker of sarcasm.

Hussain sat down. There was nothing else to be achieved with this witness.

Stapleton got up to re-examine. 'Just one question, Mrs Hodges. Does it also follow then that you couldn't tell if the driver was asleep?'

'Well, that's right. I just couldn't see the driver at all.'

'Thank you,' replied Stapleton, then sat down and whispered, 'touché,' across to Hussain.

Anderson had a sinking feeling. He should've realised there wouldn't be any case-winning revelations. He was a barrister after all. There were rarely any surprises in a trial like this.

'Miss Stapleton,' said the judge, looking at the clock. 'I think we have time for one more witness before the short adjournment.'

'As Your Honour pleases. I call Sandra Granger.'

The atmosphere changed immediately. A sense of apprehension descended over the courtroom. The mother of the girl that died was coming into court. The usher guided a diminutive Mrs Granger into the witness box. Nervously she surveyed the scene. Taking the bible in her right hand, she proceeded to repeat the oath. 'I swear by almighty God that the evidence I shall give shall be the truth, the whole truth, and nothing but the truth.'

'Would you give the Court your full name please?' asked Stapleton.

'Sandra Granger,' she whispered, overcome by the occasion.

With a sympathetic smile, the judge intervened: 'I know it's very difficult for you, Mrs Granger, but I must ask you to keep your voice up and direct your answers across to the jury. They need to hear what you say.'

'Sorry,' came a loud whisper.

Stapleton began again: 'I'm going to ask you about the events of the 24th of January of this year. I don't think there's any dispute that you left home at about 4.50pm. Is that right?'

'Yes.'

'Where were you going?'

'My mum's. Molly's nana's.' Her face twisted, already locked into the horrendous memories of that fateful day. 'It were only up the road – Warrington. Just a few junctions. Not far at all.'

'Who was with you on that journey, Mrs Granger?'

'Tom – my husband, and Molly.'

'Who drove?'

'Me. I locked the front door but had to go back. Forgot me purse, wanted to buy some flowers for Mum.' She paused, then admitted: 'If I hadn't forgotten it, we wouldn't have been there at that time, would we? Just a few seconds earlier and we'd 'a' been all right.' The witness broke down.

The judge interjected: 'Would you like a glass of water, Mrs Granger?'

Consumed by sorrow, she didn't hear. 'Why couldn't I bloody remember it?' She shook her head.

Stapleton gently moved her on to the crucial part of her evidence, which had to be elicited before the witness was good for nothing. 'Could you see the driver of the vehicle as it careered into the side of you?'

'Yes, very clearly,' she replied, speaking more distinctly than before, sensing the importance of this piece of testimony.

Stapleton leaned across her lectern towards the witness. 'Could you see his face?'

All in court held their breath.

'Yes.' Then she volunteered: 'He had his eyes closed. As if he were asleep.'

'Asleep?' Stapleton repeated for emphasis.

'Yes. And just before he hit us, he woke up.'

'Woke up?'

'Yes, opened his eyes. But it were too late to do owt.' Full of rage, she glanced across at the defendant.

The jury followed suit.

Stapleton had what she needed, so didn't prolong the agony for Mrs Granger by going through the blood and guts of the aftermath. In any event, it wouldn't win her any friends on the jury. 'Please wait there, Mrs Granger. The defence advocate may have some questions for you.'

Hussain was going to have to completely discredit this witness to have any chance of an acquittal. His stomach was in knots as he got to his feet. He sensed the animosity of the jury. He gulped. Then: 'So, Mr Anderson's vehicle came at you from behind and to the side?'

'Yes.'

'How were you able to see his face, Mrs Granger?'

'I could see it in my rear-view mirror.'

'In your mirror, surely not?'

'I'm quite sure.'

'From the angle at which the vehicle approached?'

'Yes.'

'Was Mr Anderson wearing his spectacles?' Hussain asked, holding up a pair of reading glasses.

The witness hesitated. She looked to Stapleton for an answer.

Silence.

Eventually: 'Yes, he was.'

'Sure?'

Another pause, then: 'Yes.'

'As sure as you were about his eyes being closed?'

'Yes,' came a more emphatic reply.

Hussain put the glasses on his own face. In a quiet, gentle voice: 'Mrs Granger, John Anderson has never worn glasses.'

No reply from the witness.

The judge could barely contain his anger at Hussain's disingenuous approach.

Once the witness had gathered herself, jutting out her chin she declared: 'I'm not a liar.'

'Oh, I know, Mrs Granger,' Hussain replied. Gently, he said, 'It's just grief.'

She gave him a double-take, unsure of what he was insinuating.

He didn't need to push it any further. The jury understood.

The courtroom fell silent. Hussain sat down.

Stapleton decided not to re-examine. Best left well alone.

The judge glanced up at the wall clock behind the dock. 'I think that's a convenient moment. 2.15, members of the jury.'

Once the jurors had left court, the judge vented his anger: 'Mr Hussain, I'll not have cheap circus tricks in my court. Do you understand?'

'Yes, Your Honour.'

'You misled that witness. Pull a stunt like that again and you'll be up in front of the SRA for professional misconduct. Do I make myself clear?'

'Yes, Your Honour.' It had been worth the rebuke. If he

hadn't raised a doubt with Sandra Granger, it would've been game over.

Once the judge had risen, Anderson followed Hussain out onto the landing and into a conference room, closely followed by Adey.

Anderson caught DI Taylor's eye, who was watching events unfold outside the courtroom. They both nodded. Anderson sensed an understanding, even sympathy from Taylor for his predicament.

Once inside the conference room, Anderson exploded. 'What the hell is going on? Arrested for murder? Jesus!'

'Look, John, I really can't do this now,' Hussain replied. 'My head is full of the case – your case.'

Before Anderson had a chance to respond, Stapleton was knocking on the door. 'Sorry to interrupt. Can we have a quick chat about this afternoon's batting order? Robing room in five?'

Hussain agreed. Once Stapleton was out of earshot: 'I haven't even spoken to Safa since I was released.'

'Are you on police bail?' asked Adey.

'Yes, while they continue their enquiries.'

'So you're still a suspect?' Anderson observed.

'Yes.'

'Then I want some answers or you're off the case.'

'That's your choice, John, but I can't do this now. I've got to focus on the experts for this afternoon. You'll just have to trust me, like I trusted you. Come round to the house tonight, both of you, and I'll explain everything.'

It was enough to placate Anderson for the moment, apart from one question: 'Just answer me this: did you kill Waqar Ahmed?'

'No, I didn't.'

Anderson couldn't sustain his sense of outrage, particularly in light of all Hussain's efforts in court that morning. He would wait for a full explanation. He owed Hussain that much.

CHAPTER 54

The Crown began the afternoon with collision investigator Lionel Henbury. Hussain knew that as a trained police officer he was bound to be partisan, hence extreme caution was required, since as an expert witness he was entitled to give opinion evidence.

Once he was sworn, Stapleton began to take him through the gory details of the crash site and then, crucially, the movement of Anderson's vehicle. 'How did you ascertain the direction of travel prior to impact, officer?'

'I was able to look at the track of damage, post impact.'

'For the ladies and gentleman of the jury, you mean the spread and angle of the debris in relation to the final resting place of the vehicles after the crash?'

'Yes, that's right, and I also considered the eyewitness evidence from the written statements of those who saw the vehicle.'

'Was there any evidence of the defendant's car taking evasive action prior to impact?'

'No, all the evidence suggests a gentle drift involving no driver input.'

'Any skid marks on the road, officer?'

'None.'

'Thank you, please wait there.'

Hussain got to his feet. 'Officer, it's important to be fair and objective in the presentation of your evidence, isn't it?'

'Of course.'

'Mr Anderson was driving a Volvo that day, wasn't he?'

'He was indeed.'

'That vehicle is fitted with ABS brakes as standard.'

'I believe so.'

'You know don't you, that in vehicles fitted with ABS one doesn't see skid marks even where there has been hard braking?'

'That's correct.'

'So why didn't you tell Miss Stapleton that?'

'She didn't ask.'

The jury tittered.

Not the great point that Hussain had hoped for and he was still stuck with the drifting. He decided to cut his losses and sit down rather than draw attention to the weaknesses in his case.

Stapleton took the next witness, sleep expert Professor Hawthorn, through his report, emphasising the important areas. Hawthorn was a tall, thin man, approaching the end of a long and distinguished career. His shambolic hair had the freedom of a life spent in academia. His confidence in the box revealed that he had given evidence many times before. Hawthorn was in no doubt that Anderson had fallen asleep at the wheel. As with the last witness, the defence had no expert that could counter his opinions and so Hussain would have to rely on cross-examination alone – at a critical stage of the case.

Stapleton finished in chief by blocking an escape route for the defence: 'Professor, we know there was a passenger in the vehicle. If the defendant was asleep, wouldn't she have noticed? Tried to grab the wheel or something? It's just that we know there was no sudden change to the direction of travel, just the drifting that the jury have heard about.'

'She may have noticed eventually, prior to the impact, but what many people don't know is that a reasonable reaction time for a human being is 1.5 seconds. That is the time between the hazard occurring, i.e. noticing the driver is asleep, and actually doing the evasive act such as hand touching steering wheel. It takes time for the brain to decode the information and send a message to the hand. If the vehicle was travelling at sixty miles per hour it covers twenty-seven metres every second.'

'So,' Stapleton interrupted, 'the vehicle could have travelled some forty metres in the wrong lane without time to take any evasive action, even if the passenger was aware of what was happening?'

'Exactly.'

Satisfied the jury had the point, Stapleton sat down.

Hussain got to his feet. 'You were instructed by the Crown Prosecution Service to compile a report on this collision, were you not?'

'Yes, that's right.'

'So you knew that a prosecution was being considered?'

'Yes.'

'The obvious issue to consider was sleep?'

'Yes.'

'If nothing else, because you are an expert on sleep?'

'Well, yes.'

'I make no criticism, Professor, but it is a fact then, from the very beginning of your analysis, you were searching for evidence of sleep? Anything that could support that theory?'

'I can assure you I took an entirely objective view of the evidence.'

'Of course, but your whole report comes from the perspective of sleep – in other words, can the facts fit sleep?'

'Well, yes.'

'What's your point, Mr Hussain?' interjected the judge.

Hussain cut to the chase: 'If you had been asked whether the evidence from the crash was consistent with a seizure, for example, you would have to say yes, wouldn't you?'

'I can't comment on that, I'm an expert on sleep.'

'But Mr Anderson wasn't taken from the vehicle asleep, was he?'

'No, he wasn't.'

'You are relying on the movement of the defendant's vehicle – the arcing or drifting – being consistent with a lack of braking, which you say suggests sleep?'

'That's right.'

'That evidence alone does not distinguish between sleep and any other state of unconsciousness.'

'Well, no. If there was evidence of a pre-existing medical condition I would have to revise my findings.'

'Is there any evidence?' asked the judge, already aware of the answer.

'No, Your Honour, although there rarely is in these cases.'

'Are *you* giving evidence now, Mr Hussain?'

'No, Your Honour.' Hussain turned back to the witness. 'Professor Hawthorn, there is no evidence that Mr Anderson was tired, is there?'

Stapleton cut in: 'No *medical* evidence of tiredness.'

The professor followed her lead: 'There's no medical evidence of tiredness. One has to look at the surrounding

210

facts, such as the evidence of Sandra Granger.'

'Yes, thank you, Professor,' said Hussain, eager to change the subject. 'And there is evidence that the defendant had a cup of coffee shortly before the crash. Surely that would have prevented sleep?'

'Well, firstly we don't know how much he drank. That is critical in answering what effect it would have had. But secondly, and perhaps more importantly, coffee does not act as a stimulant until at least twenty minutes after it's consumed. We see this a lot after people stop at the services on the motorway due to tiredness, grab a coffee and continue their journey. They then fall asleep a few minutes later.' Hawthorn was in full flow. 'The point I make is this – from what I've read the defendant consumed the coffee at most, twenty minutes before the crash. Sadly, it didn't have time to stimulate him.'

'But do you agree with this proposition, Professor?' asked Hussain. 'Because Mr Anderson had just drunk a coffee he would have assumed himself to be awake and fit to drive?'

'I can't speculate about that, I'm afraid, but I can say this: if someone falls asleep, there must have been a moment, before sleep occurred, where the driver felt tired and should have pulled over. Sleep doesn't just happen out of the blue.'

Hussain sat down and instinctively turned to Anderson who gave a nod of appreciation, but both men knew the professor's last answer had been most unhelpful.

Day one of the trial was over. Hussain hurried off to the robing room to discuss matters with Stapleton for the following day, but not before reaffirming his promise to explain things later.

Anderson and Adey set off on their train journey back

to Manchester. The long silences weren't uncomfortable anymore, almost expected. They both relived the expert evidence in their heads, trying to find answers that weren't there. Anderson was certain there was so much more to discover. What was it? Would he ever know the truth?

Or was he just going mad?

Adey paid for a cab from Victoria back at the flat.

Anderson stood in Adey's lounge, staring aimlessly out of the window across Manchester, ignoring the piece of paper stuck on the glass, and its contents. The gentle tapping of Adey's fingers on her laptop had become such a familiar sound that he hardly noticed anymore.

'I give up!' she shouted, slumping back in her chair.

'What is it?'

'The ghost of Heena Butt. I've searched everywhere. This woman doesn't exist, not with that date of birth anyway. It's never happened before. You can always find them somewhere, whether it's on the electoral role, benefit claims, or even a dating site. With her there's nothing.'

Anderson joined Adey at the table and tried to come up with new lines of enquiry. 'OK, so all we know is that she had a library card?'

'And yes, amazingly she didn't need any ID to get it. She gave a fake address, I've checked it out.'

'So we know she needed access to books?'

'Computers more like.'

'Right, of course,' acknowledged Anderson.

'So what else would she definitely need to exist?'

'A place to sleep,' Adey replied immediately. She'd obviously spent hours considering these questions. 'She didn't own a property but she might have used hotels. It's impossible to check every hotel and hostel even in Manchester, let alone England. And that's even if she used the name Butt.'

'What if she was in Manchester more long-term? She could've been renting. It's very hard to rent anywhere nowadays without ID – all these new money laundering regs.'

'Maybe,' nodded Adey. 'I'll put it on my list.' She checked her watch. 'Come on. Let's go. He's had long enough to speak to Safa. I need to know what the hell's going on.'

CHAPTER 55

Hussain was tight as a drum. He showed them into the kitchen where Safa was hiding her face at the sink, wiping the tears from her puffed-up eyes. She managed only a muttered welcome to the visitors. Hussain invited them to join him at the table. After a few seconds of intently clasping and unclasping his hands, he spoke.

'The police recovered a debtors list in Waqar Ahmed's things. My name was on it.'

They digested the information.

'But you represented him on legal aid,' said Anderson, jumping to a conclusion. 'So you were taking cash on top?'

'No,' replied Hussain, irritated by the assumption. 'I owed *him* money.'

'What? You owed money to your own client?' Anderson couldn't decide which scenario was worse.

'How much?' asked Adey, without making any judgement.

'Twenty grand.'

'Twenty grand! What for?'

Hussain stared down at his hands. 'Shahid.'

'Shahid?' repeated Adey in surprise.

'Who is Shahid?' asked Anderson.

A tear ran down Hussain's cheek. 'My son. My beautiful, beautiful son.' He was lost in thought. Then: 'He died of leukaemia, last May. The twelfth.'

'Just before the Banji case?' Anderson asked.

Hussain nodded.

Anderson remembered a difficult drugs case in which he had bullied and insulted Hussain throughout to hustle his way to a conviction. He shuddered at the realisation his opponent had been mourning the recent death of his child. 'I'm so sorry.'

'There was a new treatment in America. Our only hope. We had to try everything.'

On seeing Hussain overcome with emotion, Safa sat down and continued the story. 'We had no money. The house was mortgaged, everything we had went on keeping the firm afloat, and with all these legal aid cuts…'

Anderson asked, 'So you borrowed it from Ahmed?'

Hussain hung his head in shame. 'Yes.'

'I bet Ahmed jumped at the chance to have a hold over you.'

'Did you tell the police?' asked Adey.

'No. I went no comment. If I'd told them I defended a gangster whilst in his debt, I'd be struck off. It's a blatant breach of the code.'

'Taz!' exclaimed Adey. 'Better that than a life sentence for murder.'

'No, you were right,' said Anderson, surprising himself at how pragmatic he had become lately where the law was concerned. 'Say nothing. If that's all they've got, you're free and clear.'

'It is,' replied Hussain.

'I'm so sorry about your son. Both of you, I had no idea.'

'But Safa,' asked Adey, 'why do you blame Anderson?'

Anderson thought he'd already worked it out: 'Because

Ahmed called in the debt – for defending the man that prosecuted him?' Anderson paused while he thought it through. 'And so he'd been putting pressure on you to withdraw?'

'Yes,' lied Hussain. Never had he felt so ashamed.

Adey took Safa's hand. 'And poor Safa couldn't understand why Tahir wouldn't dump the Anderson case?'

'Yes,' she said defiantly. 'I'm sorry, but Taz should put his family first.'

'Well, it doesn't matter now – he's dead,' said Hussain with some relish.

Reflecting further, Anderson wasn't so sure. 'That debt meant he owned you, Tahir. If we've worked that out so will the police. It's not just the debt; they can attribute motive to you. Motive to kill.'

CHAPTER 56

Anderson made the morning train journey to Bradford alone. Adey had explained at breakfast that she had some enquiries to make, and Hussain was going by car. Anderson didn't want to put him off his game by getting a lift and asking a million questions about the case. He knew from experience, Hussain needed a clear head.

Bradford Interchange. Anderson followed the hoards off the train to make the short walk past the Victoria Hotel to the court. His phone bleeped – a text. He fished it out of his coat pocket. His fingers struggled to find the keys in the cold Yorkshire air. It read: YOU ARE GOING TO DIE.

Anderson gulped. With everything else he'd put the last call to the back of his mind. Instinctively, he looked around him at the crowds, the faces. Were they commuters or was one of them out to get him? He pulled the collar of his coat up around his neck and quickened his step.

The court building was a welcome sight, despite Anderson's dread of what might unfold there. Once he was beyond the metal detector he read the text again. There was a mobile number from which it was sent. He forwarded the text and the number to Adey. He could feel someone watching him. Paranoia? No. Standing by the lifts – Sam Connor. Waiting to be spotted, he gave Anderson a nod of acknowledgement. What was he doing here? Had he just sent the text? As some kind of sick joke? No, of course not, he reasoned, pulling himself together. His old colleague had come to give evidence for the prosecution.

Anderson took the stairs to avoid him.

Hussain was pacing up and down outside the courtroom. On seeing his client he hurried over, full of ideas about the day's cross-examinations. 'You know today is all about Stapleton getting witnesses to say how tired you were on the day of the crash, because of working on the Ahmed case?'

'I know,' Anderson sighed.

'I've got to go in hard. Put it to them they are lying out of jealousy, ambition, rivalry.'

Anderson agreed. 'But be careful not to lose the jury. Nothing gratuitous.' Anderson was finding it hard to stay positive. 'I don't think we are ever going to know the truth of what happened. Maybe Waqar Ahmed took that with him to the grave.'

'Come on, my friend. You mustn't think like that. And remember, the burden is on the prosecution to make the jury sure of guilt. We don't have to prove your innocence.'

They heard the tannoy: 'All parties in Anderson to Court One immediately.'

The courtroom was packed. Journalists filled the press box – a chambers colleague giving evidence for the prosecution would add human interest for the readers.

Anderson scanned the public gallery for a friendly face. Only strangers. Had one of them sent him the text, he wondered?

'Your Honour, members of the jury,' announced Hannah Stapleton, 'I call Matilda Henley-Smith.'

The usher led Tilly into court. Less wet behind the ears

than Anderson remembered, but still very attractive – the jury would like her. She confidently repeated the oath whilst scanning the courtroom so as to know her audience. Brief eye contact with Anderson, but no acknowledgement.

Stapleton moved quickly through the preliminaries to the day of the crash. 'So you were with him pretty much all day?'

'Yes.'

'And how did he seem?'

'Tired,' came the reply, without the slightest prick of conscience.

'Just a moment,' said the judge. 'I'm making a note.' He wasn't going to let the jury forget that one.

'Miss Henley-Smith,' Stapleton continued. 'Why did you come to that conclusion?'

'He just seemed very run down. Exhausted. We went for a coffee after court, to recharge his batteries.'

Anderson listened open-mouthed as this demure young girl sought to destroy him, seemingly without a second thought.

'The case had really taken it out of him. It was very demanding. And I think he had some personal problems at home.'

Hussain turned around to see Anderson shrug. How could Tilly have known about his home life? She was deliberately poisoning the jury against him.

Stapleton continued: 'You were in fact one of the last people to see him before the crash. How did he seem when he left Starbucks?'

'Still tired, and distracted by something,' she offered, feigning regret at having to give such a damning answer.

'But he did drink a coffee, didn't he?'

'I'm not sure that he did. I remember him getting up to leave and knocking the cup all over the floor.'

'Oh, I see.' Stapleton glanced off to the jury. 'Thank you, Miss Henley-Smith. Please wait there.'

Hussain got to his feet. Feeling the pressure: 'Difficult trials were nothing new to John Anderson, were they?'

A hesitation, then: 'No.'

'He grew up with this pressure and did these trials week in, week out, didn't he?'

'I don't know.'

'But of course, you didn't see him do any other trials, did you?'

'No, I don't think so.'

'No?' emphasised Hussain. 'Because you were a pupil. You'd hardly seen anything of the courtroom, had you?'

'Well, I—'

Hussain followed up with: 'As you'd never seen Mr Anderson at work before, you have no idea how he comes across during a case. It might be that he would always seem tired to you?'

'I suppose so. He might yawn after court in every case he does.'

The jurors laughed.

Tilly Henley-Smith had raised the stakes; Hussain had no choice but to go for the jugular. 'Why did you go for that coffee?'

'He asked me. You don't say no to a senior member of chambers.'

'Weren't you worried?'

'Worried?'

'That Sam Connor, your pupil-master, would be jealous?'

Buying time to think, she repeated: 'Jealous?'

'Yes.' Hussain shot the witness a mischievous smile.

She didn't answer.

'If we were to see your emails, would they reveal that you were in a relationship with Mr Connor?'

Tilly's face lost its rosy pallor. Was Hussain bluffing? Had he read them? He couldn't use them if he'd hacked in, but to deny the affair would be perjury.

Judge Cranston rescued her: 'Mr Hussain, what possible relevance could this witness's personal relationships have to whether your client fell asleep whilst driving or was in some other way distracted?'

'It is our case that the witness is not being entirely truthful about the defendant's tiredness – or lack of it – she has animus towards him which I must explore further.'

'Very well,' replied the judge, convinced Hussain was making a big mistake pursuing this line with the young witness.

'Were you in a relationship with Sam Connor, Miss Henley-Smith?'

She waited for the judge to rescue her again.

This time he didn't.

'That's not why I'm here,' she said, trying to stop herself moving around in the box. A dead giveaway. 'I'm not answering that.'

'I'm afraid you have to, Miss Henley-Smith,' said His Honour. 'I will stop Mr Hussain if he oversteps the mark.'

'So, I will ask you again,' said Hussain. 'Were you in a relationship with Sam Connor?'

Reluctantly, she replied: 'Yes.'

'Now let's go back to my question that started all this off: weren't you worried that Connor would be jealous if you went off for coffee with his leader?'

Unsure of how to answer: 'No.'

'Thank you. Now, you are a barrister, aren't you? An officer of the Court, are you not?'

'I am.'

'You are under oath, Miss Henley-Smith. Think long and hard before answering my next question. Is the reason you weren't worried because Connor knew you were having a coffee with Anderson?'

There was no escape. With an air of defiance: 'Yes.'

'Was there some agreement with Mr Connor that you would take Mr Anderson for a coffee?'

'Anderson suggested it.'

'But that was just good fortune. You had agreed with Connor to keep him busy anyway, hadn't you?'

Eventually, with a nervous glance across at the prosecutor: 'Yes.'

Hussain had guessed right. 'Why, Miss Henley-Smith?'

The sanctimonious young barrister had disappeared to be replaced by an embarrassed little girl. 'Connor didn't want Anderson going back to chambers.'

'Why not?'

'It was all to do with a junior brief on a murder. Orlando West, our Head of Chambers, had promised it to Anderson. They were supposed to have a meeting about it after court. Connor thought West would switch the brief to him if Anderson didn't show.'

The jurors' shock at her duplicity smashed around the courtroom. Their fickle loyalties were shifting.

Hussain took advantage: 'So you and your lover were trying to damage your leader's career whilst he was in the middle of prosecuting a difficult trial?'

'It was just chambers politics. Happens all the time.'

'Really? Did your pupil-master, Sam Connor, tell you that?'

'No,' she replied.

'So who else in your chambers stabs people in the back?'

'No one.'

She was beaten.

'Did you or Connor do anything else that day to ruin John Anderson?'

'No!'

'Did you have anything to do with that crash?'

'Mr Hussain!' exclaimed the judge. 'That's a step too far.'

'It's all right,' said Tilly. 'I don't mind answering. I had nothing to do with it and I don't know anything about it, other than what I read in the newspapers.'

'No further questions.' Hussain's disgust was evident for all to see.

A shamefaced Tilly slunk out of court.

Anderson was buoyed by Hussain's hatchet job, but would the jury just see it as a sideshow? At least Hussain had muddied the waters.

'Perhaps that's a convenient moment for a break, Your Honour?' suggested Stapleton in the hope it would allow time for Connor to be tipped off before he walked into the same trap.

'I think we'll have one more witness before the jury stretch their legs,' replied the judge.

Hoping now to play down Connor's evidence, Stapleton

rushed him through in chief, moving swiftly on as every laboured assertion about Anderson's tiredness grated on everyone in the courtroom.

Hussain couldn't wait for his turn. When it came, he wasted no time: 'He wasn't tired at all, was he?'

'I've already answered that,' Connor replied.

'You did very well out of Anderson's downfall, didn't you?'

'I don't know what you mean.'

'Let me spell it out for you. You took over the Ahmed case as leader, didn't you?'

'Yes, but it wasn't a responsibility I wanted thrust on me like that.'

'And that big murder brief? What was it called?'

'I don't know. Which brief do you mean?'

'You know, the one Anderson was going to do, but got switched after the crash?'

As if it had only just occurred to him: 'Harrison?'

'That's the one,' said Hussain. 'Harrison.'

'It was just Anderson's bad luck. I had nothing to do with the decision.'

'You said in your witness statement that you saw Anderson in Starbucks with Tilly as you walked past.'

'Yes, that's right.'

'Where were you going?'

'What?'

'Where were you going?'

'Home, I suppose?'

'But why go that way? You rent a parking space behind chambers, don't you?'

'Er, yes. I can't remember where I was going, it was weeks ago.'

224

'Were you even there? Did you just want the police to think he was having an affair – sling a bit of mud in Anderson's direction? '

'No! Of course I was there. How else would I know they were in Starbucks?'

'Maybe Tilly told you? You had a plan, didn't you?'

'What plan?'

'To stop Anderson from going to chambers so you could get the Harrison case?'

'That's ridiculous!'

'You were in a relationship with Tilly Henley-Smith, weren't you?'

Connor opened his mouth to deny it but before he could get his words out a voice shouted, 'Enough!'

Everyone looked to see Anderson on his feet. Hussain had never had a cross-examination interrupted by his own client before.

'No more questions,' Anderson said quietly.

Reluctantly, Hussain nodded. He understood. Connor was a chambers colleague when all was said and done. Anderson couldn't allow the destruction of a career over a secret affair and personal ambition. Hussain sat down. Anderson never ceased to surprise him.

A confused and flustered Connor stared over at Anderson, then at a tearful Tilly as she came into court and sat in the gallery. It clicked. Anderson had just saved him from a charge of perjury. And his career.

CHAPTER 57

A breakthrough at last – Adey had rung every estate agent in Manchester, posing as a bailiff trying to trace a debtor, Heena Butt. Adey's persistence had paid off. The Indian manager of a low-end rental agency in Fallowfield was keen to share his gripe. He disclosed that Butt had paid three months' rent upfront in cash, but was now two weeks behind. The agent had been unable to make contact. He didn't have a phone number for her though he'd gone round a few times but she wasn't in. Obviously unaware of her death, he'd assumed she was giving him the run around. More than happy to divulge her address to a voice on the other end of the phone, Adey couldn't believe her luck.

'And if you see her, tell her I going in with key in seven day.'

'I will,' Adey assured him.

'Landlord very cross. Bad for my business.'

Adey tried to seem interested.

'I take all possessions and sell. Then she will be sorry,' he went on.

After what seemed like hours of moaning and complaining, Adey was able to end the call. She'd already left her place for Fallowfield.

The one-bed flat was on Thornton Road, spitting distance from the Curry Mile. Long roads of Victorian red-brick terraced houses, some split into flats. She soon located the cheap, chipboard front door, then peered through the letter box. Stairs leading up to the living space.

Adey took the key made from the imprint of the one in Butt's handbag. She put it in the lock. It fitted. She stopped and reflected for a minute. This was a big call – interfering with a police investigation. Compromising the forensics. Sneaking into a dead person's home. Adey had inherited her mother's superstitious disposition. It just felt plain wrong.

She pulled out her phone and rang DI Taylor. 'You'd better come. I've found Butt's flat.'

Sitting at his desk, Taylor almost choked on a mouthful of Hula Hoops. 'What? How?'

'Never mind that. Bring the key from her bag. I'm sure it'll work. I'm on Thornton Road, in Fallowfield.'

'But I'm supposed to be going over to Bradford to give evidence in the trial.'

'Then you'd better hurry up,' said Adey, predicting that his curiosity, if nothing else, would make him drop everything.

'All right. I'm in Longsight. I will be there in twenty.'

In fact, he was there in ten, with the key. Taylor didn't like it when the defence were one step ahead of the investigation. He saw her waving from the pavement and managed to squeeze his Astra into a space right outside. Before he was even out of the car he asked, 'So how did you find it?'

'Good old-fashioned police work,' she teased. 'Ringing round rental agencies.'

Taylor was impressed, and embarrassed he hadn't tasked that job. Not that Armstrong would've approved what was, on the face of it, a very expensive wild goose chase. 'OK,' he said. 'Let's go and have a look.'

He pushed the key into the lock.

CHAPTER 58

Tilly held her face up to the shower head, hoping the jets would wash away the humiliation of what happened in court. She was angry at having been exposed – she'd always been the one to control situations, hide her duplicity. Nobody's fool, she'd always found it easy to use people to achieve her own ends. Had all the tools since school days: beauty, brains and guile.

She stepped out and patted the towel on her face. Catching sight of her firm body in the mirror, she moved her hips, checking all was still well with her best asset.

She heard the sound of a key in the lock. She'd have to do something about that. Dropping the towel on the bathroom floor she paraded to the top of the stairs. Why not let him see what he'd never have again? An added punishment. His suffering would make her feel a little better.

The front door opened.

Connor stood at the bottom of the stairs, gawping at her magnificence. 'Why didn't you wait, Tilly?'

'I want my key back.'

'Why? What do you mean?'

'You're toxic. Everyone's going to be talking about what happened today. I'm just praying I'm young enough to be forgiven. Hoping they'll think you took advantage of me.'

Always slow to catch on, Connor said, 'I don't get it?

We've got each other. Someone's already told my missus. And the kids won't take my calls. I love you.'

Tilly let out a sardonic laugh. 'You're a fat, second-rate barrister who I was unfortunate enough to have as my pupil-master.'

'Tilly, please?'

'I messed up – backed the wrong horse. You're going nowhere. You've peaked. It's all downhill for you now and I'm not coming.' Then she added with a snigger, 'Not that I ever did.'

Each word caused Connor a physical pain. He cut a ridiculous figure in his pinstriped suit and cashmere coat, being dismissed by someone almost young enough to be his daughter.

Tilly went back into the bathroom. Before shutting the door she called down to him: 'Leave the key on the stairs and piss off.'

'You can't speak to me like that.'

She didn't bother to respond. It was over.

Connor placed the key on the bottom stair. Then, feeling worthless, he left.

CHAPTER 59

Having just opened it, Taylor instinctively shut the door, but the stench had already filled their nostrils.

Adey wretched, then asked, 'What the hell's that?'

Taylor knew what she was thinking. 'Don't worry, it's not a body. I know that smell well enough. Come on,' he said, raising a cuff over his mouth and going inside.

After a few seconds of preparing herself, Adey followed him up the stairs.

He'd already opened a window in the kitchen and was tying up a bin liner. 'Takeaway,' he explained. 'Must've been rotting all these months.'

As the smell subsided Adey scanned the room. Chipped Formica worktops and old lino, curled up at the corners.

Taylor pulled some plastic gloves out of his pocket and handed Adey a pair before opening the cupboards. Salt and pepper and a few tins. 'Heena Butt certainly wasn't living the high life,' said Taylor.

'I'd say financially, she was on her arse.'

Taylor grinned on hearing the expression. He went into the bedroom and started going through the drawers. Nothing personal, just a few items of clothing. Thinking out loud: 'Nothing to identify her. No evidence of a life.'

An Ikea wardrobe, screaming out for an Allen key, listed heavily to the right. Covering her hand with the sleeve of her jean jacket, Adey opened it. Full Muslim dress, including burkas, hung neatly from hangers. 'She was a strict Muslim?' Adey couldn't work it out. 'Or a fetish hooker? For punters that liked the full garb?' she suggested, not really believing it.

'Possibly,' he replied. 'Then she wasn't on the job with Anderson.'

'How do you know?'

Taylor joined her and ran his gloved hand over the outfits. 'She was in jeans and a jumper when they pulled her from Anderson's car.'

'Really?' asked Adey, realising that she'd never sought to clarify what clothes Butt had been wearing. She'd only seen the naked post-mortem photos.

'Yes, I checked with the hospital. They weren't retained. Had to cut them off her. Covered in blood.'

Adey was relieved that as far as Anderson was concerned, the prostitute angle didn't seem to have any foundation.

'And why no ID?' Then Taylor caught himself. Working with the defence? Sharing ideas? What was he doing? Adey Tuur had a strangely disarming effect on him. Taylor remembered his position, and hers. 'Right, that's it. Nothing else to see. Come on,' he said, ushering her towards the stairs.

'Hang on. What's the next step? You going to have the place tested for prints? DNA?'

Taylor laughed. 'My boss would never approve that. It's not relevant to the offence – the driving.'

'But we need to know who she was. How can you leave it like this?'

'Don't be so naive,' Taylor snapped, more annoyed with Armstrong and his damn budget than with Adey. 'Who's

232

going to pay for it? Neither the jury, nor the taxpayer need to know who's been in this flat.' He winced, realising he sounded like his DCI.

Adey continued to protest as Taylor got into his car: 'If Anderson gets potted, I hope you can live with yourself, *detective.*'

'I'll cope, love.'

The glib reply infuriated Adey.

Taylor turned on the ignition, then lowered the electric window. 'Has it occurred to you that Anderson might be guilty? Maybe his prints are all over that flat.'

Adey refused to accept it. She'd switched from being sure of his guilt to being sure of his innocence. There was no evidential basis to justify the change of heart. It was something more powerful. An emotional attachment. Blind faith. She wasn't prepared to give up on Anderson, and if the police wouldn't investigate, she would just have to take matters into her own hands.

Adey decided to walk across to Victoria Park to follow up the remaining lead. She'd spent a great deal of time analysing the data recovered from Heena Butt's phone. Of the four numbers in the contacts, three were no longer in use and all seemed to be pay-as-you-go. The fact that phones seemed to have been ditched suggested only one thing: criminality.

Adey had finally managed to hack into one network provider's records and, as luck would have it, the one number still in use was on that network. Most of the phone usage was cell-sited to the Victoria Park area, particularly when in contact with Butt's number. Adey took a walk around to see if anything jumped out; a long shot, but she was out of ideas.

She walked past Manchester Royal Infirmary on Upper Brook Street. Was this the link? Possibly, but the cell-site was slightly further along. After wandering down a few side streets she walked along Upper Park Road. Out of nowhere, rising up before her, Manchester's Central Mosque. On seeing it she knew. It fitted perfectly with the cell-site. Adey was sure from the call patterns that Butt must have attended this mosque and known someone else who did.

Time was running out for Anderson. She had no choice but to ring the number.

'Hello?' The voice was male, Asian.

Adey took the plunge: 'Oh, hello, who is this?'

'Who are *you*?'

'I'm a friend of Heena Butt.'

'How did you get this number?'

'I haven't seen her for ages. Is she OK?'

Silence. Then: 'Where are you?'

'At the mosque.'

'I will meet you there tomorrow at eleven and I will explain. OK?'

'I'm very worried, can't we meet today?'

'No, I'm sorry, not today.' He hung up.

Adey breathed out. What was she doing? Who was this guy? And why the hell was she putting herself in danger by agreeing to meet him?

She decided not to mention it to the others.

CHAPTER 60

The last prosecution witness was the officer in the case – Taylor. Hussain was apprehensive about cross-examining a detective who, days ago, had interviewed him on a charge of murder.

Once Stapleton had established the basics of the defendant's arrest and charge, she tendered him for cross-examination.

Hussain began: 'There is one very important unanswered question in this case, isn't there, officer?'

'What's that?'

'Who was the lady that died in the defendant's car?'

'It's certainly unanswered. No disrespect to the deceased, but I don't know if it's important. We think her name was Heena Butt.'

'You are assuming that from a library card found in her belongings?'

'That's right.'

'Do you know anything else about her at all? Her job, anything?'

'Afraid not. Her flat was located today, but it took that part of the investigation no further forward.' Taylor was almost sympathetic to the defence on this. He was an old-school bobby. He more than anyone was uncomfortable with knowing nothing about the deceased, whether or not it had any relevance to the issues for the jury. 'Believe me, we've tried.'

Hussain chose not to belittle him in front of the jury, or even to point out that it was the defence who found Butt's flat. It wouldn't help Anderson. 'What about her phone? We know some numbers were extracted – four, I think? What enquiries did you make?'

'Yes, they were all pay-as-you-go, unregistered. We rang the one number that was still in use and left a message. No one called back. That's as far as we could take it.'

'That's odd isn't it? Three of the four numbers in her contacts no longer in use. Could that indicate a criminal network was operating?'

'Pure speculation,' interrupted the judge. 'Don't answer that, officer.'

Hussain moved on: 'Did you check missing persons for a Heena Butt?'

'Of course. There was no match. I should add that we used the date of birth on the library card and ran a trace through the electoral role and all other lists at our disposal. Nothing.'

'Possibly a foreign national then?'

'Maybe, but she didn't enter our borders using that name – we ran a check.'

'So you haven't found anyone that knew her?'

'No, unless you count Mr Anderson, of course.'

On the face of it, the officer had done all he could. Time to change tack. 'Would you agree that Mr Anderson had a lot of enemies – because of his job as a prosecution barrister?'

'Quite possibly.'

'He even reported receiving anonymous threats by phone whilst awaiting trial?'

'Yes, that goes with the job. His and mine.'

'You didn't find out who that person was?'

'No, sir.'

'This note was found in the deceased's handbag: "John Anderson, Spinningfields Chambers – 05 man." Have you any idea what that means?'

'No, sir, we don't.' Taylor's frustration was evident. 'Look, if you are trying to say someone else was responsible for this car crash, then I need to know in what way? Give me something to go on.'

The judge peered at Hussain over his spectacles. 'Is that what you are saying?'

'It is, Your Honour, but we cannot provide that information because the defendant has no recollection of events.'

'Ah, yes of course,' came His Honour Judge Cranston's cynical reply.

'And why doesn't Mr Anderson know who his passenger was?' said Taylor. 'If that's true then it makes it very difficult for us to investigate his claims that he didn't fall asleep or get distracted somehow.'

Hussain decided to cut his losses and sit down. He would have to rely on the Crown's unreliable evidence of tiredness from Tilly and Connor, and a good performance from Anderson in the box. Or was that wishful thinking?

Once the judge had risen for the day, Hussain went over the day's events with his client in a conference room. Anderson was wired. Too much to consider: Tilly, Connor, the text message, the prospect of giving evidence the following day. The pressure on both men was becoming unbearable. Anderson was a day or two away from years in prison, locked up with countless men he'd put there. Hussain imparted some advice to his client: 'Get a good night's sleep tonight, John. You could be in the box for some time. Need your wits about you. Remember, don't answer back with a question. Don't be arrogant, the jury will hate that. And you need to come across as scared – terrified even.'

'That won't be hard,' Anderson replied. 'Could we get verdicts tomorrow?'

'Possibly. Certainly speeches and summing up.'

'Might try and see the boys tonight. Might be my last chance for a long time.'

'If the worst happens, they could visit you?'

'Definitely not!' Anderson snapped, then apologised. 'I couldn't bear for them to see me like that.' He sighed. 'Thanks for everything, Tahir. I'll see you tomorrow.'

Hussain watched what was left of John Anderson shuffle out and down the stairs. He knew then that a guilty verdict would finish him. Not just his career, but the man.

A light smattering of snow coated the square outside the courts. Anderson took deliberate steps to avoid slipping. The crisp evening air stung his ears.

Bradford Interchange was bustling with commuters heading back to Halifax, Ilkley, Huddersfield and the surrounding towns. A row of makeshift stalls, manned by undernourished Asian men selling second-hand shoes, lined the entrance. Up the escalator and onto the platform, the 5.13 was about to leave. He hobbled alongside the train and in through the first door. Standing room only. Once inside the relative peace and quiet of the carriage he realised his mobile was ringing. A feeling of dread. Was it him again? The display revealed a number – the same one. 'Hello, what do you want?'

'Another bad day at the office?'

The voice was unfamiliar, but definitely Mancunian and possibly the same person that rang before. As with the text, Anderson was at the station. Was he here on the train, watching? He took in the myriad of faces. He shouted into the phone: 'Who are you?'

A few passengers looked over at Anderson.

The caller responded with laughter. Then: 'Mr Anderson, I wanted to be the person to tell you.'

'Tell me what?'

'Your children are dead. I ate them.'

Anderson's blood ran cold. Everything slowed down. The words tripped across his brain, again and again. No! He terminated the call. Hands shaking, he rang Mia. Was he awake or in a dream? A nightmare? Ringing out. Directed to voicemail.

He rang again.

Waiting.

At last, she answered.

'Mia, it's John.'

'Oh, hello. What do you—'

'Where are the kids?'

'Sorry?'

'Where are the kids?'

'Don't speak to me like that.'

'I'm sorry, please.' Trying to control himself: 'Are they OK? What are they doing?'

'Playing in the garden. We had a bit of snow.'

'Check on them, please. I'll wait while you do it.'

Sensing the urgency, Mia's tone changed to one of concern. 'Why, what is it?'

239

'Just do it!'

'You're scaring me.'

Anderson could hear Mia open the back door. 'Boys, can you come in for a minute?'

He pushed the phone hard against his ear. Was she talking to them?

Mia's voice: 'Boys, where are you?'

No response.

'Can you see them?'

'No.'

Anderson's body began to shake.

'John, they're not here!' Panic. 'Where are they?'

'Oh my God. No, please. God, no.' Anderson slumped against the compartment door.

'John?'

He tried to think. 'Ring the police. Someone's been making threats.'

'What? Who? Why didn't you tell me?' She yelled out: 'Angus! Will! Oh, it's all right. They *are* here, on the Xbox.'

Relief. Anderson's face cracked up. Dropping his hands, he slid down the side of the carriage until he hit the floor. His head fell into his free hand. After a few moments he put the phone back to his face. 'Don't bother to pack, just get in the car and take the boys. Go to—' He checked himself and instinctively looked around him at prying eyes. 'Just go away for a few days. Call me when you are out of town.'

'But, John?'

'Just do it.'

'OK.' She hung up.

Anderson put his hands over his head, pressed his fingers into his scalp and let out uncontrolled guttural groans.

Some passengers moved away. Those sitting at a safe distance gawped.

He closed his eyes. Jumbled thoughts, daydreams, faces; Angus and Will, Adey, Waqar Ahmed, Tredwell, Heena Butt's lifeless body. Little Molly Granger. Overload.

'Mr Anderson, are you all right?' DI Taylor patted him gently on the shoulder.

Anderson stared at him, face blank.

Taylor helped him to his feet just before the doors opened – Halifax. A mass exodus of commuters freed up some seats. 'Come on, sit down over here,' said Taylor.

Snapping out of the initial shock, Anderson blurted: 'Officer you must help me, I'm begging you, for my children.' He gave a rambling account of the call and the text that morning.

Taylor had to slow him down a few times, just to make sense of it. Anderson was utterly convincing. One only had to look at him. If it was an elaborate lie, why do it after Taylor had already given evidence? This was real all right, and threats towards children was a different matter. More than just turning up at the zoo. And knowing what he did now about Martin Tredwell, Taylor resolved to step up all efforts to find him.

It took the rest of the train journey, but Taylor managed to bring Anderson back from the edge of the abyss. He calmed him with the logical point that it was all a wind-up by some disgruntled former defendant. After all, the boys were alive. Taylor spent the rest of the journey distracting him with small talk. He couldn't help but think how odd it all was – to be counselling the defendant in a case he had investigated. No doubt about it, he liked Anderson. There was a question he couldn't resist though: 'One thing I can't understand: you are so establishment. You come from a dynasty of legal royalty. Why use someone as shady as Tahir Hussain to defend you?'

Anderson's intense gaze held Taylor's for a moment. 'He turned out to be the best friend I've got.'

CHAPTER 61

The lift was broken again. By the time he'd walked across Manchester and made his way up to Adey's flat, Anderson was exhausted. The smell of Adey's cooking welcomed him.

'I thought I'd do a traditional Somali dish for you,' she shouted cheerfully from the kitchen. '*Cambuulo*, it's made from azuki beans.'

Anderson's eyes welled up. Any gesture, even a hot meal, meant so much. A bundle of emotions, he was at breaking point.

'Jesus, you look terrible, what's happened? Hussain said you had quite a good day with Tilly and Connor?'

Anderson updated her, his voice giving out several times.

Without thinking she pulled him into her arms.

For the first time in his adult life, John Anderson cried.

'Let it out,' she whispered. It felt alien to her, to hold someone. She gave Anderson a rare smile, took his hand and led him to the bedroom.

'What about the azuki beans?' he whispered.

She laughed. 'Don't worry, they have to boil for hours.'

That evening John Anderson forgot everything, and afterwards, at long last, they both slept soundly.

CHAPTER 62

'Knock once more,' Taylor said to the team of officers outside number four on the second floor. The run down Victorian building in Burnage, converted into bedsits, was well known to the police. Any property in Manchester with a landlord who accepted cash and asked no questions attracted all sorts of itinerants and illegals.

Still no answer.

'Right, force it,' he ordered.

The door smashed open and the officers went inside.

Taylor knew that smell – death.

They found Tredwell in the lounge, hanging from a beam, wearing only underpants. Eyes bulging out of his disfigured face and tongue dangling from his mouth, Taylor thought he resembled a toad. An upturned stool lay on the floor.

Taylor touched Tredwell's foot. 'Stone bloody cold. I want to know how long he's been like this and I want all forensic results by morning. Clear?'

'You'll be lucky, gov,' muttered Waters.

Taylor knew only too well what a strain there was on resources at GMP. 'All right then, prioritise any weapons. Blood and DNA. If he killed Ahmed, I want to know about it as soon as.'

CHAPTER 63

'Get that down you, gov,' said Waters the next morning, putting a coffee on the desk.

A bleary-eyed Taylor hardly acknowledged the gesture. Chasing phones for Anderson, and now this development in the Ahmed murder. Another all-nighter; the missus wouldn't be happy. At least he'd booked the week in Marmaris. Hotel with a pool. He remembered how the kids went mad when they saw the brochure. Never used to plan anything, but for some reason the Anderson case had altered his outlook, made him realise how things can change in the blink of an eye. He shook his head in disbelief. Not even a murder and yet it had affected Taylor so profoundly.

Waters took a call. He shared the information with Taylor: 'There's a lockdown, searching now.'

'Good,' Taylor replied, getting wearily to his feet and taking a swig of coffee. 'I'd better get over to Bradford and let everyone know the latest. I want to be updated the minute you find anything.'

'And last night's corpse?'

'As soon as the post-mortem is done, bury him.'

'OK, gov.'

'By the way, well done for getting the billing so quickly – these things never go unnoticed.'

Waters acknowledged the compliment. Unlike Taylor, he liked and respected his boss.

'Got a minute?' DCI Armstrong called out to Taylor on his way out.

Taylor let out a surreptitious sigh and changed direction.

'Come in, shut the door.'

Taylor obliged. Was it a bollocking or just checking up on him? He couldn't stand being monitored all the time. He wasn't a kid.

'Congratulations on the Ahmed case.'

'Thank you, but none necessary,' replied Taylor, surprised at the praise. 'After all, we were too late to get our man.'

'That's not down to you, or MIT. What about Anderson, how's that going?'

'As expected.' Taylor's monosyllabic response made it obvious he was keen to make tracks.

The DCI nodded. 'No surprises then?'

'Only the phone calls, but they are unrelated. There's something about the case I just don't like.'

'What?'

'I dunno, call it a copper's nous.'

DCI Armstrong gave a condescending smile. 'Why is it every detective hits his mid-forties and starts going soft?'

'I've just never done a case before that's gone to trial when we only know half the story.'

'The half we need to know – the driving. I know he was one of the good guys, but the long arm of the law touches us all.'

'Anderson's team have found Butt's flat. It hasn't helped us to formally identify her. Our lack of resources is allowing them to steer this case.'

246

Armstrong appeared concerned. 'Did it come out in court?'

'Well, yes, but not that they found it. Hussain spared me that indignity.'

'You know I haven't got the resources to send you on some wild goose chase.' Armstrong paused. 'And anyway, sounds like we got away with it. Least said, soonest mended.'

'There's nothing here, gov, is there? No disclosure they haven't had I should know about?'

Armstrong scoffed. 'Relax, officer. No smoke and mirrors here.' Then: 'That'll be all,' as if dismissing him from the headmaster's office.

CHAPTER 64

Nothing was said. They both hated goodbyes. Not even a clinch at the door before Anderson set off. What was the point of acknowledging it might have been their first and last night together? In fact, nothing had been discussed at all. The age gap, their different histories, the fact Anderson was technically still married. Was it just two desperately lonely people reaching out? Needing comfort? To be held? Or was it more than that? There was too much going on to think things through.

A concerned Hussain greeted Anderson on the landing at Bradford Crown Court. Adey had updated Hussain about Anderson's latest trauma with the anonymous caller. 'Mia and the kids OK?'

'Yes. Shaken up, but they're fine.'

'Any more calls?'

He shook his head.

'Come on, Taylor wants to give us a load of info.'

'What about?'

'No idea.'

Hannah Stapleton chaired the meeting in the conference room, with Taylor and the CPS lawyers standing behind her. 'There have been a few developments. I don't think they're disclosable because they don't assist your case, but because you are obsessed with conspiracy theories, and out of courtesy if nothing else, we are going to disclose some information.'

Hussain and Anderson exchanged glances.

'First of all, Tahir, you are no longer a suspect in the Ahmed murder.'

The tension lifted immediately. Anderson placed a hand on his friend's shoulder. 'That's great news.'

Stapleton continued: 'A man you will both know was found dead this morning. Hanged himself. Martin Tredwell. As you know, DI Taylor is the OIC in that case. They believe Tredwell killed Ahmed.'

'How so?' Hussain asked Taylor directly.

Taylor got the nod from Stapleton. 'We found a mixed DNA profile at the murder scene, matching Tredwell. Once we'd located his latest address, we found a kitchen knife that matched the wounds on Ahmed's chest. Obviously been cleaned thoroughly, but ingrained in the wooden handle was a speck of blood, invisible to the naked eye – Ahmed's.'

Anderson was still catching up: 'Tredwell killed himself?'

'We think so.'

'Why?'

Taylor shrugged. 'Who knows? Crazy, wasn't he?'

Hussain and Anderson stood silently, taking it all in.

'Tell them about the phone, officer,' said Stapleton.

Anderson guessed: 'It was Tredwell who made that call yesterday?'

'No, actually we don't think so,' replied Taylor. 'He'd been dead at least twenty-four hours, probably longer. My team worked all last night on the number Mr Anderson gave me. We've been trying to do some cell-siting. It isn't an exact science, but when a mobile phone makes a call the signal usually goes via the nearest mast or cell-site.'

'We understand the science, officer,' Anderson replied, desperate to know his findings.

'When that number called your phone it went to a mast next to Her Majesty's Prison, Manchester.'

'Strangeways?' exclaimed Anderson.

'Yes. We got them to instigate a lockdown and they found the sim card only an hour ago, behind some grouting in the showers on E wing.'

'We're going to need names of everyone on E wing,' demanded Hussain.

'Forget it,' replied Stapleton. 'That is highly sensitive and besides, any prisoner could use someone to conceal items on another wing. There are over 1200 inmates in Strangeways. We've only told you this to put Mr Anderson's mind at rest. DI Taylor's hunch that these crank calls were down to someone he prosecuted appears to have some merit. And we wanted Mr Anderson to know, before he gives evidence – so that he can concentrate – that this person is safely behind lock and key.'

Anderson appreciated the sentiment. 'Thank you.'

Stapleton got up to leave. 'We'll let you discuss matters and if you want I will recall DI Taylor.'

Once the prosecution team had left, Anderson spoke first: 'It's a mistake to have Taylor recalled, that's why Stapleton offered.'

'I agree. We can't demonstrate any link to your driving within these new revelations, it would look desperate.

'Yes, let's stick with the Crown's paucity of evidence on tiredness.' Anderson thought again for a moment. 'You know what really scares me on top of everything else, Tahir? That psycho is waiting for me in Strangeways.'

'Try not to worry about that. If the worst happens, you'd probably go to Leeds from this court – Armley.'

That was some comfort to Anderson. He couldn't believe they were talking in these terms. Prison, surely not?

The usher knocked on the door then opened it. 'Ten-thirty, into court please. Oh, and there's a gentleman here.'

Orlando West barged past her. 'Hello, old chum,' he said, giving Anderson a hearty pat on the back and ignoring Hussain completely. 'Your character witness here, ready to go.'

Anderson thanked his old pupil-master, feeling guilty for wondering whether he would actually show up.

'Got to be in Liverpool for twelve. Abandoned my junior on a murder. I've spoken to Hannah, she's agreed to interpose me first thing, if that's all right with you, John?'

Anderson redirected the question to his lawyer.

Hussain agreed.

Anderson just had time to make a quick call to Mia. There was no point staying at her mother's any longer if this guy was locked up.

She was relieved to hear the news, and although the call was rushed, Anderson was surprised that she hadn't yet bothered to ask about the trial. Was she really that uninterested in his fate?

'All parties in Anderson to Court One,' came through the tannoy.

As Anderson went through the door to the courtroom, Hussain pulled him back. 'One thing, John, when you're in the box.'

Anderson registered Hussain's anxiety. 'What?'

'The lie in your police interview. I know it's unlikely, but Stapleton might spot it. She might ask if you lied.'

'I know.'

'I can't tell you to say you only remembered about Tilly in the second interview. That you didn't lie.' Hussain hesitated. 'But if you admit the deception, the jury might not forgive you. You know that, don't you?'

Anderson ushered his lawyer into the courtroom. 'Don't worry, Tahir. I'm sure she won't ask about it,' he said, failing to reveal that such concerns had been on his mind too.

West was magnificent in the box. Earnest and charming, he described his former pupil in glowing terms. Even Hussain thought so. As godfather to Anderson's wonderful children, he emphasised his friend's great integrity, honesty and sense of fair play, values he had held dear all his life. Stapleton didn't even cross-examine. It was the perfect platform for Anderson to give evidence.

West gave him a confident wink on his way out of court.

Then Hussain finally said the words Anderson had been dreading for weeks: 'I call the defendant, John Anderson.'

The jury scrutinized Anderson as he made his way to the witness box. The usher put a bible in his trembling hand. 'I swear by Almighty God that the evidence I shall give…'

The same thought kept rattling around his head – he had absolutely no recollection of the drive home. What was he supposed to say? He caught sight of the Grangers sitting in the public gallery.

All eyes were on John Anderson.

Hussain began by steering the client through his career, careful not to overplay it or adduce anything of Anderson's privileged background. Then they came to the fateful day.

Anderson described going for a coffee with Tilly and how he left to watch his son play football – the last thing he could remember. He said that he wasn't tired; long days and late nights were commonplace, something which he had always handled with great ease. Hussain asked the usher to show Anderson the post-mortem photograph of Heena Butt. Anderson insisted that he'd never seen her before. He explained to the jury how he saw her face every night in his sleep and how he would never forget it.

'It's the Crown's case, Mr Anderson,' Hussain asked with a final flurry, 'that you are making this all up. You knew Miss Butt, you were tired and you knew you were tired. That you are pretending you can't remember anything. Is that true?'

Anderson directed his answer straight at the jury. 'No, it is not true.' With his voice cracking up, he added: 'I cannot remember that journey at all and I wish I knew why.'

Hussain sat down, elated at how well it had gone in chief. The jury had seen the real John Anderson. A sincere and broken man. Only the hardest of hearts could have failed to connect with the defendant.

Hannah Stapleton QC rose slowly to her feet, pulling her gown up around her shoulders and gently adjusting her wig. She knew this was where cases were won and lost. 'Orlando West is an impressive man?'

'Yes, he is.'

'And a close friend of yours?'

'Yes,' Anderson replied, full of emotion, recalling how West gave his evidence in support.

'He thinks you are a man of great integrity. An honest man?'

Anderson blushed.

'In fact he doesn't really know you at all, does he?'

Where was this going? 'What do you mean?'

'When you were first interviewed by the police you said the last thing you remember was leaving court?'

Oh no! Anderson could feel the hairs on the back of his neck stand up. He knew what was coming. 'Yes, I did.'

'When, in your second interview, you were presented with evidence of someone seeing you with Tilly at Starbucks, you claimed that piece of information had slipped your mind, but then you remembered it?'

'Yes.'

'Do you believe in the criminal justice system, Mr Anderson?'

'Yes I do.'

'Did the oath that you took today mean anything to you?'

'Yes it did.'

'So, remembering that you are under oath, answer me this: did you lie in your first interview? Did you pretend that you couldn't remember going to Starbucks with Tilly because you didn't want anyone to know you were having a cosy tête-à-tête with a pretty young barrister?'

Anderson didn't answer. He looked across at Hussain, who was willing him to lie.

Anderson wrestled with his conscience. *It doesn't matter, you're innocent. Just lie. You're home and dry. A white lie. The end justifies the means.*

'Well, Mr Anderson?' Stapleton pressed.

Finally, John Anderson gave the only answer he could: 'I panicked. I'm sorry.'

'You lied?'

'Yes.'

Game changer.

Hussain looked heavenwards and closed his eyes.

'Did you tell Mr West that you lied to the police?'

'No, I didn't.'

'He doesn't really know you like we do, does he?' She cast a conspiratorial eye across to the jury.

Anderson didn't reply.

'Mr Anderson?'

Silence.

'Not only are you in fact a liar, you lied in this very case, didn't you?'

With a hint of irritation at Stapleton's persistence: 'Yes, I've accepted I lied.'

'And you expect the jury to believe that you can't remember anything else?'

Anderson could only shrug.

'You remember what suits you, when it suits you, don't you, Mr Anderson?'

Whispers amongst the jury.

Hussain was crestfallen.

Everyone in court, including Anderson, knew the importance of what had just happened.

It would take a miracle to save him now.

CHAPTER 65

Whoever he was, he was late. Adey paced up and down. She wanted to make it to Bradford for the verdict. She wondered how Anderson was doing in the box. Her mobile rang. 'Hello?'

'Walk to the Curry Mile, wait outside the Sanam Sweet Centre.'

He wanted to meet her near the office. Was he just making sure she was alone?

Ten minutes later she was there. Her phone rang again.

'Walk to Whitworth Park and sit down.'

Adey didn't like it one bit, but agreed. Already this had the feel of something dangerous. After ten minutes of waiting on a bench and thinking everyone she saw was him she heard a voice from behind her.

'Hello, I am Shezaad.' An Asian man, early-thirties with a beard sat down beside her. In traditional Pakistani dress, he wore *shalwar* trousers and a long *kameez* shirt under a donkey jacket.

Adey wasted no time: 'How is Heena?'

Shezaad smiled. 'You know she is dead.'

Lying was pointless. 'Yes, what happened?'

Shezaad fiddled with a ring on his finger. After letting out a deep sigh, he began: 'She was my girlfriend. We were to be married. I loved her very much. But I know nothing of the world, only of Islam.'

Adey was already sceptical.

He went on: 'I found out after she died that…' He paused, repulsed at the forthcoming revelation. 'That she had been working as a prostitute.'

'Who told you that?'

With a mixture of anger and sorrow: 'It doesn't matter now.'

'It matters to me. Who told you that?'

Shezaad politely ignored the question. 'My heart is broken.'

'So why didn't you come forward – speak to the police?'

'I could not. I was here illegally, so was Heena. We are from Pakistan.' After a moment he continued: 'The man in the car was a customer. I could not be the one to ruin her reputation.'

Adey jumped up. 'This is bullshit. I don't believe you. You delayed seeing me because you had to find out what to say to me. Who do you work for?'

'I've told you the truth.'

Adey began walking away, then whipped her phone out and held it up to take Shezaad's picture.

'What are you doing?' he shouted, putting a palm up to the lens.

She backed away.

Shezaad lunged at her, taking hold of an arm and grabbing at the phone.

Adey kicked him hard between the legs.

He buckled.

Taking her chance, she ran without looking back. People she passed stopped and turned in curiosity at a young woman running for her life through Rusholme.

Only back at the Curry Mile, in the apparent safety of the crowds, did she stop to flag down a passing cab. Breathless, she only just managed to splutter the words: 'Bradford Crown Court, quick as you can.'

The cabby gave his customer a double take. 'That'll be a hundred quid, at least.'

'Just drive.' Once they were on their way she checked her phone for the photo. Relief – she had a clean shot. Who the hell was he? And why didn't he ask her name?

Unless he already knew all about her.

CHAPTER 66

The jury had heard all the evidence. HHJ Cranston rose for ten minutes to allow the advocates time to prepare for their closing speeches.

Hussain collared Anderson as soon as they were outside the courtroom. 'Why?' He was exasperated. 'Why couldn't you lie? You would have been acquitted.'

'But I wouldn't have been John Anderson anymore. I had to be true to myself.'

Hussain shook his head and said: 'You are one stubborn bastard, John.' Hussain had the utmost respect for his client. Despite everything, he had maintained his principles, even though it would probably cost him everything.

The photo of Shezaad came through on Hussain's iPhone with a short note of the encounter. They disclosed it to Stapleton who in turn showed it to Taylor. No one on the prosecution team recognised him or claimed to have any knowledge of him. Taylor called Shezaad's number which, unsurprisingly, was now switched off.

Hussain found it unnerving that even at this late stage of the case they were getting new information. 'What do we do, John?' he asked his friend. 'Do we try and ask the judge for time to investigate this further, or get on with speeches?'

Anderson mulled it over. 'There's nowhere else to take it. Let's just get on with it.'

Hussain could see Anderson's fighting spirit ebbing away. The trial had taken its toll.

'All parties to Court One.'

The press box and gallery were full. Taylor had to pull rank to get a seat.

Stapleton's speech was masterly, feigning regret for inviting a conviction of an otherwise law abiding individual. How tragic it all was, but their duty was to find Anderson guilty. She focused on the lack of any positive defence and Anderson's lie in his police interview. She made only passing reference to Sandra Granger's dubious evidence of sleep. After twenty minutes, she retook her seat, confident of victory.

Hussain's speech was longer and full of emotion. He dealt superbly with the lie, turning it on its head, making the point that Anderson couldn't lie to the jury, which demonstrated his honesty and innocence. He highlighted the lack of evidence of tiredness, coming only from a couple of jealous colleagues, and a mother twisted by grief. The expert evidence was dismissed as vague and inconclusive. He finished on the greatest mystery of the case: 'Members of the jury, you will remember this case in six months from now. You will even remember it in six years. And when you do, you will still ask yourselves: who was Heena Butt? They never did tell us.

'When you see on the television or read about terrible miscarriages of justice, people being released from jail after many years of imprisonment for something they didn't do, you may ask yourselves: what are those jurors who convicted him thinking when they see these news stories? Are they thinking: why were we so sure? Why didn't we see the signs? Why didn't we hear the alarm bells ringing?

'Members of the jury, in this case, the alarm bells are ringing out loud and clear. You cannot be sure of guilt. The only proper verdict, on both counts, is not guilty.'

Anderson was deeply moved, not just by Hussain's speech, but his whole approach to the case. He'd given it everything, and prioritised his client above all other things. Anderson could have asked for no more.

Still half an hour before the short adjournment, HHJ Cranston decided to get on with his summing up so the jury could retire before lunch, and hopefully deliver verdicts by close of play.

First, there was a matter he raised with counsel in the absence of the jury. 'Have either of you given any consideration as to whether the lesser alternative of causing death by careless driving should be left to the jury? I am minded to if there's no objection from either party?'

Both advocates requested five minutes to consider their respective positions.

Anderson and Hussain disappeared into a conference room. 'Tahir, you know what happens when there are two counts?'

'Yes, the jury compromise and convict on the lesser count.'

'Which is why the judge wants it on the indictment. Guarantees a conviction for at least death by careless.'

'It's tempting though, John. You need to think about it. Maybe twelve months, eighteen max. You'd only serve half that and you'd be in open conditions within weeks.'

'But my career would still be over and we'd never know what really happened.'

'We'll probably never know, whatever you decide. Like

you said, Ahmed's gone and maybe even Tredwell had something to do with it. You mustn't lose focus. The primary objective is to get the best result for you.'

'Sorry to break up the party, chaps.' Stapleton barged into the room. 'It's your lucky day. In light of the judge's comments, I've taken instructions from the CPS and the OIC; not only do we consent to death by careless going on the indictment, we will accept a plea to it and bin the dangerous.'

Hussain was delighted.

Anderson was more cautious: 'What would Sandra Granger have to say about that?'

'It's not her decision, is it?' Stapleton replied.

'Why would you accept careless?'

'Contrary to what you might think, Mr Anderson, I am a fair prosecutor. We are not baying for blood. We accept you went for a coffee to wake you up. You wouldn't have known it takes twenty minutes to kick in. The facts fit a careless. We all make mistakes, we just have to pay for them, one way or another. Have a chat and let me know.'

Hussain sat down and chucked his wig on the table. 'Sit down, John.'

Anderson joined him.

'John, as your lawyer, I have to advise that it's a no-brainer. A very generous offer. You've admitted lying to the police. This is the reward for all our hard work. It justifies your decision to have a trial, and if you plead guilty now, the first time the lesser offence was offered, you'd get full credit, maybe even a suspended sentence.'

It was a big call.

Anderson was unsure of what to do. Eventually: 'It just doesn't feel right. We've come this far.'

Tahir knew Anderson well enough now to predict what was coming next.

'No, I've decided. No deals, no compromises, no death by careless on the indictment. All or nothing.'

CHAPTER 67

The summing up was fair. No judge wanted to find himself appealed in London for bias. HHJ Cranston made it clear that the jury's task came down to one question: had the prosecution proved, so that the jury were sure, that Anderson had fallen asleep at the wheel or been distracted so that the vehicle crashed? There was no issue that his driving caused Heena Butt's and Molly Granger's deaths and so, if he drove dangerously, it followed that John Anderson would be guilty of causing death by dangerous driving. 'What is dangerous driving, members of the jury? Well, the legal definition is driving that falls *far* below the standard of a careful and competent driver. No more, no less.'

At 1.05pm, the jury bailiffs were sworn and the jury filed out to begin their deliberations.

'I will not take a verdict before 2.15,' indicated the judge, who had plans to go for lunch at his club now that his summing up was done.

Anderson shook Hussain's hand outside the courtroom and thanked him for all his efforts.

Keeping the truth from Anderson was more agonising for Hussain with each passing day.

'Mr Hussain, can I have a word?' asked the usher. 'The judge would like you to join him for lunch at the Bradford Club.'

Hussain thanked her then rolled his eyes at Anderson. He detested members' clubs of any sort, particularly when it involved social contact with the judiciary. 'Protocol – he's only invited me because he can't ask Hannah without the defence being present.'

'You'd better go then. Need to keep him happy. I used to hate that sort of thing.' Then with a sheepish grin: 'Nevertheless, I always went – a right crawler.'

'I remember,' Hussain replied with a wink. 'Sure you'll be all right?'

'Yes, I'll be fine. Go.' Anderson sat down on one of the seats on the now deserted landing.

He had never felt so alone.

CHAPTER 68

The Bradford Club – upstairs in an old building in the centre of town; a small bar and a shabby dining room was the home of most of the Bradford judiciary at lunchtime. A last, fading remnant of the grand old days when Bradford was the wool capital of the world.

The judges hung on Stapleton's every word. Still a looker at forty-eight, she flirted outrageously while they guffawed and leched. Ignored, Hussain remained silent throughout the lunch. Unconcerned with their chatter, his mind was elsewhere.

As the coffees were handed out, Cranston deigned to speak to him: 'Terribly sad all this. Met his father a couple of times. Nice chap. Must be awfully disappointed.'

'I was surprised not to see him at court,' said Hussain. 'You know, supporting his son.'

Cranston sneered at Hussain's remark about a brother judge. Then: 'I heard about that other matter you were suspected of. I hear it's gone away, for now?'

'Yes, they had the wrong man. Seems to be happening rather a lot lately.'

Cranston didn't like Hussain one bit. No concept of how things were done. Didn't revere the judiciary at all. 'Hadn't you better get back?' Cranston said through a faux smile, then added: 'If he's convicted, I won't be adjourning for reports. I'll sentence today.'

'But of course, judge,' Hussain replied. '*If* he's convicted.'

CHAPTER 69

He cut a lone figure, thought Adey as she made her way over to Anderson. 'Hello,' she said.

'Hi, are you OK? Hussain told me what happened.'

'I grew up in Moss Side – course I'm OK.'

'Not to mention Mogadishu.'

A wistful smile. 'I heard it didn't get us anywhere. I'm sorry.'

'Listen, I know you tried everything, and then some.'

She believed in him, completely. That was enough for Anderson.

'I'm glad you came, Adey. About us…'

She'd been waiting for this.

'I don't know what will be left of me when I get out. Prison changes people. We've both seen that.'

She thought of Bahdoon and who he used to be. 'Let's cross that bridge when we come to it. Isn't that what pompous lawyers say?'

They both forced a smile.

'All parties to Court One immediately.'

Verdict.

This was it. 'Good luck, John.' Adey could hardly get her words out. 'Aren't quick verdicts usually acquittals?'

Anderson shrugged.

The landing was soon full of press and public, jostling to get into the courtroom.

Someone was calling out: 'John! John!'

Anderson stopped at the door of the court to see who it was.

Out of breath and panting, his brother, Stephen Anderson, marched across the landing. 'John, I rang the court, they said you'd get a verdict today. I'm sorry I couldn't get here before – work.'

'I understand. I'm amazed you could get up here at all. I keep seeing you on telly giving some opinion about the latest government policy. It's great to see you doing so well.'

'I'm sorry about Mum and Dad. You know what they're like.'

Anderson nodded.

'But I wanted you to know, whatever happens, I'm here for you. Whatever you need, let me know. Anything.'

Holding back the tears, they hugged.

Anderson was ready to face the music.

As Anderson was about to enter the courtroom, Hussain came up the stairs, still pulling on his gown.

Anderson waited for him. 'I just wanted to say thanks again for everything, my friend. Win or lose.'

'But I persuaded you to have a trial, John. Will you still thank me if you are convicted?' he asked anxiously.

Anderson smiled. 'Of course. It was the right thing to do. I could never have lived with myself. I needed to know what actually happened. You earned me a "careless". I made the decision to reject it, not you.'

'But we still don't know what happened.'

'But at least we tried.'

'Yes, I tried my best – you know that, don't you?'

'Of course.' Anderson sensed something more. 'What is it, Tahir?'

'It doesn't make any difference now, but you have a right to know.'

'Know what?'

The usher came out of the courtroom: 'Mr Hussain, didn't you hear the tannoy? Can I ask you to bring your client in immediately, we have a verdict.'

'We're coming,' he replied. 'Just a moment.'

The usher glowered at him, then went back into court.

'Ahmed was blackmailing me.'

'I know, about withdrawing from the case?'

'I didn't give you the full story. He actually wanted me to defend you and to lose the trial.'

'What?' Confused, Anderson took a few seconds to process the information.

Hussain could see his client's disappointment.

Anderson recalled how Hussain was instructed. 'That's why you came to Bradford to see me at the prelim? Ahmed sent you?'

'Yes, but I wanted to defend you. I could've just let you plead guilty.'

'And Adey?'

'She has no idea.'

Anderson was too shocked to be angry, which made Hussain feel even worse. 'Why are you telling me now?'

'Because you became my friend. It was easier to keep it from you when I didn't know you. I'm sorry.'

'Did Ahmed have anything to do with the crash?'

'I don't know. Really. I challenged him several times. He admitted nothing. And you know, there's no evidence against him.'

The usher came back out and this time physically pushed them through the door.

The courtroom was at bursting point. Even the judge

270

was surprised when he came in. Counsels' rows were full of barristers from other courts, eager to see the outcome.

Anderson was oblivious to the hoards of people, still reeling from this new revelation.

When everyone was seated, the jurors came into court and took their seats.

A prison officer, standing next to Anderson in the dock, nudged him to his feet.

The court clerk addressed the jury: 'Would the foreman please stand?'

A middle-aged man with glasses stood up. He had the appearance of being educated. Maybe that was a good sign, thought Hussain.

'How do you find the defendant on count one, guilty or not guilty?'

Hussain prayed for an acquittal.

The courtroom held its breath.

'Guilty.'

Gasps from the gallery.

Guilty? Anderson's legs gave way.

The dock officer, used to such events, pulled him back up and held Anderson until he could bear his own weight.

'How do you find the defendant on count two?'

'Guilty.'

Anderson's ashen face was blank.

The judge wasted no time: 'A custodial sentence is inevitable. The defendant's previous character has been well demonstrated during the trial so I see no need to adjourn for a pre-sentence report from the probation service.'

Anderson could see the judge's mouth was moving, but he could take nothing in.

271

'Anything you'd like to say, Mr Hussain?'

In shock, Hussain struggled to get his words out. Never had a verdict mattered so much to him. 'No. Your Honour is aware of the Sentencing Council guidelines in this case?'

'Yes, I am. Mr Anderson, this is a very serious offence that led to the death of a young woman and a five-year-old child. Nothing will bring them back and no sentence I pass on you can ever be measured against the loss of life. In my view you ran a cynical defence when it was obvious to all, including the jury, that you fell asleep whilst driving. Although I can't hold your right to have a trial against you, I cannot afford you the credit that would have been due on a guilty plea. I must also conclude that you show no remorse for this crime. Taking into account the guidelines of the Sentencing Council, the total sentence is five years' imprisonment, to run concurrently on each count. Take him down.'

The dock officer cuffed a shell-shocked Anderson and pushed him down the stairs inside the dock that led to the cells, and into another world.

PART III

CHAPTER 70

Adey dropped a file onto Hussain's desk. 'Con at four in Peter Hawkins. Crim damage.'

Hussain pushed it to the side and carried on daydreaming. Nothing had been the same since *R v Anderson*. Neither of them could focus on other cases. Even the possibility that the firm might go under couldn't shake them into action.

Only Adey had seen Anderson since the verdict – ten minutes afterwards in the court cells before he was transported to HMP Armley. Hussain hadn't been able to face him.

Anderson had made it quite clear he was to be left alone and had refused all visits since. As with any recently convicted prisoner, hope was hard to endure. Rather than discuss frivolous appeals with his legal team, Anderson wanted to get his head down and serve the sentence. As a criminal lawyer, Anderson would know there were no grounds of appeal. No misdirections on law by the judge. No irregularities in the trial process.

Adey couldn't stop worrying about him. How would he cope with the shock of jail in his already fragile mental state?

Hussain had the same concerns, coupled with an overriding sense of guilt. He'd persuaded Anderson to plead not guilty, and then lost the case. Adey had told him a thousand times it wasn't his fault, but he wouldn't be persuaded. Four weeks on and the memories of the trial – of Anderson – hung in the air, haunting every aspect of their days.

'Peter Hawkins, not that toerag. Can't you see him?' Hussain protested.

'Sorry, I'm seeing my brother.'

Any further disagreement was cut short by the arrival of a visitor.

Sam Connor shut the door behind him, shook the rain off his umbrella and stood sheepishly before them. 'I've been a bloody idiot.'

Adey made towards him. 'You sent a man to jail. A man I believe to be innocent.'

'I'm sorry.'

'I'm sorry,' mimicked Adey. 'Is that all you can say?'

Hussain raised a hand to stop her. 'What do you want, Mr Connor?'

'To help. I want to help.'

'Why?'

Before Connor had a chance to answer, Adey started again: 'It's a wind-up.'

'It's not, I swear to you. I want to make another statement, saying that I got it wrong about Anderson being tired.'

'Got it wrong?' scoffed Adey. 'Lied, more like.'

'It's difficult to explain. I thought I was doing the right thing. I kind of convinced myself he was tired. I can't believe it now.'

Hussain was more curious than angry. 'The right thing?'

'Yes. I know it sounds stupid but Orlando West kept telling me I had a duty to say it.'

276

'West?' Hussain shot Adey a sideways glance. 'Go on.'

'He kept saying we couldn't be seen to be covering up. Had a duty to the court and the criminal justice system. I was weak. West gave me an excuse to bury Anderson, so I could have his practice.' With eyes cast down: 'And I took it with both hands.'

Hussain was sceptical. But why make the effort of coming to Rusholme to say all this? 'Why would West want to stick the knife in?'

'I don't know. It's all about back-stabbing and chambers politics with him. You know, divide and rule. He created a culture of ruthless ambition in chambers; I lived by it for years.' Connor shook his head. 'I've been doing a lot of thinking since the trial.'

Adey had no sympathy. 'Too late.'

'Why now?' asked Hussain.

'I can't live with myself. He saved me from a charge of perjury, after what I'd done to him. If I make a new statement maybe we can get leave to appeal on the grounds of fresh evidence?'

Adey was still fuming. She could hardly bear the sight of him. Hussain, more measured, was thinking it through. 'It's very weak on its own. What about Tilly?'

'Not a chance. Chambers refused to give her a tenancy – because of all this.'

'But your seniority saved you, I suppose?'

Connor turned crimson.

'Anyway, Anderson would never let you risk your career. You'd have to convince him first.'

'He refused my visit.'

Hussain exhaled deeply. 'Not just yours.'

'Worst of it is,' said Connor, 'he asked me to defend him, and I said no. Should've been flattered.'

No one offered words of comfort.

Connor lingered despite the uncomfortable silence. He had something else to say. 'Then let me help with an appeal. Let me read the papers. A fresh take on things.'

Adey burst out laughing. 'You must be joking!'

'Hang on, Adey,' said Hussain. 'Anderson's in jail and we've got no grounds of appeal. How could things get any worse?'

'But why should we let him read them?'

'Because pride is not a reason to say no.' Hussain picked up the file and handed it to Connor.

'All right, but the brief stays here,' said Adey. She led him into the boardroom and made a point of leaving the door wide open so that she could keep an eye on him. 'No documents leave this room. Oh, and I'll take that witness statement first, just in case you change your mind.'

Connor put pen to paper in a carefully worded document, not quite accepting that he lied in the box, but that he might have been a little overzealous in his description of Anderson's tiredness, out of a desire to be impartial. The Court of Appeal would be hard pushed to accept the statement as fresh evidence, but from Connor's point of view, at least he could save his own skin, and that had to be his first priority.

Hussain got nothing done that afternoon, aware of Adey's eyes boring into him. Each time he dared to look up he was met with a disapproving glare. He was beginning to regret letting Connor see the papers. But what if they'd missed something?

'The deceased!' exclaimed Connor, running out of the boardroom waving a post-mortem photograph of Heena Butt. 'I've seen her before!'

Both Adey and Hussain stopped what they were doing and replied in unison: 'Where?'

Shaking his hands in the air, Connor replied full of frustration: 'I can't bloody remember.'

'Then try harder,' demanded Adey.

CHAPTER 71

The hatch opened.

Anderson raised an arm: 'I'm fine.' Better to announce it than make the officer come into the cell and see for himself. On suicide watch since arriving at HMP Armley, these hourly checks served only to remind Anderson of the fragility of his state of mind. He wondered whether he would have the same thoughts that came to him on the platform at Wilmslow station.

Nights were worse. The sounds on the wing created a permanent state of panic. Strange howling noises, shrieking and banging. A constant reminder of the madness and badness that inhabited Armley prison.

Anderson had the luxury of a single cell as his former profession was likely to engender negative feelings in any potential pad-mate. Although a great relief to Anderson at the beginning, the loneliness had become unbearable. Repetitive days of doing nothing. Paradoxically, although he craved company of any sort, during association he cowered in the cell, eyes fixed on the door, too afraid to even go out on the landing. What if they recognised him or didn't like him? Paralysed with fear, he suffered further dramatic weight loss and nervous exhaustion. At least he wasn't in Strangeways where half the prison knew him, and where one man in particular was waiting for him.

He'd stopped counting the days until his release. What was the point? Nothing to come out to, only disgrace. His night with Adey felt like a dream. Had it really happened? What could she possibly have seen in him?

Hours spent staring at the same whitewashed walls, Anderson was retreating further into himself, shutting down. A dangerous method of blocking out the realities of the world around him.

He curled up in a ball on his bed, knees tight to his chest, haunted by jagged memories of what he'd lost.

Numb.

CHAPTER 72

Adey had been to Strangeways hundreds of times, not just to see her brother, but also clients. It never got any easier. She hated the place. The sounds, the smells, everything about it, even the name. Renamed HMP Manchester for political reasons after the infamous riots of 1990, all Mancunians still knew it as Strangeways.

Sitting, waiting for Bahdoon, she thought of Anderson, of how he might be coping in Armley. If only he'd call or send a letter, just to say he was all right. It was different for Bahdoon; he'd spent his teenage years in and out of institutions. All his friends were in jail. Bahdoon's problem had always been fitting in on the outside. Too scarred by all the violence he had witnessed in Mogadishu, with only a sporadic education and no job prospects, he drifted into crime and found the support for which he yearned in a local gang, The Rusholme Cripz. There was a certain irony in that his name, Bahdoon, meant 'the one who looks for his clan'. At seventeen, he carried a firearm and played his part in the neighbourhood turf wars with rival gang, Dem Crazy Somalis.

As a result of the lengthy terms of imprisonment handed out to twelve members of the notorious Gooch Gang in 2009, the fight over the void which had opened up was bloodier than anything that had gone before. Bahdoon was caught on CCTV carrying out a drive-by shooting which left a young man dead. In 2011, he started a life sentence with a minimum term of eighteen years.

Adey blamed herself for her inability to keep Bahdoon on the straight and narrow. Truth was, once he'd discovered crack cocaine, all her efforts had been futile.

'Hello, sis.' Every inch of Bahdoon was rippling muscle. Not the scrawny young man of a few years ago. Working out passed the time.

'Been in the gym, I see? How are you?' she asked with a beaming smile. Adey always tried to appear happy on visits. No point turning up with the weight of the world on her shoulders. That wouldn't help him. But it made the relationship with Bahdoon feel artificial; neither wanted to worry the other, so prickly small talk was inevitably the order of the day, leaving them both feeling cheated by the end of each painful visit.

'Girl, you got yourself a man yet?'

Always the same opening line – Adey ignored it. Why did he have to tease her?

'Then maybe you stop wasting your time coming?'

'You know I'd always come. Why do you say these things?'

Bahdoon clicked his tongue and sat back, arms folded. Sometimes he acted like a child. He'd never had the chance to grow up, find himself. Thought he was man enough to shoot someone, in fact he'd been too immature to think through the consequences.

'So how've you been?' Adey wasn't going to give up that easily. There was a tension in all their contact, a side effect of so much going unsaid.

'Got moved to E wing. I'm in seg. Me likes da quiet. I'm chillin'.'

'Segregation? Why?'

'Screws heard some bruvas wanted to wet me up, so they moved me.' Bahdoon chuckled, seemingly unperturbed by the danger.

'At least they told you.'

'They 'ad to. It's da law. Got a duty, innit.' Bahdoon clicked his tongue again. 'Me thought you was da lawyer. You not know dat shit?'

Adey refused to rise to it, changing the subject. 'I need a favour.'

Bahdoon was taken aback. Adey never asked for anything.

She took a piece of paper out of her pocket – Anderson's list of the people he prosecuted that went to prison. 'I need to know if these people are in Strangeways and on what wing.'

Bahdoon clicked his tongue. 'A bruva can get in a lotta shit for asking them kind o' questions.'

'Do you think I'd ask if I wasn't desperate?' Adey was fired up too. 'I've never asked you for anything. There are people in here you'd kill for and you can't even do this for your own sister?'

Bahdoon glanced off, registering the irony. 'Why d'ya want to know?'

Adey didn't answer.

After a long silence: 'All right, sista. Me see what I can do.'

'Thank you.' She hated putting Bahdoon in danger but with Connor unable to remember where he'd seen Heena

Butt, the anonymous caller was their only lead. Adey slid the paper across the table.

Bahdoon shook his head. 'You know I can't just take that? There's rules, girl.'

Having failed to notice in her desperation to help Anderson, Adey was suddenly aware of the prison officers monitoring everything.

Bahdoon gave an imperceptible nod to an inmate on the other side of the room, who moments later was on his feet gesticulating and swearing at his girlfriend. As the officers rushed over, Bahdoon put the paper in his pocket.

Seconds later all the visits were terminated.

CHAPTER 73

Anderson paced up and down the tiny space. Four steps each way. Becoming more frustrated by the minute, he couldn't take his eyes off the envelope. A letter from Mia, he recognised the handwriting. Pride of place on his pillow, unopened. He was afraid. Afraid of himself. He might not cope with what was inside. A reminder of the world outside. He snatched at it and threw it in the bin, then minutes later took it out and placed it above the sink. Torture. This process had been going on for hours. He thought of tearing it into minute pieces, but knew he'd spend days trying to put it back together.

He could bear it no longer. After several deep breaths, he opened it. Disappointment. No letter from Mia, just a document – a photocopy of her application for a decree nisi. How cold and clinical, he thought. Another envelope fell out. It read: 'Dad'. Already affected, he opened it. Two pieces of paper, the first a drawing by Angus, his youngest. Immediately, he could discern himself holding Angus's hand. Both standing by a red sports car, probably a Ferrari. He held the picture, his face alternating between smiles and sobs. Placing it gently on his pillow he read the letter, in Will's handwriting:

Dear Dad,

*We won another match today and I nearly scored a goal!
I wish you could have seen it. I got in a fight. I've got a
black eye. Mum is angry but I think it looks good. A
boy at school said you are a criminal who's gone mental.
I know that's a lie isn't it? I know you wouldn't do bad
things. I miss you so much Dad. When are you coming
back?*

Love Will

Anderson's tears fell onto the paper. His whole body began
to shudder. Then he let out a roar from somewhere deep
within, joining the chorus on the landing. Shouting and
screaming he hurled things around the cell, banging on the
wall until he had nothing left. Exhausted, he collapsed on
the bed and closed his eyes.

Once the rage had subsided, the only emotion that
remained was disgust. Disgust at his self-pity. At blocking
out what his boys were going through.

John Anderson clenched his fists tight and stood up, then
hammered on the cell door.

Eventually, a prison officer came and opened the hatch.
'All right, all right, what is it?'

'I want a transfer – to Strangeways.'

CHAPTER 74

The journey across the Pennines, crammed into a sweatbox, had taken forever. Anderson could hardly move his bad leg, but it was worth it – he felt sure the answer was there.

Securing a transfer had been easier than expected. Shouting about his European Convention right to be near his family and threats of judicial review soon did the trick. The governor was more than happy to offload a problem-causer with legal training. And as a vulnerable, there was only one place for him – E wing.

John Anderson had a plan and it gave him strength.

Hussain and Adey first saw Anderson sitting in a glass booth on legal visits. He looked so gaunt, they hardly recognised him. Both hid their shock, just relieved to be back in contact. Hussain gave Anderson a hearty handshake. Adey was a little more reserved, unaware of Anderson's current feelings towards her.

Anderson spoke first: 'Tahir, I know you did everything you could, and I'm grateful you took over the case and that we fought it. OK?'

'Thank you, John.' Hussain felt a burden lifted. Holding back the tears, he nodded his appreciation.

Unaware of why Anderson's remarks were of such importance to Hussain, Adey got straight to the point: 'Why the transfer?'

Anderson began: 'I've got to work on the basis that our

mystery caller is responsible. We've got nothing else. And he's here, probably on E wing. I reckon he must've been controlling Butt. Find him and we uncover the truth about her. So I need to smoke him out.'

'That's a dangerous strategy, John,' said Hussain.

Anderson shrugged. 'We haven't got much choice. And I've been thinking, this psycho has one massive weakness – he wants me to know it was him that put me here. He can't help himself. That's why he rang and texted me. With me here, he won't be able to resist it.'

'Please be careful, John.' Hussain had never seen Anderson so determined.

'My brother is here on E wing,' said Adey.

'Your brother?' Why had she never mentioned him?

'Bahdoon Tuur. He's doing life for murder. Gang violence.' She tried to say it matter-of-factly, but her embarrassment showed through. 'I asked him to find out if anyone you prosecuted was here.' She took a sheet out of the file and showed it to Anderson.

He pored over the list. 'This is great.'

'He had to stop after people started asking questions, but he managed to get a look at a list of everyone on E wing.' She pointed to some names. 'There are seven people you prosecuted on the wing right now.'

Anderson drew breath. A sobering thought.

'Two of them are still serving the same sentence. Four of them were released and were out for years before committing new offences.'

'So you're saying discount them, either because they could have come after me years ago or they were inside at the time of the crash?'

'I guess so,' Adey replied.

'Unless it was organised from inside, that's why he used Butt?'

'Maybe. I'm checking them all out. The only one that was out at the time of the crash for a short time was Peter Almond, but the profile is all wrong – mortgage fraud.'

'I remember, on his mother?'

'That's right. He's back in on a confidence fraud.'

'Please keep digging, Adey. He's in here.'

'OK,' Adey replied. 'But you need to watch your back, John.'

Anderson appreciated the concern etched into her face. It had been a while since he'd experienced that kind of connection with someone.

'John, there's something else,' said Hussain. 'Sam Connor came to the office, full of remorse. He's made a new statement, saying he made a mistake.'

'Really? Does he mean it?'

'I think so, Adey's not so sure. He wants to help with the appeal.'

'Good, let him, but forget the statement. That's not what this case is about.'

'That's what we thought you'd say. He's read the file now and he recognises Butt.'

'Jesus! From where?'

'He can't remember.'

Anderson's excitement subsided. 'She must be an ex-client. Get him to check the chambers computer.'

'He has. Nothing under that name.'

Anderson mulled over all the new information. 'What made Connor change his mind?'

'Mainly guilt about stabbing you in the back, but here's the thing. He tried to put it on Orlando West.'

'West?'

'Yeah. Said West drove the whole thing, out of some kind of higher duty to the administration of justice.'

Anderson was astounded. 'West told him to lie?'

'He didn't quite go that far. West nudged him in the right direction. Certainly didn't talk him out of it.'

'But West's evidence was brilliant!'

'I know. Maybe he was just covering his tracks?'

A prison officer banged on the door of their booth. 'Five minutes, please.'

Conscious of Adey's presence, Anderson had one more matter to raise: 'Mia has served divorce papers on me.' Careful not to show any emotion: 'Did we ever find out who that man was?'

Adey answered: 'No. I went back a few more times but never saw him again. Either it ended or they started being more careful.'

The officer knocked again and broke up the conference.

Anderson had a lot to think about. He also had seven potential enemies waiting for him on the wing.

CHAPTER 75

DI Taylor had been summoned to Armstrong's office. What had he done now? Taylor couldn't stomach the man. This DCI was all about the career, not the policing. Not the victims of crime. Taylor had watched him sucking up to the right people over the years, hence his meteoric rise. Many believed he'd make chief constable of GMP. After all, he had a golf handicap of three.

'You wanted to see me, gov?' Taylor hovered in the doorway of Armstrong's office.

'Yes, come in, Taylor. Heard Anderson's been transferred to Strangeways?'

'You're joking? Poor sod. He'll have a lot of enemies in there.'

'His request apparently.'

'What?'

The chief wanted to know more: 'Had anything from the defence about an appeal?'

'No, nothing, gov. They're out of time now.'

'Unless they go on fresh evidence?' Armstrong's landline rang. He answered it. 'OK, thanks.' Turning his attention back to Taylor: 'Right, that'll be all. Got a car waiting, off to London for a meeting.' Had to show off. He rushed out, leaving Taylor standing there.

Taylor noticed the DCI's diary was open on his desk.

Something made him gaze down at the page for a moment. The entry for that afternoon read: 'Anderson', with an address in London underneath. Taylor castigated himself, not wishing to be the kind of copper that spied on his colleagues. He tried to put it out of his mind.

But it was too late – he'd seen it now.

CHAPTER 76

Anderson's cell was similar to the one in Armley; he was again the only occupant. Drained and disorientated, he'd not slept well on his first night. Still recovering from the journey in the sweatbox, compounded by nightmares of past cases. His first waking thought was of Orlando West. Had he really tried to get him convicted, or was Connor up to something? He ate the breakfast pack, delivered the night before, and tried to remember the case details of those who were on his wing.

6.30pm. The jangle of keys. Anderson's door was being unlocked. Association. A rush of anxiety. If he was going to advertise his presence, he had to leave the sanctuary of his pad and mix with other prisoners. He touched Angus's drawing one last time, steeled himself and headed out onto the landing. Almost frozen with fear, telling himself this was what he wanted, he took a few steps along the spur of E wing. Too afraid to make eye contact, he didn't recognise anyone, but felt everyone staring and nudging him as he passed.

'Hey, my learned friend,' echoed off the walls from the landing above. 'How's it going?' The voice broke into laughter with others joining in. News travelled fast.

A fat man with ginger hair blocked Anderson's path then held out his hand. 'Pleased to meet you,' he said jovially.

Anderson took it gratefully. Had he made a friend already?

The man didn't release his grip. He squeezed tighter. 'Terry Sykes.' In a more sinister tone: 'Hello, Mr Anderson. You put me in this shithole for a stabbing I never done. Remember?' Anderson tried to pull his hand away but didn't succeed, until the man whispered in his ear, 'Watch your back.'

Heart racing at a hundred miles an hour, Anderson did an about-turn and walked back to his cell. Everyone knew he was here.

He spent the rest of association sitting on his bunk, eyes fixed on the door. A few prisoners walked past, or peered in and chuckled.

At last, 8.45pm. Breakfast pack and lock up. Once the cell door was secured, he breathed a sigh of relief. Now he could think. He remembered prosecuting Sykes. More than five years ago, Sykes had put a knife into a prostitute's eye in a row over money. Definitely sick enough to bear a grudge, but Anderson's instincts told him this guy didn't have the wherewithal to arrange a hit. Not this sophisticated, anyway.

The dangerous monotony of prison life went on. The constant expectation of violence made time drag and pushed Anderson's mental strength to the limit.

It was Angus's birthday. He hadn't spoken to either of the children since before conviction. However painful it would be, he had to ring. Unfortunately, the phone was on the other side of the landing. Anderson counted down the minutes until association, then as soon as his door was unlocked he set off on the journey across the landing, ignoring the whistles and insults.

'Give him a dig,' someone shouted.

To Anderson's relief, no one did. He made it to the

phone – no queue. He entered the pin that allowed him to ring his authorised numbers, and dialled.

'Hello?'

'Hello, is that you Angus?'

'Daddy! It's Daddy!'

'Happy birthday, son.' Anderson could hardly speak.

'When am I going to see you, Daddy?'

'I don't know, son. Not for a while. But when I do, I'll bring a big present with me, OK?'

'OK. Will's not here.'

'Tell him I love him very much. I love you both.'

'OK, bye.'

Anderson wiped his nose. Composed himself. Any sign of weakness on the return journey would be disastrous. He made it back and threw himself onto the bed. He wanted to cry his eyes out, but would have to wait until lock up. Curled up, he turned towards the wall. He almost jumped out of his skin. Someone had written on it in black ink:

I GAVE YOU ENOUGH ROPE TO HANG YOURSELF

Whoever it was must have come in whilst he was on the phone to Angus. In a fit of anger, Anderson jumped off the bed and ran out onto the landing. 'You bastard!' he shouted at the top of his voice. 'My name is John Anderson. I'm waiting, if you've got the guts to face me.'

Someone shouted back: 'What's eating *her*?' which caused raucous laughter.

Anderson went back into his cell, lay on the bed and buried his face in the pillow. Then, remembering his boys, he sat up. Eventually, he got off the bed and touched his drawing and Will's letter – both on the wall above his sink.

Suddenly, from behind him: 'Long time no see?'

Anderson turned and saw him standing in the doorway. Bearded, a white man, but in traditional Muslim dress. Anderson knew many inmates converted to Islam to get better food but, despite his colour, he looked the real deal. Anderson didn't recognise his face, only the voice, from the phone calls.

Sniggering, the male held up an arm and pushed his head to the side, mimicking a hanging.

'Who are you?' Anderson asked.

'I did this to you. It was me.'

'Why?'

From under his *kameez* the man produced a shiv – a makeshift knife. Two razor blades melted onto a toothbrush, the double blade designed to make stitching the wound nigh on impossible. 'I'm going to kill you.'

It was now or never. Anderson charged forward, reaching out for the arm that held the shiv. They grappled. Anderson was no match for his sinewy opponent, fuelled by hate. Anderson reeled back, dazed from a head butt. Forced to the ground, the man was soon on top of him with the shiv now on Anderson's throat. 'Say goodbye to your kids.'

This was the end. Anderson closed his eyes.

A shrill scream. Cracking bone.

The weight on Anderson's chest was removed. He opened his eyes. A huge black arm gripped around the attacker's neck, with the other holding him in a half nelson. The shiv lay on the cell floor.

Bahdoon Tuur released the captive whose right arm,

broken, fell limp to his side. Weeping and muttering threats of revenge, he left.

Still shaken, Anderson got to his feet and offered his hand to his saviour. Bahdoon ignored it, more interested in putting the shiv in his pocket.

Anderson wasn't put off by the rebuff. 'Thank you. Who are you?'

'Tuur. Me sista asked me to look out for ya.'

'Adey?'

He nodded. 'Shouldn't you be asking *his* name?'

Anderson was still absorbing what had just happened. He dusted himself down. 'Yes, who is he?'

'Mohammed Mohammed. A total mental.' Bahdoon made to leave. 'And before you ask, I didn't see nothin'.'

Anderson could hardly take it all in. Was he suffering some kind of delayed shock? He decided to go back to the phone while he was still holding it together.

It felt good to hear Adey's voice. He gave her a watered-down account.

Adey's obvious concern was tempered by her relief that Bahdoon had been there. She was heartened he'd kept his promise to look out for Anderson. Adey had the list of E wing inmates in front of her. 'That name's on it, but you've never prosecuted him.'

'I know it's him. Please find out all you can. Then can you and Hussain come for a visit?'

Adey was already opening up her laptop.

CHAPTER 77

Anderson's appearance had improved considerably. Not just because they were getting somewhere; Hussain, unprepared to take more risks, had called the prison to demand his client be put on full seg. No governor wanted a death in custody on their hands.

As a result, the strain on Anderson had decreased markedly. Nothing to do but sit in his cell studying the case papers and some law books Adey had sent in.

'What have you got for me?' Anderson asked as soon as he was in the booth.

Adey noticed the tram lines on his neck left by the shiv. 'Plenty,' she replied. 'A man called Michael Doran changed his name by deed poll to, wait for it, Mohammed Mohammed, after converting to Islam in 2009.'

'Doran? I know that name.'

'You were part of the team that prosecuted him in 2003 for a series of horrendous stranger rapes. Dragged women off the street at night.'

'Always in a graveyard?'

'That's the guy. He'd knock them unconscious first.'

'I remember, it was horrific. Southern cemetery, just off the Parkway, before it turns into the M56. They'd come round and discover not only had they been raped but they'd had their nipples and vulva sliced off.'

'Yes. He got life with a minimum rec of ten years.'

'He can't still be serving – he's not wearing prison issue?'

'That's right, he's on remand. Believe it or not, he got paroled last year, claimed he was a changed man, had found Allah. Got arrested fleeing the scene of another rape on January 31st this year. Been awaiting trial ever since.'

'That's a week after the crash!'

'Makes me shudder to think what might've happened in your cell last week,' said Hussain. 'He committed that offence whilst out on licence for a life sentence. He's never getting out now, so he had nothing to lose by killing you.'

No one spoke as they all digested that chilling thought.

Anderson broke the silence: 'What do you know about his new matter?'

'Only what I've told you,' Adey replied. 'I can't get anything because it's pre-trial, but leave it with me.'

'OK,' said Hussain. 'What now? Mohammed is never going to admit to anything.'

Anderson was already on it. 'We find another route. Write to the CPS asking if the police hold any intelligence that links Mohammed aka Doran to the crash. Or to me. Or any prior intention to do me harm.' Anderson was thinking out loud: 'We have to find something new, a link. We need fresh evidence to get leave to appeal.'

Hussain leaned across the table and patted Anderson's arm. 'Hang in there, my friend, we'll find it.'

CHAPTER 78

Taylor groaned when he read the letter from the CPS. He felt uncomfortable at any mention of this case. Wished it would just go away. 'Have you seen this?' he asked Waters.

'Yes, gov. Got to give his lawyers full marks for effort.'

Taylor read an extract out loud: 'Do the police hold any intelligence on Mohammed Mohammed, aka Michael Doran, that links him to the accident on 24th January or to John Anderson?'

'I've already run a check. There's nothing and obviously we got nowt on our file.'

'Poor bastard. Says Mohammed attacked him and claimed responsibility for the crash.'

'Like that would stand up in court!' Waters scoffed. 'Smacks of desperation to me.'

'I remember the case, only just out of uniform. He's a real sicko.'

'Me too,' said Waters. 'Can't believe he got parole. He's back in now, thank God. And from what I hear the evidence is so strong on this new matter, he won't see the light of day again.'

'Who's the victim?'

'Eighteen-year-old girl, been out celebrating her birthday, apparently. Chopped her bits off.'

Taylor grimaced. 'I'd better run this by Armstrong.'

He felt guilty knocking on the DCI's door. He didn't need his input; he wanted to test him, his own colleague – a superior. Not normally Taylor's style.

'Come.' Detective Chief Inspector Armstrong looked up from his desk. 'What is it, Taylor?'

'Had some correspondence about the Anderson case,' he replied, passing the letter to his boss. 'Thought I should dot the i's and cross the t's.'

'So what do you want from me?' Armstrong snapped, irritated at being drawn into the disclosure process.

'Just checking we haven't got anything on this guy, Doran, that links him to Anderson, other than the fact Anderson prosecuted him in '03?'

'Is there anything on the file?'

'No, gov.'

'Anything from NCIS on the computer?'

'No.'

'Well, there's your answer.'

Such a firm response put his mind at rest. 'Right, thanks, Chief. I'll say we are not aware of any intelligence.' Taylor opened the door to leave.

'Hang on, Mark.'

Taylor stopped.

'Better put we do not *hold* any intelligence.'

Taylor's mouth went dry. 'Why not say *not aware*? Are we? I mean, what's the difference?'

'You know lawyers. They try and pick everything apart. Best to be precise.'

'Yes, gov.' That didn't answer Taylor's question.

Now he was deeply troubled.

CHAPTER 79

Anderson had been pacing his cell all morning waiting for the legal visit at 2pm. He prayed their letter to the CPS had turned up something.

Hussain gave him the bad news. 'Sorry, John, they said no intelligence held on Doran.'

Anderson sighed.

'But Adey has something.'

'You're not going to like it,' she said anxiously. 'Doran's current matter. I did some digging and I've got details on the modus operandi.'

'Go on,' said Anderson.

'She was drugged first. In a club. Rohypnol.'

'Rohypnol?' Anderson sat back in his chair and closed his eyes for a moment. 'Of course! Rope – it's street slang for Rohypnol. *I gave you enough rope to hang yourself.* Doran drugged me.'

Hussain was ahead of him: 'I reckon so – slipped it into your coffee in Starbucks. You flake out on the drive home.'

'And it wipes the memory,' Anderson added. 'But what about Butt?'

'We can't work that out. Maybe she administered the drug somehow, but no drink container of any sort was recovered from the vehicle – we've been back over the search records.'

303

'So how do we prove it?'

'That's the bit you're not going to like,' said Hussain. 'A blood sample was taken at the hospital and tested for alcohol, and a standard screening for drugs, cocaine, etc., which of course were negative. But no test for Rohypnol. Why would they? And no one thought to preserve the sample.'

Anderson shook his head.

Hussain continued: 'Rohypnol is only detectable in the blood for seventy-two hours max, so—'

'No point giving a sample now.'

'Correct.'

'OK then,' said Anderson, remaining positive. 'We bang in grounds of appeal with what we've got.'

'Which is what?'

'Doran attacking me – and the Rohypnol.'

'John,' said Hussain gently. 'That's just a theory. It's not evidence. Leave to appeal will be refused.'

'What about Sandra Granger, can't we argue she lied in the box?'

'That was a matter for the jury, not the Court of Appeal. You know that,' said Adey. 'And when you read the transcript, which is what the judges will have, it doesn't come across like that.'

Hussain agreed. 'You had to be in court to see she was lying.'

'Then we go to London and renew it before the full court. Try and turn something up once we're there.'

'Come off it, John. If we go with nothing we will lose, and we can never come back. Let's wait.'

'Wait for what, Tahir? It's now or never. Besides, I can't take much more.'

'Then we use Connor. It's weak but at least it's something new.'

'He's really prepared to stand up in court and say he lied?'

'More mistaken. He'll look an idiot but escape a perjury charge. Like I said, it's not great but it gets us into court.'

Out of options, Anderson agreed.

'What other witnesses will we require at the hearing?' asked Adey, ever the practical member of the team.

'Just the OIC, I suppose,' Anderson replied.

'I want West,' said Hussain. 'I don't trust that man, never have. I think he knows something.'

'He was just a character witness, what do I tell him?' asked Adey.

'Flatter him,' suggested Anderson. 'Tell him the court places great store by his opinion of me. He'll lap it up.'

'All right then,' said Hussain, bringing the meeting to a close and trying to sound positive, despite the hopelessness of the appeal. 'See you in London.'

Anderson took both their hands and held them firmly. 'Thank you.'

CHAPTER 80

Taylor read the letter again. *Requested to attend the Court of Appeal.* Even though the single judge had refused leave, they were still going to renew the appeal before the full court. In other words, they had nothing.

He couldn't get Anderson out of his head. What he must be going through.

'Are you all right, gov?' Waters asked, peering over his computer screen. 'Seem very quiet today?'

Taylor suddenly stood up and grabbed his jacket off the back of the chair. 'Back in an hour.'

'Where you going?'

'If anyone asks, say you haven't seen me.'

'Hello, Sandra love. How've you been?'

'Oh, hello, Mr Taylor. I mean Detective Inspector. Come in. Would you like a brew?'

'Yes, please.'

Tom Granger joined Taylor in the lounge whilst Sandra made the tea.

'How are you coping, Tom?'

'You know. Up and down.' He glanced around the room. 'House is so quiet now.' His vacant gaze came back to Taylor. 'You got kids?'

'Two girls. A right load of trouble.'

They smiled weakly.

Sandra put the mugs down and joined her husband on the settee.

'How are you managing, Sandra?'

'It's the anger. I can't get rid.'

'I know,' Taylor replied.

'Bet you see a lot of bereaved families in your job?'

'Yes I do, but I've got no answers. Suppose you just have to try not to become bitter. Must be hard, I know.' He took a sip. 'I wanted to tell you that he's appealing. It's on Friday, in London.'

Sandra looked at her husband.

He filled the sudden silence: 'Never been to the Smoke.' Then, reflecting further: 'Do we go?'

'There's no need, you're not required to give evidence.'

'Oh, I see. Has he got a chance?'

'Not really. He needs some fresh evidence. Like someone to admit they lied in the first trial. He's just clutching at straws.'

This time Tom gave Sandra a furtive glance. Now she avoided eye contact.

'Sandra?' asked Taylor gently. 'Your evidence was very important in the trial. Might've tipped the balance.'

She watched Taylor now.

'Yours was the only direct evidence that Anderson was asleep.'

'I'm glad I could help. Did what I could,' she replied.

'I remember when I came here and took your statement, you'd already been told Anderson was asleep.'

'What you trying to say?'

'I wondered whether that clouded your memory?

307

Whether you did actually see him asleep?'

'What? You're saying I lied?' Defensiveness turned to anger. 'That bastard killed my Molly.'

'I know,' Taylor said softly. 'But it wouldn't be right, to Molly's memory, if it wasn't the truth.'

'But he were guilty?'

'Maybe. But once we cut corners, make things up, the wrong people start getting convicted. Got to be done right.'

Sandra jumped up. 'He was driving the bloody car, weren't he? I think you should go.'

Tom stood up and placed a hand on his wife's shoulder. 'Sandra, hang on a minute, love.'

'I want him out, now.'

'OK, I'm sorry. I'm going.'

Taylor realised his visit had been a big mistake.

CHAPTER 81

'Hello, Mother,' said Anderson. 'This is a nice surprise. Dad not with you?'

Still adjusting to the surroundings, she replied, 'You know what he's like.'

'Regrettably, I do.'

'He doesn't know I'm here.'

'Very brave of you,' he said.

'Is it awful, John?'

'No, it's not that bad,' he lied.

'John.' She paused. 'I thought you should know. Your father's stopped paying the school fees.'

'What? Just when the boys need stability more than ever?'

'I'm sorry. This appeal was the final straw. He sees it as another embarrassment.'

'I never even wanted them to go to private school.' Anderson longed to be on the outside, so he could help manage the transition, look after them.

'I'm so sorry.' Ashamed of her husband, she changed the subject. 'Anyway, I also wanted to wish you luck with the appeal. I'll be thinking of you.'

'You're not coming?'

'Depends. Your father thinks it might look worse for him if we're not there.'

'It's always about him, isn't it?'

Nothing she could say in his defence.

'You know what, this place gives you a lot of time to think. I've realised, I just don't like the man.'

'John!' She placed a hand on his arm. 'He's your father.'

'He's a cold, selfish man. Why do you stay with him?'

All she could say was, 'I'm too old for all that.'

'And worst of it is, I'm just like him.'

'Don't you say that. You're nothing like him. He wanted you to be, and you've spent your life letting him mould you.' She cupped his cheek. 'Making the same mistakes I did.'

'Oh, Mum. I've really buggered my life up.'

'While there's breath in your body, it's not too late.'

Anderson managed a smile. 'Thanks, Mum.'

CHAPTER 82

DCI Armstrong burst into the open plan office, fuming. 'Everyone out, now!'

Stunned, the officers left what they were doing and made their way out.

'On the double! Not you.' He pointed a finger at Taylor.

Once they were alone, Armstrong launched at the DI: 'What did you think you were doing?'

'What do you mean?'

'You know exactly what I mean – accusing Sandra Granger of lying? Still mourning the death of her five-year-old daughter. Just had her on the phone. Wants to make a complaint. What were you playing at?'

'I don't think she told the truth in court,' Taylor replied, though he knew he'd been out of order.

'And who the hell are you to decide that? The jury didn't agree.'

'I'm not sure about the safety of the conviction.'

'What?' Armstrong pointed a finger at Taylor. 'And when did you become judge and jury? Getting too big for your effing boots, Taylor.'

'I'm sorry but the evidence—'

Armstrong cut him off. 'This is because I made DCI isn't it? You want to undermine me?'

'Where did that come from? I never wanted it.'

'This is going on your file.'

'My file?' Unable to control himself, Taylor got up and stood toe to toe with the DCI. 'Why does it matter so much anyway? Come to think of it, why did this case need a DI? So what if Anderson's a barrister?' Taylor's brain was ticking over. Seeing things from a different angle. 'Why was it so important to get me on this case? Who wanted me to nail Anderson so badly?'

Armstrong lost some of his bluster. 'Always have to rebel against authority, don't you? That's why you never made it.'

'What? Didn't kiss the right arses, like you, you mean?'

'You cheeky git. Right, that's it. Go home and calm down.' Armstrong shoved him in the shoulder. 'Go on, sod off.'

'With pleasure.' Taylor stormed out. It wasn't until he reached the car park that he got a sinking feeling. He'd overreacted. But why? Armstrong's offensive remarks had never got to him before.

Was it because of a dawning realisation that somehow an innocent man had been convicted?

And that he had unwittingly been party to it?

CHAPTER 83

Taylor had lost track of time. The Mickey Mouse alarm clock said 4.03am. He'd been sitting there for over an hour. He leaned into both bunks and kissed his children gently on their cheeks. Taylor often watched them sleeping when *he* couldn't. He thought of Anderson's children – without a father.

He crept back into his bedroom and slipped silently under the duvet.

'What is it, Mark?' His wife knew him better than anyone.

'Nothing, go back to sleep, love.'

She flopped an arm onto his chest. 'It's not nothing. You've not slept for three nights. Now what is it?'

Taylor turned the bedside lamp on and sat up. 'It's the Anderson case.'

'Not that again?'

'Shush, you'll wake the kids.'

In more of a whisper: 'I thought you were finished with all that?'

'I was. They're appealing, asking all sorts of questions.'

She sat up. 'And do you know the answers?'

'No, but I think there is something *to* know that's been kept from me.'

'OK.'

'I may be wrong but Armstrong has been acting strangely and I think he went to see someone recently, to do with this case. There was an address in his diary.' Taylor stopped himself. It was the first time he'd aired these thoughts to anyone.

'And?'

'It may be nothing but if I was defending I would want to know. It goes against everything I believe in, to go and leak information to the defence, and anyway it might have absolutely no relevance,' he said, trying to convince himself he wasn't thinking straight. 'But something is wrong here. I want to do the right thing.'

She stroked his forehead. 'What is it about this man?'

'I don't know.'

She waited.

'Unless he's the world's best liar, I think he's innocent. A very honourable and decent man. I did a real job on him in interview.' He shook his head. 'As good as sent him to jail.'

'Hush, you were only doing your job.' After some reflection, she asked, 'If you tell the defence this thing, will it affect your pension?'

Taylor laughed. 'Only if I get caught.'

She leaned over and kissed him. 'Then don't get caught.'

That was why he loved her.

CHAPTER 84

Adey was determined to remain professional – not let her anger show itself. Just a job, she kept telling herself. She had a perfect vantage point from Strada, a restaurant adjacent to the communal entrance of the Spinningfields apartment. Her enquiries revealed that Daddy had paid for it.

Adey didn't have to wait long before she clocked the young blond in Ugg boots and fake fur, swaggering out of the building and across the Square.

Adey followed. She'd made the decision not to go to the address to confront her. Bound to result in a door being slammed in her face. Catching her out in the open would make it more difficult for Tilly to end the conversation.

Into Waitrose on Bridge Street.

Ten minutes later Tilly reappeared, laden with a bag in each hand.

Adey crossed the road to confront her. 'Hello, Tilly.'

Tilly gave her a quizzical look. Already on her guard: 'Do I know you?'

'Part of John Anderson's legal team. We're appealing. Thought you might like to do the right thing and make a statement admitting your lies at the trial.'

'Piss off.' Tilly put her head down and picked up the pace.

Adey matched it, now walking two abreast. 'He wasn't

tired at all, was he? Sam Connor has made a further statement.' Exaggerating, she added, 'A retraction.'

Tilly pressed on. 'Leave me alone.'

'At least Connor has finally decided to do the right thing.'

'That loser?' Tilly's anger took over. She stopped. 'I've lost everything because of him. You know they didn't give me a tenancy? Chucked me out, the bastards.'

Adey laughed. 'Live by the sword—'

'Connor got looked after though, didn't he? No one threw *him* out of chambers. My career's stuffed now.'

'I'm sure you'll survive, resourceful girl like you.'

'You taking the piss?' Tilly's temperature was still rising.

So was Adey's. 'You spoilt little brat. What about John Anderson? You sent an innocent man to jail.'

'Who are you to speak to me like that?'

'You don't give a shit about anyone but yourself, do you?'

Outraged at the observation, Tilly took a step back, dropped one bag then swung the one in her right hand at Adey's head.

Adey ducked.

It hit the wall, spattering milk in all directions.

The momentum caught Tilly off balance.

Adey thrust a hand to Tilly's throat, pinning her against the wall. With the other she poked Tilly's forehead. 'Nothing in there. Just one bad mother, aren't you?'

Eyes blazing, Tilly didn't reply.

Adey tutted, then released her grip. 'Bitch, you ain't worth it.'

Leaving her shopping strewn on the pavement, Tilly hurried off up the street.

Adey kicked the wall in frustration. She didn't have the witness statement she'd come for.

This appeal was going nowhere.

CHAPTER 85

Hussain had already taken the train to Euston.

He wanted to stay the night in London so that he was fresh in the morning. Appearing before three High Court judges was nerve-wracking enough, but acting for an applicant, without leave to appeal, that he cared so much about, and with no fresh evidence, was almost too much to bear. How was he was going to find the answers in court?

Adey was going down in the morning. She locked up the office and started walking back to Hulme, so engrossed in the appeal she didn't notice the rain. Was there something she'd missed? Something she should've done? What did *05man* mean? How would Anderson cope when the appeal was dismissed?

'Evening, Adey.'

The voice came from the darkness of a shop doorway. A figure stepped into the light. She could see a raincoat with the collar turned up. DI Taylor.

'What do you want?'

'I was sorry to hear about leave being refused in Anderson.'

'Well, we're going anyway, like you give a shit.'

'I'm here to help you, so why don't you wind your neck in and listen?'

Embarrassed, Adey realised she had nothing to lose by hearing him out. 'OK, what is it?'

'This never came from me. Clear?'

'OK.'

Taylor needed reassurance. 'Do I have your word on that?'

'You trust my word?'

Taylor managed a smile. 'Yes, I do.'

'Then you've got it.'

'OK. After all that build up, it may be nothing. And let me make it plain, I know no more than you, it's a hunch.'

'Understood.'

Taylor still wasn't sure he was doing the right thing. 'I think you could be looking in the wrong place.'

'Wrong place? What do you mean?'

'You've been focusing on police-held intelligence. I saw something connected to this case that had an address on it – Thames House.'

'Thames House?'

'Yes – MI5.'

Adey could hardly believe what she was hearing. 'Are you sure?'

'No, I'm not. I've told you that.'

'But the hearing is tomorrow morning!'

'No time to waste then. I've done my bit, the rest is up to you.'

Taylor walked off into the evening drizzle.

MI5? Adey's head was in a whirl.

CHAPTER 86

The Royal Courts of Justice, a magnificent nineteenth-century gothic building on the Strand – home of the Court of Appeal.

Hussain sat in the café opposite, eyes fixed on the imposing archway, waiting for the doors to open. Butterflies in his stomach. This was his first appearance as an advocate in the appellate court. These judges were the brains of England. As an instructing solicitor he'd been a few times to sit behind a barrister and had witnessed them cut down where they stood by the superior intellects of those on the bench. This court did not suffer fools gladly. Hussain reminded himself that John Anderson had reason to be far more anxious about today's proceedings than him.

At last, the front gate was unlocked. Hussain hurried across the road, keen to spend as much time as possible with his client before the hearing. On receiving Adey's phone call the night before, Hussain had been in a state of panic. MI5? Was it really possible? Surely they needed more time to investigate this new lead?

Hussain stopped in the Great Hall and stared up at the ceiling. A visitor could be in no doubt this was the heart of the criminal justice system of England and Wales. Gothic archways leading off or up to the courtrooms. It took years to really know one's way around the countless passageways of these law courts. He scurried off to the only robing room he knew, on the right of the entrance, and began to put on his collar and bands.

Once robed, he headed back across the Great Hall towards the cells.

'Hey, Hussain?' Hannah Stapleton was marching towards him. 'What do you call this?' she demanded, waving a printout of the email he'd sent her the night before. 'MI5? Are you having a laugh?'

'Do I look like I'm laughing?'

She read from the email: '"Does MI5 hold any intelligence on Michael Doran, aka Mohammed Mohammed, that is relevant to this case?" How the hell am I supposed to action that? We're on at 10.30.'

Hussain took solace from Stapleton's tirade. All counsel, however senior, found an appearance at the Court of Appeal a stressful experience. 'Please just do what you can? Thanks.'

Hussain caught sight of Adey coming through security and took his cue to leave Stapleton, standing open-mouthed in the middle of the Great Hall. 'Have you seen West or Connor yet?' he barked at Adey.

'No, I haven't. Calm down, Taz.'

'I'm sorry.' He took a few deep breaths.

'You look knackered, are you OK?'

'I need to know if West and Connor are here. Please find them, then meet me in the cells.'

They set off in different directions.

The door to the cells was as old as the building itself.

'Yes, sir,' came the chirpy greeting from the cockney prison officer on opening up.

'John Anderson, please?'

The officer studied his clipboard. 'Not here, sir. He waived.'

Hussain began to panic. 'Waived? That's not possible. I know he would have exercised his right to attend.'

'Leave him alone. Can't you see he's nervous enough?' said the officer's colleague appearing at the door. He turned to Hussain: 'Thinks he's funny, bloody pillock. Come this way.'

Hussain followed the second man down to the cells, whilst the joker chuckled to himself.

Anderson was soon brought limping into the conference room. He slumped onto a chair. 'Another marathon in the sweatbox,' he explained. 'Had to stop at all the prisons in England on the way down, then a dreadful time in Pentonville last night.'

Hussain could see Anderson was really suffering.

'Anyway, enough of all that. Any developments?'

Hussain updated Anderson with Taylor's leak about MI5.

Like Hussain and Adey, Anderson couldn't believe it. 'I just can't see where MI5 could possibly fit into this?'

'John, let me apply to adjourn? Buy us some time.'

'No, we need to keep the pressure on. Ask Stapleton to get someone from MI5 here today.'

'John, this is suicidal.'

But Anderson was in no mood to back off now.

CHAPTER 87

Adey spotted a man, very distinguished-looking, waiting outside the courtroom – Orlando West. Never having seen him in the flesh before, she recognised him from his photo on the chambers website. He was even more imposing in real life. 'Hello, Mr West. I'm Adey Tuur from Hussain & Co.'

Their eyes met. Adey suddenly felt an odd shiver down her spine.

'I can't for the life of me understand why you think I can help?' he protested. 'Is that solicitor – what's he called again?'

'Hussain.'

'Ah, yes. Is Hussain sure the Court want to hear from me?'

Adey took a few moments to compose herself. She was in no doubt, this was the man she'd seen that night in Anderson's house, having sex with Mia. As if on cue, Anderson's wife appeared from behind a pillar. West turned immediately: 'May I introduce Mrs Anderson, here to lend moral support. What was your name again?'

'Adey Tuur.' She held out her hand, but neither of them took it. She left for the cells.

On entering the conference room, she shared the revelation: 'I've just seen Orlando West. He's the one I saw screwing your wife!'

'Impossible!' Anderson replied instinctively.

'Why?'

'I always thought he was gay.'

'Not from where I was standing.'

'Are you sure, Adey?' asked Hussain. 'It was dark.'

'Taz, I'm sure.'

'I'm sorry, John,' said Hussain. 'I know how painful this must be for you.'

Anderson sat back in the chair. 'Every day I learn something new about my old life. How could he do that to me?'

Adey had to bring Anderson back: 'You need to focus. Does this shed any light on what happened on the 24th January?'

Anderson leaned forward, acknowledging the point. She was right. 'No, there's no real evidence against him.'

Adey followed it through: 'I'm just thinking how these judges will react if Taz puts a defence character witness in the box and accuses him of sleeping with your wife.'

Even Anderson managed to see the irony. 'Not our best point.'

'I'm only putting it if it becomes relevant,' said Hussain. 'Or they'll eat me alive.'

'You'll just have to feel your way,' suggested Anderson.

'Feel my way! We haven't got a bloody clue where we're going, have we?'

Nobody replied.

'And is Connor here yet?'

'Not yet, Taz,' Adey replied.

Hussain raised his arms to the heavens: 'Allah, give me strength.'

CHAPTER 88

The courtroom was packed. Grey stone and ancient wood for décor only added to the solemnity of the proceedings. Hussain's stress levels were at breaking point. Adey, sitting behind him, gently patted his back in an effort to keep him calm.

He turned around. 'Connor?'

She shook her head.

'All rise!' Three elderly gentlemen in red robes came into court and took their seats, Mr Justice Billings in the middle, presiding.

Anderson was brought in and seated in the dock on a raised platform to the right of the judges. Able to get a glimpse at the public gallery he saw his brother Stephen, and to his surprise, even his parents. Mr and Mrs Granger sat stony-faced in front of Orlando West and Mia. Were they really lovers?

DI Taylor, sitting with two CPS lawyers behind Hannah Stapleton, made no eye contact with Anderson, or the defence team.

Hussain realised that such was the arrangement in appellate courts; he would have no opportunity to consult with Anderson during the proceedings. Anxiety levels rose again.

'My Lords,' he announced. 'I represent the appellant,

Miss Stapleton, Queen's Counsel, is for the—'

'Don't you mean you represent the *applicant*?' Mr Justice Billings cut in. 'He only becomes an appellant if this Court grants leaves to appeal. At the moment we haven't seen anything vaguely resembling arguable grounds.'

'Yes, My Lord.' Hussain's first mistake. 'Might I make a preliminary application?'

'Which is?'

'That the applicant sits not in the dock, but next to me, here in counsels' row?'

'That's highly unusual,' the judge replied with disdain.

'So is the applicant, My Lord. He was – is – a very experienced barrister, and I require his assistance to ensure that justice is done, which is, after all, the only ambition of this Court.'

'But he's been struck off, hasn't he?'

'Only because of this conviction, which we seek to quash, My Lord. This Court is the bowel of the criminal justice system in this great country; I implore it not to stand too much on ceremony.'

Hussain's pomposity raised one or two half-smiles. The judges consulted each other, exchanging whispered opinions.

Eventually: 'Very well. Dock officer, please accompany the applicant. We will rise while that is done.'

Hussain was amazed, and mightily relieved.

Once Anderson was in position, and had spread his dog-eared bundle of papers out in front of him, Sam Connor made an appearance in counsels' row. He whispered: 'That's the Court of Appeal for you – they can do what they bloody well like!'

Anderson twisted around to see his old rival.

326

'I'm really sorry, John,' said Connor.

Nothing else needed saying, the past was the past. A hearty handshake and a warm smile was enough for Anderson. He had more important things on his mind. And besides, Connor was here to make amends.

'I've remembered where I saw Heena Butt before,' Connor whispered to the defence team.

Everyone was eager to hear this revelation.

'On the morning of the crash I was in chambers early, doing those bloody schedules.'

Anderson remembered.

'I saw her in chambers. Coming out of West's room. He was showing her out.'

No, please no, thought Anderson.

'I knew it!' exclaimed Hussain.

'Shush,' said Adey, holding a finger to her lips. They were attracting the attention of the public gallery.

'That's it now,' said Hussain. 'West set you up. I'm going for him.'

'Tread carefully,' warned Anderson. 'We don't know the details yet.'

'There's one more thing,' said Connor.

'What, there's more?' asked Hussain.

Connor was nervous. Choosing his words carefully: 'I can't give evidence.'

'What are you talking about? You are the main thrust of this appeal!' Hussain's outrage was again noticed by others in the courtroom.

'I'm sorry. I've thought of nothing else. It would ruin my career. I'd never live it down.'

'You gave us your word,' said Hussain.

'I want to give evidence, but…' He shrugged. 'I'm not like Anderson. I'm weak.'

'You're a coward,' said Adey.

'Leave it,' said Anderson. He'd heard enough. Connor simply didn't have it in him.

'I'm sorry,' was all Connor could say.

The others watched their star witness slope off to the public gallery.

'Excuse me?'

'What is it?' snapped Hussain, before realising it was Mrs Granger who had spoken. She was standing at the side of counsels' row with her husband.

She looked even more gaunt than when Hussain had last seen her. Haunted.

'I want to give evidence.'

'You? Why?'

Hands twitching: 'I didn't tell the truth at trial.'

Stunned, no one knew what to say.

'I still think you're guilty,' she said, looking directly at Anderson. 'But I never saw your face before the crash.' Then, by way of explanation: 'When I made me statement I were proper angry.' She shook her head. 'So I lied. Then I just stuck with it. It were wrong o' me.' She studied her hands, fidgeting with the buttons on her jacket. Sandra Granger's anguish was plain to see.

'Mrs Granger,' said Hussain. 'You do realise that you would be admitting perjury? You could go to prison.'

She took her husband's hand. It had obviously been a matter of considerable debate in the Granger household. 'I know.'

'Right, well, thank you,' said Hussain, gathering his

thoughts. 'If you'd like to wait outside, Miss Tuur, my colleague, will come and take a statement before we call you.'

The Grangers nodded and left the courtroom.

'Quite a turn up,' said Hussain. 'I'll ask for time whilst the statement is taken.'

'A grieving mother going to jail?' said Anderson. 'We can't call her.'

'What are you talking about?' said Adey. 'This could get us a retrial.'

'I don't want a retrial. I want to finish it today. I came here to find out what happened, not to sacrifice Sandra Granger to save my own skin. She's got more guts and integrity than Sam Connor ever had.'

Adey just didn't get it. Hussain did. 'OK, my friend, I will go and tell her.'

He joined her on one of the old wooden pews, slotted between stone pillars along the corridor. 'We're not going to call you, Mrs Granger, so you have nothing to worry about.'

'Why not? I don't understand?'

'Mr Anderson feels you've suffered enough. We are not here to punish you, but to find the truth about what caused this tragedy – for all of us.'

Sandra Granger stared at Hussain, unable to comprehend Anderson's generosity.

She was mystified.

CHAPTER 89

'All rise!'

The judges came back into court.

Anderson at his side, coupled with this new information about West, Hussain was rejuvenated. 'My Lord, I call Orlando West, Queen's Counsel.'

'Orlando West?' repeated the presiding judge. 'He only gave character evidence in the trial. This Court always finds it a pleasure to hear the dulcet tones of Mr West, but we of course accept the evidence he gave the first time. There's no fresh evidence here.'

West, sitting in the gallery, sensed something wasn't right.

'My Lord, there are some new matters we would wish to explore.'

'*Explore*! This is an appeal, not a fishing expedition, Mr Hussain. Is there even a witness statement?'

'Due to the pressure of time, I'm afraid not.'

The Court was losing patience with Hussain. 'This really is wholly unacceptable.'

'I can assure Your Lordship, I will take this very shortly.'

'Very well,' said the judge. 'But let me make it clear, so far this Court is singularly unimpressed.'

Hussain lowered his gaze to acknowledge the admonishment.

West made his way to the witness box, his customary

self-assurance absent. He took the oath. The judges smiled at him, lest it be thought *he* had displeased the Court. West returned an obsequious bow.

'Here we go,' Hussain whispered to Anderson, before turning to the witness. He began: 'John Anderson was your pupil?'

'Yes, he was.'

'You took him on as a favour to his father?'

'Yes, but we were glad to have him.'

'You gave him an enviable start at the Bar?'

'That's for others to judge,' West replied, smiling at Mr Justice Billings, more relaxed now that he knew the subject matter of this examination.

'And as the years passed, you became not just his mentor, but a very dear family friend?'

'I like to think so.'

'You know so. You are godfather to his children?'

'Yes, I am.'

'You, more than most, were able to witness first hand, the utter shock and devastation that the events of 24th January had on John Anderson and his family?'

'I did.'

'My Lord,' said Hussain, switching his attention for a moment, 'I say that, meaning no disrespect to the family of Molly Granger, whose own loss is immeasurable.'

'I'm sure that is understood by all, Mr Hussain.'

Hussain refocused on his target. 'And in his hour of need, he came to you to ask but one favour – that you defend him?'

The question surprised West. Why would he ask that? 'He did, but sadly I felt it was inappropriate for me to act, because of our friendship.'

'But you *could* have accepted the brief, couldn't you? I mean ultimately, it was a matter for your own conscience.'

'My own professional judgement,' came the measured response.

'If you had known something about the events of 24th January that John Anderson did not, then of course you could not represent him.'

'Obviously.'

'If that were the case, you wouldn't touch the brief with a barge pole, would you?'

'What are you getting at?' West's reply had a sense of urgency. Flustered. What was coming next?

'Is that why you turned your friend down? Because you knew something?'

'Certainly not!'

Mr Justice Billings leaned forward: 'This is quite extraordinary, Mr Hussain. I don't know what you're insinuating, but we commend Mr West's very difficult and apposite decision.'

Time for the kill: 'Do you recognise this person, Mr West?' Hussain handed the usher the post-mortem photograph of Heena Butt.

West studied the photograph. 'This person is deceased so it's difficult, but no, I can't say I do.'

'That is Heena Butt, the woman found dead in the applicant's car. Do you know her?'

'No, I do not.'

'But she came to see you in chambers on the morning of the 24th, didn't she?'

An almost imperceptible pause before West answered: 'Well, I suppose it's possible, but I certainly don't remember it. I see countless people. As a lawyer yourself, you'll appreciate that.'

Outfoxed, Hussain was beginning to panic. In a last desperate lunge: 'Were you in on this in some way?'

'I beg your pardon?'

'Were you party to a conspiracy to set Mr Anderson up?'

West burst out laughing. 'Ridiculous!'

'To get him out of the way?'

'Why on earth would I want to do that?'

'So that you could take his place. After all, you were having an affair with his wife, were you not?'

'Do I have to answer that, My Lord?'

'So you don't deny it then?' pressed Hussain.

'No you do *not* have to, Mr West,' interjected the old judge, incandescent with rage. 'Mr Hussain, I am appalled by what I have just witnessed. Eminent Queen's Counsel, Mr West, came here to assist the defence by giving character evidence on behalf of the applicant and you trick him into the box and accuse him, apparently without any evidential foundation, of being responsible for this tragedy and having extra-marital relations with the applicant's wife.' The aged judge paused to catch his breath. Then: 'Rest assured, I will be reporting you to your governing body. You are not fit to wear that gown.'

Hussain was not only shaken by the reprimand, but embarrassed to have been outmanoeuvred so easily. He whispered to his client, 'I'm so sorry, John.'

'Don't worry,' Anderson replied, hiding his disappointment. 'He's a worthy opponent.'

They watched West retake his seat in the public gallery next to Mia. Had Connor lied to them? Maybe Adey was mistaken? He didn't know which scenario he wanted to be the truth.

Billings wasn't finished: 'I take it that concludes the live evidence?'

Stapleton addressed the Court. 'My Lord, the defence made a disclosure request of the Crown this morning, which—'

'This morning?' repeated Mr Justice Billings. 'Why on earth wasn't that done sooner, Mr Hussain?'

'Some information came to us very late, My Lord.'

He rolled his eyes at his brother judges.

'I will need five minutes with the witness, My Lord,' Stapleton continued. 'To consider any possible disclosure and then I can tender him for cross-examination.'

'And this goes to what issue?'

'I'm not entirely sure, My Lord. The defence assert that MI5 may hold some information pertinent to this appeal.'

'MI5? Were they in some way involved?'

'Not that I'm aware of.'

The judge shook his head, making his disgust at the way this appeal was being conducted abundantly clear. After a deep sigh: 'Very well, five minutes. We'll rise.'

CHAPTER 90

Hussain was glad of the respite from the judges' glowers.

Anderson brushed off Hussain's continued apologies for the disastrous cross, but inside he was distraught. They needed a miracle.

'Right,' said Stapleton, sliding along counsels' row to where the defence were sitting. 'We've managed to get someone here from MI5. His name is Saul Pennington.'

'Does he know anything?' asked Hussain.

'Only this: they were aware of Doran. They knew he was bitter about his 2003 conviction and bore a grudge against the police and lawyers involved. It's got no relevance to this case.'

Hussain wasn't prepared to just accept it. 'You'll have to stick him in the box.'

'Sure,' replied Stapleton, unconcerned about this apparently peripheral piece of disclosure.

As she moved back to the prosecution team, Anderson caught Taylor's eye. They read each other's mind – this guy, Pennington, knew more than he was letting on.

'All rise!' The judges came back into court.

Hussain was in a flap, whispering to Anderson: 'I don't know what I'm going to ask this witness.'

Anderson poured him a glass of water. Hussain snatched nervously at it, causing droplets to splash over Anderson's papers.

'My Lord,' Stapleton announced. 'I call Saul Pennington from MI5.'

Anderson, desperately trying to think of some line of cross-examination for Hussain, dabbed at the wet sheets with a tissue Adey had handed him.

Once the witness was sworn, Stapleton tendered him to Hussain, who rose slowly to his feet. What was he going to ask?

Anderson stared at one particular piece of paper from his file:

John Anderson, Spinningfields Chambers – 05man.

The water had made the ink run; the words were blurred. Suddenly, his heart skipped a beat. Could it be he had the answer? Thoughts crystallizing, he pulled at Hussain's gown, who was still trying to think of his first question. 'Would you like me to take this witness?'

'Are you sure?' Hussain was more than happy to let Anderson take the flak.

'Yes, if the Court allows it. It's the most important cross-examination of my life. I should be the one to do it.'

Hussain nodded. 'My Lord, Mr Anderson will take this witness.'

'What?' erupted Billings. 'You are the advocate, you will take the witness.'

'My Lord, it is open to the applicant to sack me in any event, and conduct the hearing as a litigant in person. Ultimately, it is his right.'

Hussain had a point. Reluctantly: 'Oh, very well, let's get on with it.'

CHAPTER 91

John Anderson winced in pain as he rose to his feet, resting an arm on the lectern to spare his injured leg the full weight of his body. Much had happened since he last conducted a cross-examination. It felt strange, not least because he was without the protection of a wig and gown. Anderson took a deep breath. Everything had come down to this.

He began: 'What is your official job title, Mr Pennington?'

'I don't really have a title as such.'

'Are you a field operative?'

'No, I'm not.'

'It's just that I want to establish how high up you are in the organisation. Are you a fall guy that knows very little, sent here to answer questions, or are you a decision maker?'

'Well, I'm part of a team but I can answer your questions.'

'Thank you, Mr Pennington.' Now the gentle sparring was over, Anderson decided to up the ante: 'It was disclosed to us today that you had information about Mr Doran, otherwise known as Mr Mohammed.'

'Yes, we did.'

'You had that prior to the 24th January?'

'Yes.'

'That he was bitter about his conviction?'

'Yes.'

'Was he making threats towards me?'

'You and a lot of other people. He's a very disturbed individual.'

'How did you come by this information?'

'He came to our attention during an undercover operation.'

'What was the nature of that operation?'

'That's very sensitive, classified information. I don't want to answer that.'

'Well, is the operation still ongoing?'

'No.'

'Were arrests made?'

'Yes.'

'So, answering my question will not compromise any operations, will it?'

'I suppose not.'

'So, I will ask you again, what was the nature of that operation?'

Pennington glanced sideways at Stapleton.

Anderson reined him in: 'There's no point looking at her, Mr Pennington. The way it works, you see, is if you have sensitive material that you don't want to disclose, it's given to the CPS and Miss Stapleton reviews whether it is disclosable. But MI5 didn't give the prosecution anything, did they?'

'No, we didn't.'

'No, you kept them in the dark. So now, unless His Lordship says otherwise, you will answer my questions, understood?'

'Yes.'

Anderson was already in control. His Lordship couldn't help but be impressed.

'So, the operation, Mr Pennington?'

'We had information that two Pakistani nationals, known criminals, were attempting to set up a terrorist cell in the Manchester area.'

'Go on.'

Pennington huffed, annoyed that he was having to divulge the information. 'They were seeking to recruit what we call "young impressionables" that attended Manchester Central Mosque. One of those they enlisted was Mohammed Mohammed, formerly known as Michael Doran.'

'Right, and can I assume you had an undercover operative who infiltrated the cell?'

'Yes. That operative heard the threats made by Doran towards yourself.'

'Anything else that might be important you want to tell the Court?'

After some hesitation: 'No, I don't think so.'

Anderson flopped onto his seat.

Relieved it was over, Pennington made to leave the witness box.

'I'm sorry, Mr Pennington,' said Anderson, getting back on his feet. 'Please come back. It's my leg, it gave way. Does that sometimes. I'm not finished.'

Pennington stopped.

'Did Heena Butt work for MI5?'

'No.'

'Are you sure about that?'

'Yes,' he replied, shifting nervously from one foot to the other.

Stapleton got up. 'I think that's enough, My Lord. Mr Anderson is fishing for evidence. The workings of MI5 are highly classified for obvious reasons. Can we let Mr Pennington get back to protecting our shores?'

'Yes, I agree,' replied Mr Justice Billings. 'Thank you for coming, Mr Pennington.'

'My Lord,' said Anderson. 'Just one question that might lead to something – if not, I'm finished with the witness and would abandon this appeal.'

Too good an offer to refuse. 'Very well, just that one matter, Mr Anderson.'

'Mr Pennington,' said Anderson, holding up a piece of paper. 'This was found in Heena Butt's handbag. I thought it read: "John Anderson – Spinningfields Chambers – 05 man". But I got the last word wrong, didn't I?'

Pennington appeared to study the document. 'I don't know.'

'It actually says "Osman", doesn't it?'

Hussain suddenly realised where this was going.

'I don't know,' Pennington replied.

'As an MI5 officer you must be aware of the famous case of *Osman v UK*?'

'Yes.' The witness was becoming more agitated.

'That case, which went all the way to the European Court of Human Rights in Strasbourg, founded a fundamental principle: that if any state agency had information that one of its citizens, whether in jail or out, was at risk of being killed, the state had a duty to tell them of the threat.' Anderson banged his fist down on the lectern. 'That's right, isn't it?'

Pennington had no choice but to answer: 'Yes.'

'We as lawyers, and you as MI5 officers, know that as an Osman warning?'

'Yes.'

Anderson leaned forward and said very slowly: 'On the 24th January was Heena Butt tasked with giving me an Osman warning?'

Pennington sighed. Eventually, almost in a whisper: 'Yes.'

'I didn't hear you.'

Louder: 'Yes.'

Stapleton leapt to her feet. 'My Lord, the prosecution were not aware of this.'

The judges were still reeling from the last answer.

Anderson had the initiative. He pressed on: 'I will ask you again, did Miss Butt work for MI5?'

'No, she didn't.' Pennington paused, then admitted, 'She worked for the Pakistani intelligence services. She was with us on secondment. Butt was an alias we gave her.'

Anderson's team scoffed. Even the judge couldn't let that one go: 'Mr Pennington, in future, make sure you are less economical with the truth.'

Pennington turned crimson. 'My Lord.'

'Please continue, Mr Anderson.'

Anderson acknowledged the judge's green light. 'So Heena Butt, real name I assume is classified, was to warn me that Doran was planning to kill me?'

'Yes.'

'Did Doran say how he was going to do it?'

'Not exactly, but he said it would involve Rohypnol.'

Anderson closed his eyes for a moment. Gasps from the gallery. Stapleton turned to her team, clearly unaware of this latest revelation. 'Miss Butt was too late, though, wasn't she?'

'I don't know what you mean?'

Anderson, flabbergasted by that lie, almost shouted the next question. 'Everything that happened to me on the 24th January, everything I described, is consistent with my being drugged, isn't it?'

'I can't answer that, I'm not an expert.'

'Come now, Mr Pennington. At the very least you should have disclosed what you knew to the police after the accident, so my blood could have been tested for the presence of Rohypnol?'

'That wasn't my decision.'

'Oh, I see, time to pass the buck.' For the first time Anderson saw the bigger picture. 'There were two courses of action open to you; the first was to disclose this at my trial, or if the information was too sensitive to disclose, explain it to the CPS and indicate that I shouldn't be prosecuted. Why didn't that happen, Mr Pennington?'

Pennington shrugged.

'Is it because MI5 knew that Doran was out on licence from a life sentence? He'd breached his licence conditions, hadn't he, by associating with criminals at the mosque?' Anderson waited for an answer.

'Technically, he was in breach, yes.'

'So you should have notified the parole board, who would have recalled him to prison. But you decided not to compromise the operation, didn't you?'

'Yes.'

'And Doran went on to cause the deaths of two people – Heena Butt and Molly Granger?'

'Yes.'

'Was it worth it? Was the secrecy of your operation worth two lives? The life of a child?'

342

Pennington didn't reply.

'You knew that if I wasn't prosecuted, people would want answers as to why.' Anderson turned and pointed to Mr and Mrs Granger. 'In particular, the parents of Molly Granger.'

Tears were streaming down Mrs Granger's cheeks.

'You couldn't risk it getting out that you'd kept quiet about Doran's criminal activities, so I was sacrificed?'

All Pennington could say was, 'It wasn't my decision. I know there were discussions about what to do.'

'I bet there were,' Anderson seethed. 'And then a week after the crash, Doran raped and mutilated an eighteen-year-old girl, didn't he?'

'Yes.'

'Now there was definitely no going back. It could never get out, could it?'

'What do you mean?'

'The first decision not to arrest Doran could possibly have been justified as being in the public interest – national security. But once he'd caused two deaths, you had to take him out. Not doing so was a fatal mistake?'

Pennington nodded: 'Yes.'

'So the Doran saga was buried. And that meant it had to be hidden from all parties in *R v Anderson*.'

'It wasn't that simple.'

'What do you mean?'

'After the offence on the 31st, on the eighteen-year-old girl, he was locked up anyway. And we assumed you knew about the Rohypnol – you'd have the blood tested, so we wouldn't have to disclose anything.'

'Why on earth would you think that?' Anderson fumed.

'Well, because Butt had given Orlando West an Osman

on the morning of the crash – the 24th. Told him about Rohypnol. He was your leader in the Doran case. He'd had the same threats.'

Silence smashed around the courtroom.

Everyone stared at West, who was still sitting in the gallery. Mia, distressed, did the same, then stood up and staggered out of court. West appeared frozen to the spot.

Anderson couldn't believe what he was hearing. His closest friend had known all along; watched him go to jail. Lied in the witness box.

Anderson had to stay focused. 'But when you realised West wasn't going to share that information, you still kept your mouths shut and watched me drown?'

'I have to accept that.'

Anderson handed the usher the photo Adey had taken of the man who chased her. 'Mr Pennington, who is this?'

He glanced at the exhibit. 'An MI5 operative.'

'Even during my trial you were still trying to put my lawyers off the scent, weren't you?'

Pennington hung his head in shame.

'Mr Pennington, I spent seventeen years prosecuting criminals for my country. I gave it everything, day in, day out; it's an ugly business. Always at risk of someone trying to take revenge. Screws up your relationships, your life.' Anderson's voice broke up. 'You were supposed to protect me. Look at me, Mr Pennington.'

Pennington raised his head.

'I was abandoned in the blink of an eye, like I was nothing. I demand to know who made that decision?'

Pennington could keep it in no more. 'It wasn't MI5. It was a hot potato right from the start. We couldn't authorise the continued freedom of a psychopath like Doran. Had to be referred up, to the Home Office. *They* decided to keep the CPS in the dark throughout your trial.'

'Of course,' said Anderson. 'It was a political decision. How high did it go?'

'It's not for me to say, but we had it signed off. It's all on file.'

'Let me see it.'

Pennington glanced up at the judge, who responded by saying, 'Show him.'

Pennington opened his briefcase and took a document out of a folder. The usher took it and handed it to Anderson.

John Anderson couldn't believe his eyes.

After a few seconds he handed the document back to the usher, who in turn returned it to Pennington. In a complete volte-face, Anderson said, 'My Lord, I wonder whether it actually matters who it was? Before I go any further, I invite the Crown to consider whether they oppose this application for leave to appeal?'

After some urgent whispering between the CPS lawyers and Stapleton, she got to her feet. 'Neither do we oppose the application for leave nor the subsequent appeal against conviction.'

'Very wise, Miss Stapleton.' His Lordship muttered a few words to his brother judges, then: 'We grant leave and we quash this conviction. There will be no retrial. It seems plain as a pike staff that Mr Anderson was drugged. A written judgement will follow.' Mr Justice Billings addressed Anderson: 'A brilliant cross-examination. I hope you haven't lost faith in the criminal justice system, Mr Anderson? We need more advocates like you at the Bar.'

Anderson could hardly take it in, let alone consider his future.

'And, Mr Hussain, you showed great courage in the face of stiff criticism.'

Hussain was almost sure the old judge winked.

As people left their seats and began to file out of the courtroom, His Lordship added: 'Just a minute, dock officer. As sad as it makes me to say it, Mr West will have to be taken down to the cells for the moment. Is there a police officer here?'

Taylor stood up. 'Yes, My Lord. I am the Officer In The Case.'

'Very good. No doubt you would wish to arrest Mr West for perjury?'

'Yes, My Lord.'

'Perhaps you could arrange for his transportation from the cells to a police station for interview.'

Taylor bowed. 'Yes, My Lord.'

'And, Mr Anderson, I think you may have to go back down momentarily, to be processed before your release?'

'Yes. I'm familiar with the procedure, My Lord.'

'Very good. We'll rise.'

Two prison officers took hold of a shell-shocked Orlando West and escorted him out of court.

Case closed.

CHAPTER 92

Only Adey, Hussain and Anderson remained in the courtroom, staring at each other.

Adey broke the silence: 'Well, that went well.'

They all laughed.

Anderson grinned at Hussain. 'We've come a long way, you and I.'

'We have indeed.'

'Words are not enough, Tahir. You believed in me when no one else would.'

'Stop it, you're embarrassing me,' he joked. Then more seriously: 'And anyway, I did it for my boy, for Shahid.' With a tear in his eye: 'Something good in this world of shit.'

Anderson smiled at his friend.

Composing himself, Hussain went on: 'John, I've been meaning to ask, have you ever thought about joining a solicitors' firm? Try your hand at defending for a while? You're good at it. Forget silk. How do you like the sound of Hussain & Anderson – has a certain ring to it?'

Anderson laughed off the offer. 'Too old to learn new tricks, I'm afraid. Think it will always be the independent Bar for me.' He turned his attention to Adey and held out his hand. Didn't seem enough somehow.

Connor came bursting into the courtroom, without a hint of embarrassment at his earlier cowardice. 'Come on,

John, everyone's waiting. Got a table at The Delaunay. And by the way, just spoken to a few of the main players in chambers – they want you as head.'

Everything was happening so fast. Like he'd never been away. 'Give me a couple of minutes, Sam.' Anderson turned back to his lawyers. 'You'll both come, won't you?'

Hussain started the excuses: 'Not really my scene. Got a load of work to catch up on now this is over.'

'Me too,' said Adey. 'There's a train from Euston we can catch in half an hour. You go, John, your old life is waiting for you.'

Anderson hesitated for a moment. The prison officers came back into the courtroom before anything else could be said. 'Come with us please, sir?'

A last glance at his friends. Friends? No. What was he thinking? They were just his lawyers. Anderson, more than anyone, should have known that.

He chuckled at his brief descent into sentimentality.

CHAPTER 93

Anderson followed the prison officer along the cell corridor. He'd seen and smelt enough whitewashed walls to last a lifetime. The odour of jail would never leave him. A chaotic blend of damp, urine, canteen food and disinfectant. Anderson still couldn't quite believe it. A free man. Exonerated. His career back on track. Who knows, maybe even silk next year? Surely they owed him that much?

He wanted to laugh. Cry. Shout.

Life felt good.

Then, gradually, a dark cloud descended over him. A feeling of melancholy. Now that the initial euphoria had subsided, the realisation remained. The realisation that so many of those that he held dear had cared so little. Had even wanted to destroy him.

Who was John Anderson? Why had his judgement about people been so wide of the mark? Had he forged friendships purely for convenience? For the advancement of a career?

He stood by the senior prison officer's desk, motionless, contemplating these things whilst forms were filled in and Anderson's few meagre possessions were handed to him in a sealed plastic bag.

He caught sight of Orlando West across the corridor, sitting alone in a visits room. Staring into space, absent of any animation, West seemed different somehow. Smaller.

Anderson turned to the officers and said, 'I just need to say goodbye to someone.'

The officer in charge didn't bother to reply, engrossed in signing off the paperwork.

Anderson walked over to the booth.

West saw him approach. As Anderson opened the door, without making eye contact, West said, 'Come to gloat, have you?'

Incredulous at the comment, Anderson shook his head. 'No. I want to know why?'

West said nothing.

Anderson persisted: 'You knew all along. Watched me suffer. Let me go to jail. That day in the robing room when you offered me the Harrison murder, you said there was something else you wanted to tell me in chambers. It was about the Osman warning you'd had that morning, wasn't it?'

West remained impassive.

'But you never got the chance to tell me, did you? And after the crash you kept it to yourself.' Anderson shook his head at the full realisation. 'An opportunity too good to miss. To get rid of me.'

West was unmoved.

Now full of emotion, Anderson said, 'I thought we were friends? That I was like a son to you?'

West turned to Anderson and gave a sardonic smile. 'Are you really that naive? We're all out for what we can get.'

Taken aback, Anderson replied, 'Are we?'

'It helped my career to take the great Howard Anderson's son under my wing. Act as your mentor. And it suited you to treat me as such. A symbiosis.' West looked away again.

Cold and detached, he had no interest in Anderson's need to dissect their relationship.

Anderson needed more answers. 'And all this was just to clear your path to my wife. That was it?'

West became irritated by the exchange. Suddenly, full of energy, he got up and stood face to face. 'And why not?' Holding up a clenched fist: 'If you want something, you take it.' He took a step back and laughed. 'That was how your father always conducted himself.' With contempt for the man standing before him, he added: 'You really aren't your father's son after all, are you?'

'What about honour? Integrity? We all want to be judges. It's not just a career. We have to live righteously, don't we? You sit as a Recorder. How can you pass judgement on people, send them to prison when you have no moral compass?'

'It's just a career, you fool. Like any other. Prime ministers don't get the job because they care more about society than other politicians. They're just the most ambitious. Prepared to crush those in their way to the top.'

Anderson pitied him. A greedy, selfish life.

He could now see how West's ideology had seeped into the bricks and mortar of Spinningfields Chambers. Without noticing, they'd all become infected. Connor, Tilly and others, even himself.

A prison officer touched Anderson's arm: 'Time to go, sir.'

Anderson let out a sigh. He saw his life for what it was. So many wasted years. Blind to what really mattered. 'Goodbye, Orlando.' Nothing else to say.

West turned away.

Anderson was guided up the steps that led to the main entrance. The officer took the key on a chain from his pocket and opened the door.

Freedom.

Detective Inspector Mark Taylor was walking towards Anderson, on his way to the cells to arrest West. Taylor stopped and held out his hand. 'Congratulations.'

Anderson shook it. 'Thank you. I know what you did.'

'It's the least I could do.' Neither spoke for a moment, sharing in the joy that justice had finally been done. Then Taylor said, 'The Grangers wanted me to give you their sincere apologies. And their thanks.'

Anderson smiled wistfully. 'Not necessary. They were let down by the system. Our system.' He set off down the corridor towards the Great Hall.

Taylor called after him. He needed to share something else. 'Mr Anderson?'

Anderson stopped and turned.

'This case has changed me, you know. Made me see things more clearly.'

Anderson nodded. 'Me too.' Then he added, 'There's still time left, detective.'

'Yes. Yes there is,' Taylor replied.

CHAPTER 94

Anderson's parents were waiting with Stephen in the Great Hall. 'That's my boy!' said Howard, hands raised in triumph.

Never had anything sounded so hollow to John Anderson. He stared with incredulity at the man he'd spent a lifetime trying to emulate. Heartbroken, he said nothing. No point highlighting the hypocrisy to the person who had pushed him to plead guilty, offered no support, but thought only of himself. Howard Anderson would never change.

Things were different now. The old John Anderson had died in prison. This new man didn't need the approval of his flawed father. From now on, John Anderson would live by his own values and pursue his own dreams.

Anderson's mother moved to hug her son, then thought better of it. 'We're all so happy, John,' she said, through a haze of Prozac.

Mia bounded over and threw her arms around him. 'I'm so relieved, John. I knew you were innocent.' Then, doe-eyed: 'I've been such a fool, John. Can we start again? Make it work this time?'

So much had changed. A thousand thoughts ran around Anderson's head. 'I'm so sorry, Mia.'

An affectionate smile. 'It doesn't matter now, John.'

'It does. We should never have married. It wasn't love for either of us. Not back then, or now.'

Her expression changed to one of surprise.

He tried to explain: 'I didn't know who I was. Too busy trying to be someone else – living up to other people's expectations of me instead of my own. I'm sorry.'

Her eyes narrowed. Anger rose up: 'What? *You* don't love *me*?'

Before she had a chance to say anything else, Anderson said, 'Thank God for the boys. We are truly blessed.' Looking around him at the familiar faces, those he supposedly knew best – loved the most – Anderson realised he was with the wrong people.

He resolved there and then, never to make that mistake again.

EPILOGUE

Hussain and Adey had managed to get table seats. With broad grins, they watched the train pull out of the station.

Winning always felt good. Still hadn't sunk in.

But they would miss Anderson. Quite a guy.

Hussain spotted Mr and Mrs Granger coming through the carriage looking for their seats.

Seeing them and remembering their loss, then his own, had a sobering effect on Hussain.

Mr Granger stopped. Embarrassed and unable to make eye contact, he said, 'Thank you.' Then: 'I'm sorry. We just needed to know what happened.'

Hussain was choked. He stood up to address him. 'I know, Mr Granger. You have nothing to apologise for. I understand your loss. I really do.'

'I know. Detective Inspector Taylor told me. I'm sorry.'

Hussain smiled ruefully. 'I think we both have to try and move on now, don't we?' He paused, then: 'What else can we do?'

Granger nodded, then set off down the carriage after his wife.

'This seat taken?'

'No,' replied Adey, before realising that John Anderson was sitting down beside her.

'I've been thinking,' he said. '*Anderson* & Hussain sounds better, don't you agree?'

'Maybe,' conceded Hussain, his face beaming. 'What made you change your mind? A run-down solicitor's office in Rusholme is a big comedown from a barristers' chambers.'

Taking Adey's hand in his, Anderson replied, 'I like the staff.'

Adey squeezed tightly.

Hussain chuckled. He approved.

Anderson gazed out of the window at the jumbled buildings of Camden flashing by as the train sped out of the city. Senses heightened after the monotony of prison, he had to close his eyes to savour the moment. Only the comforting rattle of the train forging onwards and the warmth of Adey's hand.

He felt a new emotion.

Contentment.

Hussain's voice broke in: 'By the way, you never told us whose signature was on the document?'

'Yes,' said Adey. 'Was it someone very important?'

Anderson didn't reply.

'Come on,' pressed Hussain. 'Just between us? Whose career did you save?'

Eventually, eyes still closed, he replied, 'In confidence?'

'Of course,' Hussain replied.

'A junior minister. Stephen Anderson. My brother.'

'What?' Hussain and Adey replied in unison.

Anderson opened his eyes. 'A chip off the old block.'